"Triana's masterful, gripping storytelling will not let go."
— Scream Magazine

"*Full Brutal* rocked my world! It's one of the most powerful hardcore horror works of modern times."
— Edward Lee, author of
Header and *The Bighead*

"*A must read.*"
— Rue Morgue Magazine on *Growing Dark*

"Kristopher Triana's work is a volatile mixture of visceral noir and twistedly disturbing passion play that invades the reader's psyche and exposes the raw and throbbing nerve hidden within. His prose is un-apologetic and totally without restraint or mercy. There's no denying it. Triana is the Master of Extreme Horror!"
— Ronald Kelly, author of
Fear, The Saga of Dead-Eye, and *Southern Fried & Horrified*

"Kristopher Triana is without question one of the very best of the new breed of horror writers."
— Bryan Smith, author of
Merciless and *The Killing Kind*

"Whatever style or mode Triana is writing in, the voice matches it unfailingly."
— Cemetery Dance

"One of the most exciting and disturbing voices in extreme horror in quite some time. His stuff hurts so good."
—Brian Keene, author of
The Rising and *The Complex*

THE PRETTIEST GIRL
IN THE GRAVE

KRISTOPHER TRIANA

GRINDHOUSE PRESS

Grindhouse Press
PO BOX 540
Yellow Springs, Ohio 45387

Grindhouse Press logo and all related artwork copyright © 2023 by Brandon Duncan. All rights reserved.

Cover design by Squidbar Designs © 2023. All rights reserved.

Grindhouse Press #093
ISBN-13: 978-1-957504-05-6

For Mona

"We have been force-fed for so long the shudders of a thousand graveyards that at last, seeking a macabre redemption, a salvation by horror, we willingly consume the terrors of the tomb ... and find them to our liking."

—Thomas Ligotti,
The Conspiracy Against the Human Race

ONE

THE GIRLS MET IN THE cemetery.

It wasn't the easiest place to get to, but a thin trail had been preserved, mainly by kids who went out there to party when there wasn't anything better to do. The young had to make their own good times in a small town like Greenwalk. It offered little entertainment for the underage. But while local teens sometimes went to the old, decrepit graveyard, few were bold enough to go all the way in, as the girls would tonight.

Bella stepped over the exposed roots of a red maple, the combat boots she wore merely for fashion now serving their intended purpose. She ascended the hillside with ease. Exercise wasn't exactly her thing, but being seventeen, staying fit came with little effort. Rose, on the other hand, was the active one. As the star forward of the school basketball team, she'd been guaranteed a full ride college scholarship, and though the odds were stacked against her, she was on the right path to compete in the NCAA. It was one of many differences that had been pulling the two friends apart during their senior year.

"Watch your step," Bella told the others.

Rose avoided the roots by leaping over them altogether. Bringing up the rear, Celeste struggled, grabbing onto tree branches for support. She was the bulkiest of the trio, but while her thick legs gave her strength, her added weight slowed her down. Her black hair fell across her face. She blew at it, making the green streak flutter away.

"Need a hand?" Rose asked.

Celeste glowered. "I can do it."

Rose gave Bella a look. She hadn't meant to patronize Celeste, only assist her, but Celeste was overly sensitive when it came to any statement that could be construed as a commentary on her weight. Even when Bella had once tried to tell Celeste she wasn't as heavy as she thought she was—which was true—Celeste had shut her down.

The girls pressed on, Rose walking alongside Bella. Her natural blonde hair was a white stream in the moonlight, reminding Bella of the waterfalls in nearby Tunxis State Forest. She'd loved the falls as a kid. Those years seemed like another life entirely.

"God," Celeste groaned, "are we there yet? I feel like we've been hiking for hours."

Bella almost asked if she needed a break, but decided against it. "Aubrey said it's a mile and a half from the road. The trail levels out just a little further north. At least it's not snowing."

"How do we even know we're going north?"

Rose nodded upward. "There's the north star. It's not the brightest one in the sky, but it's visible tonight."

Celeste gave her an incredulous look. "Are you sure, though?"

"Pretty sure. Besides, look at the trees. In areas without much water, the mossy side faces north."

Celeste smirked. "Who're you, Paulina Bunyan?"

"I was a Girl Scout, okay? Pardon me for knowing things."

Sensing Rose's aggravation, Celeste backed down, despite her general cynicism. Bella did her best to keep the peace between her two friends from different worlds.

"Chill out, guys. We're almost there."

Under any other circumstances, she never would have put Rose and Celeste in the same place. Rose was an overachiever in academics as well as athletics. Uncommonly tall with lean muscle, she was strong without coming off as butch, and was popular at school. Despite all her admirers, she'd had the same boyfriend since junior high, and was the kind of girlfriend every parent hoped their son would find. She listened to Regina Spektor and Adele and loved movies starring Paul

Rudd. Therefore, Celeste saw Rose as a "basic bitch", her favorite term for girls she considered generic embarrassments to feminism, even though Celeste herself was a stereotype in her own right. A quintessential emo, Celeste adorned herself in clothes from Hot Topic and proudly listened to classic goth bands like Siouxsie and The Banshees and Joy Division, though Bella knew she still enjoyed the modern new wave of My Chemical Romance and Paramore. Celeste also spouted nihilistic musings more likely found in a meme than a philosophy text. She was a mopey slacker when it came to school, but extremely creative with a real gift for charcoal drawing and playing the piano.

Each girl represented a different era of Bella's formative years. Rose had been her best friend growing up. They lived on the same street, went to the same schools, and were only a few months apart in age. Bella never had Rose's interest in sports and never even considered joining The Girl Scouts, but they shared many other interests, such as reading fiction and following fashion, and were both excellent students. They'd been like sisters, and it pained Bella that their friendship seemed to be withering now that she'd embraced a goth lifestyle. Rose tended to blame Bella's change in interests on Celeste, and there was a fair amount of truth to that, but Bella hadn't followed Celeste against her will. She'd simply grown to relate to gloomy music in a deep and profound way, especially since her parents' marriage began to fall apart. Bella had her own problems too, with boys and uncertainty about college, and that only added to the emotional release being a goth provided her. She wasn't as fatalistic as Celeste, but depression weighed heavily upon her most days, and she found catharsis in wearing black, reading Anne Rice, and writing poetry in her journal most people would see as macabre, which is why she kept it under lock and key. She didn't want her mother to read it. It would just give her another reason to worry. Mom tended to overreact. That's why Bella lied about where she and Rose were going tonight and didn't mention Celeste at all. Like Rose, Mom's opinion of the gloomy girl was less than complimentary.

"Look," Bella said. "I think I see it."

She stopped. The three girls came side by side. The trees thinned here, and a cool breeze caused Bella to hug her leather jacket tighter around her like a sleeping bag. The clearing was a bramble of weeds and thorns gone brown from the start of winter, and the soft, blue light cast down from the heavens made deceivingly long shadows of the tiny tombstones. The clearing before them was circular, with a knee-high wall of stacked river rocks surrounding it, though the barrier had crumbled in spots.

"Wow," Rose said. "I honestly thought this was gonna be bullshit."

"Aubrey doesn't lie," Celeste said.

"I wasn't saying that. I just can't believe there's a graveyard this deep in the woods, even if it is an abandoned one from the nineteenth century or whatever."

"Yeah. It's kinda cool."

"How come I've never heard of this before?"

Bella shrugged. "I hadn't either. It's just old and forgotten, I guess."

Celeste drew a bottle of Sprite from her coat, but when she opened it, Bella could smell the vodka. Sipping it, Celeste offered the others a drink, but they declined.

"Just don't let Aubrey see you with that," Bella said. "You know she wants us sober for this."

"Yeah, yeah, yeah."

"It's so small," Rose said, looking around the plot. "There can't be more than twenty graves."

Bella took a step forward. Her friends fell in behind her. She scanned the area without entering the cemetery itself. "I don't see the others." She drew her phone from her coat pocket and checked the time. Two minutes to midnight. "They must not be here yet."

A waft of sweet-smelling smoke drifted past. Bella turned, seeing Celeste puffing on her vape pen. Another gust of wind caused Rose to fold her arms despite wearing a hoodie and her team's letterman jacket. The gust moved a cloud across the face of the moon, robbing them of its glow.

"Told you we should've brought a flashlight," Rose said. "We should at least use the ones on our phones."

"Aubrey said not to," Bella said.

"Do you always do everything this Aubrey chick says?"

"C'mon. You said you'd keep an open mind about this. I did *your thing*, remember?"

Corrected, Rose didn't retort. The *thing* Bella had gone along with was supposed to be for her benefit, a ridiculous snowboarding double date with Rose, her boyfriend Tyson, and his pal Colin. Clearly, Colin was a tool Rose had used in her effort to steer Bella "back on track."

He was a nice, good-looking guy and certainly matched what had once been her type. But her taste in music wasn't the only thing that had changed. Rose knew that, and it irked Bella that her friend wouldn't accept it. She didn't even like snowboarding anymore, let alone jocks like Colin. She'd sooner swim Lake Superior than date a guy who wore his baseball cap backwards. Besides, she had a crush on someone else.

Rose owed Bella, and Bella was cashing in tonight. Aubrey insisted they needed six girls for whatever this was. Bella and Celeste were in, as was Savannah. Together, they were the goth girl quartet, always down for something macabre or mysterious. But they needed two more people, and they had to be female. Savannah said she had someone she could bring along, and when Aubrey looked at Bella, expecting her to have more options than the misanthropic Celeste, she agreed to bring a friend.

But she'd practically had to beg.

"A séance in an old cemetery?" Rose had asked, raising an eyebrow. "Are you being serious right now?"

"Not a séance," Bella insisted, a little embarrassed. "Well... I mean, yeah, sort of like that. But not, like, super cheesy."

Rose shook her head. Nearly six-foot-one, she towered over Bella, making her feel like she was being frowned upon by a parent or teacher.

"Jeez, Bella," Rose said. "Halloween was months ago."

"It's not like that."

"Yeah, well, whatever it's like, forget it. I know you're going through a goth phase right now but—"

"It's not a *phase*. It's a life choice."

Insulted, Bella turned her back on her friend.

"Okay, okay," Rose said, putting her hand on Bella's shoulder. "I didn't mean it to be judgmental. I can understand being goth . . . but isn't a séance in a graveyard a little much? I mean, you don't really believe in ghosts, do you?"

Bella sighed. "No. Of course not."

"Then what is this all about?"

Bella didn't know what to tell her, for she didn't quite understand it herself. Aubrey was always vague. At twenty, she was the oldest of their clique, and considered herself some sort of leader, and Celeste and Savannah only encouraged it, as well as her grandiose delusion of being some sort of queen of darkness. Though Aubrey sometimes struck Bella as odd even for a goth, she still looked up to her, and therefore indulged her. Tonight, she was even going so far as to follow her.

There was a rustle in the brush, and a shadowy form came from the other side of the cemetery. Celeste gasped, clutching her vape pen to her chest.

"Oh shit!" she whispered. "Is that a bear?"

"Nah," Rose said. "They're mostly hibernating by now."

"*Mostly?*"

"Well, sometimes if they have enough food sources, they don't."

Bella squinted. "It looks like more than one thing. But definitely too small to be bears. I think it's the others."

Rose leaned forward for a closer look. "Yeah. Must be them."

"Why wouldn't they use the trail?"

Rose shrugged. "I dunno. They're your friends, Bella."

Three figures entered the deadening, two roughly the same size and shape, donned in all black, with the third much smaller and dressed practically. They were slender forms, young and female. As the clouds broke, Bella recognized Aubrey and Savannah, but not the girl tagging along. Aubrey waved—not like a friend, but like a priest summoning a child forward.

Always with the drama, Bella thought.

She hated to admit it, but Rose was right when it came to the line between gothic and corny. Sometimes she felt the way Aubrey straddled it was awfully cavalier.

The two groups approached, crossing into the cemetery to become one. Aubrey wore her leather trench coat with the spiked shoulders and the tiny chains that wrapped around the arms—a coat Bella would kill for. A black bag was slung over her shoulder. A natural brunette, her long hair was so close to black she didn't bother to dye it like her friends did. She had large, almond eyes that reminded Bella of a Siamese cat, and moved just as gracefully and predatorially as one. Behind her, excessively pale Savannah looked like a poltergeist in the light of the moon, the zebra stripes of her hair matching the *Beetlejuice* choker around her neck. She held the smaller girl by the wrist.

Where has this one come from? Bella wondered. *She looks like a middle-schooler.*

The girl's eyes were wide, gazing at the surrounding woodland like a first-time tourist. Bella guessed her to be around ninety pounds.

With her Ugg boots and jacket by The North Face, all she was missing was a yoga mat and an avocado cookbook to complete her white girl motif. She looked less like a friend of Savannah's and more like a virgin sacrifice.

Not that they were into that sort of thing.

Bella walked among the small, flattened grave markers—tombstones crumbled to fragments and stone nameplates jutting out of the earth like shrapnel. Aubrey gave Rose the once over, then flashed Bella a knowing smile.

"Hey, Aubrey," Celeste said.

Aubrey nodded, barely acknowledging her. She kept her attention on Rose, sizing up the physically imposing girl. But while a towering figure, Rose was always gregarious no matter who she was meeting, and her kind smile had a way of making most people instantly comfortable around her.

But Aubrey wasn't most people.

Bella introduced them.

"Hi," Rose said with a small wave.

Aubrey smirked. "Charmed." She turned to Bella. "Now we have six."

"Yeah," Bella said, waiting for more that didn't come. "For what, though?"

"All in due time."

Savannah came forward, tugging the wide-eyed girl along. "This is Marnie." The girl smiled but looked away, bashful. "She's my little sister. We snuck out!"

"Oh," Bella said, not knowing what else to say.

"She just turned fifteen," Savannah said. "Old enough to be initiated, right?"

"I'd say so," Aubrey said. "As long as she's willing."

Marnie finally looked up, and in her eyes Bella saw a familiar desperation, the same yearning to be accepted by older girls any fifteen-year-old feels. Marnie was just excited to be out after dark with her big sister, and was therefore ripe for molding, so eager to please she'd be as malleable as Play-Doh.

"Um, yeah," Marnie said, gushing. "Sure, Aubrey."

Aubrey looked to Rose. "And what of you?"

Rose crossed her arms. Bella could practically hear the laughter Rose was holding back. She'd known Aubrey for all of thirty seconds and already decided she was utterly absurd. She gave Bella a quick glance, just enough to tell her *I'm only doing this for you*, then nodded.

"Sure," she said. "I'm game."

TWO

HOLLY COULDN'T REMEMBER THE LAST full day she'd enjoyed without her back hurting. She didn't even have to do anything to set it off. Sometimes she'd just get out of bed and it'd be kinked up. Other times it seemed like a knot formed slowly throughout the day, making it so all she could think about was the warm bath and glass of wine waiting for her at home. The tub was nothing special, and the wine came in a box, but this ritual kept her from attempting a social life.

She removed the warm rag from her eyes and took another sip of chardonnay.

Christ, she thought. *Is this what it is to be over forty?*

She was always tired, always achy, always in a malaise. Her post office job was unfulfilling and repetitive, and yet it exhausted her of other people to the point she just wanted to go home and seal herself away from them. She rarely even saw her friends anymore. Everyone was busy with their families and careers. The close girlfriends she'd had in her thirties were now just photos on social media. Holly wouldn't have anyone to go out with even if she wanted to.

THE PRETTIEST GIRL IN THE GRAVE

This also made it harder to meet a guy. Without a friend to set her up or a house party where she could meet new men in a comfortable setting, Holly found the concept of dating both exhausting and terrifying. She knew she had to move on, but where was she supposed to meet someone new? She didn't want to scroll through dating site profiles like she was trying to pick out a movie. Besides, she'd be too nervous to actually go out on a date with someone she hadn't met face to face beforehand. It just wasn't how she did things. Or at least, not what she'd done when she was last on the market.

Well, she'd been put back on the shelf after nearly twenty years of marriage but wasn't on a display in a high-end store the way she was when she was young and firm. Now she sat on a virtual Goodwill rack for those desperate and foolish enough to want to give love one more go. And the same went for the sort of men available to a forty-five-year-old single mother in a small town. The good ones had either been taken or broken, leaving only the scraps of scraps, the human equivalent to cold French fries at the bottom of the takeout bag.

But God, how she was sick of taking care of herself. Her vibrator had been working overtime even before Justin moved out. Long before the idea of divorce even entered her mind, she and her husband had grown sexually distant. Emotional distance soon followed, and by the time she managed to vocalize her unhappiness to Justin, it was too late. By then, nothing would have changed her mind about leaving him. Now she was realizing you didn't bounce back from a failed marriage the way you did other dead relationships, and the dating scene after forty was a mortifying wasteland. She didn't want Justin back—she wasn't even warm to the idea of a new husband—but she wanted *someone* in her life. Yet looking at dudes her own age, Holly was flabbergasted. They weren't guys, they were men—*old* men. They had bald spots and gray in their beards, the abs long gone, the pecs deflated. It was as if she were looking at the dads her friends had had when she was a teenager, and it disturbed her. So much time had passed while her attention had been on other things. Was she really the female equivalent of these men?

Then she'd look in the mirror only to have it confirmed. Her upper arms flapped when she raised them. Laugh lines had turned to crow's feet. Gravity had taken a toll on her bust and backside, and there was a small ring of fat around her midsection that made her belly stick out just above her groin, a companion piece to her c-section scar. And she had more than a few gray hairs of her own. The

Holly she knew had been abducted by this strange woman who looked entirely too much like her mother, and it left her feeling dazed, busted, afraid.

Forty-five. Officially middle-aged. And alone.

Pulling the drain plug with her toes, the tub gurgled as it sucked down the used bathwater. Holly finished her glass of wine and wrapped herself in a towel.

You're not totally alone, she told herself. *You have Bella.*

Her relationship with her daughter was hardly something to celebrate these days. Bella was going through a rebellious, despondent phase that mirrored the one Holly had gone through at that age. But explaining that similarity to Bella would be impossible. It made Holly snicker sometimes, the way her daughter thought she'd personally invented the combat boots and slip dress combo. Holly had rocked Doc Martens with pleated skirts and fishnet stockings way back in the Jurassic era of the '90s, doing everything she could to look like Courtney Love and Juliette Lewis. By comparison, Bella's goth garb was tame. All the things her daughter thought made her an individual had been lifted from Generation X—her *mother's* generation—and she didn't even realize it, or at least didn't acknowledge it. If she did, would she finally think her mother was cool or would she decide those things were now lame by association?

Holly put on her sweatpants and an ancient flannel that couldn't be beat for comfort. She stepped into her fuzzy slippers, one of which had the old battle scar of a cigarette burn from when she'd briefly returned to the habit. Looking at her outfit, Holly mocked herself.

"Foxy lady."

She went downstairs and refilled her wine glass only partway. Glancing at the clock on the oven, she was shocked to see it was already midnight. It felt like she'd just begun winding down from another long day of work, and now she had just eight hours before the alarm would get her up to go in again.

I'm gonna call out, she told herself, knowing it was a lie but wanting to imagine the possibility, to believe in a work-life balance, even if just for a moment. But she was a single mom now. Justin hadn't been much of a provider even when they were married. She'd not asked him for alimony, but had hoped he would at least be reliable with child support, especially since he'd be saving money by moving in with his mother. Holly had been kidding herself thinking she could count on him for even that. Justin was far too trapped by the deadly trio that takes all the manliness out of men—weed, video games, and porn. He was a selfish Peter Pan who couldn't take criticism any better than he could clean up after himself. For so long she'd waited for him to mature, but he was mentally stuck in his twenties, no more of an adult than when they'd first met. It was a marvel she'd stayed with him as long as she had, but she'd needed someone.

Holly thought of Bella now as she sat up in bed with a *Golden Girls* rerun on the TV. Her daughter was going on eighteen, in her senior year and aimless. Ennui weighed on Bella like a wet, wool coat, but she made no effort to ease it by occupying herself. Holly extended her curfew in the hope her daughter would go out and party a little. Maybe meet a boy—or who knows, maybe a girl? Bella had her share of male suitors, as her grandmother called it, but had never had a serious boyfriend. She was on birth control because of her heavy, painful periods, but Holly believed she was still a virgin. Her daughter was pretty, and not just in her mother's eyes, but a lack of confidence slowed her down. Holly worried Bella had failed to launch, and seeing her now, with her grades slipping and her mood deteriorating, she feared her daughter was doomed to make the same mistakes she had. Holly wanted better for her daughter than to marry young and be tied down to a lazy, irresponsible leech of a husband. And while Bella had always brought her great pleasure, Holly often wondered what her life would have been like if she'd waited a little longer to have children.

Seeing Rose Peterson grow up as bright in personality as she was in wit made Holly happy, but she wondered what Trisha Peterson may have done that Holly hadn't with her own daughter, even though she knew it was unfair to think that way about herself. She also tried not to think about Trisha if she could avoid it, or her husband, Sawyer. But it pleased her that Bella and Rose were still friends after all this time and were out together tonight. Holly told her daughter she could stay out until one, something previously unheard of. She needed all the help she could get.

Finishing her wine, Holly switched off the light and let the voices on TV lull her to sleep, the voices of dead women.

THREE

"WE'RE GOING TO PLAY A game," Aubrey said.

Bella resisted the urge to roll her eyes. Her new friend sounded like the bad guy from those *Saw* movies. In the middle of the cemetery, Aubrey stood inside a circle formed by the other girls, each on a spot she'd marked with a tealight candle. Using a stick, she drew lines from one girl to the next, forming a star in the dirt, then walked into the pentagon at the center.

Bella looked to the others. Rose was expressionless, but Bella knew her well enough to know what she was thinking. Even when they were kids, Rose thought horoscopes and tarot cards were inane nonsense, so this pentagram must have seemed like an oversized Ouija board to her. To Bella's left, Celeste was stoic but attentive to Aubrey's every move, anxious to be called upon. Savannah and her sister completed the bottom points of the star. Savannah smiled mischievously while Marnie looked lost, like she'd regressed to an even younger version of herself.

"Okay," Aubrey said. "It starts with each of us answering the same three questions. You have to be completely honest in your answers."

"Like truth or dare?" Celeste offered.

"Sort of, only dare isn't an option, and the questions are set in stone."

"Who came up with them?" Rose asked. "You?"

Aubrey flashed her cat eyes. "No. They're old questions specific to this cemetery."

Bella wondered how Aubrey knew this, but didn't dare ask. The graveyard was so small and insignificant, a mere pile of rocks in a less-traveled forest. It wasn't tended to or visited by distant descendants of the departed. People in town didn't mention it. Bella only learned about the place when Aubrey brought it up this week, insisting they go for something special, something she kept vague.

"I'll ask the first question of each of you," Aubrey said, "and then I'll give my answer too."

She paused for theatrics, looking at each of the girls with a closed-mouth grin. She spun slowly, arm outstretched like the hand of a clock, and closed her eyes, humming. When at last she stopped, she was pointing at Bella.

Aubrey opened her eyes. "Bella, what are you afraid of?"

Bella's shoulders grew tight. "Is... I mean, is that one of the questions?"

"Yes. Tell us. And remember, you *must* be honest."

Or else what? Bella thought, then pushed the thought away. There were plenty of things she feared—most too personal to share. How intimate was her answer expected to be? And why did she have to go first? The others would have time to think about their answer while she was being put on the spot.

"We're waiting, Bella," Aubrey said. "Don't overthink it. Just say the first thing that comes to your mind."

I'm afraid for my future, she thought.

"Bees," she said instead. "And hornets, wasps. Anything with a stinger that can fly."

Aubrey stared her in the eyes, and Bella couldn't tell if she was satisfied or pissed off by her answer. She didn't exhale until Aubrey turned her attention to Rose.

"Rose. What are you afraid of?"

Bella couldn't imagine Rose fearing anything and was curious what her answer would be.

"Losing, I guess," Rose said.

"Losing what?" Aubrey asked.

"Just, like, in general."

"So, you really mean *failure*."

Bella tensed, seeing Rose's nostrils flare. Aubrey's smile didn't falter.

"Fine," Rose said. "But maybe *afraid* is a strong word to use. It's more like I work my ass off to avoid failure. That way I don't have to be afraid of it."

Aubrey nodded. "Still counts."

She turned to Celeste, who answered before Aubrey could repeat the question.

"I'm scared of motorcycles. Being on one, I mean."

"You're afraid of crashing?"

"Yeah. My uncle died in a bike crash. He flew onto a fence and a post went right through his chest. I just feel safer in a car."

The sisters were next.

"I'm scared of getting pregnant," Savannah said.

Celeste snickered, but one glance from Aubrey shut her up.

"I do not want another human being growing inside me, ya know?" Savannah said, flashing her oversized grin. "Plus, it *destroys* your body. To hell with all that. That's why I make guys use a rubber even though I'm on the pill. I love my body too much to wreck it."

Beside her, Marnie flushed at her sister's confession. Then it was her turn.

"Um," she said, stalling.

"First thing that comes to mind," Aubrey reminded her.

"I, guess, um . . ."

Boys, Bella thought. *You're scared of boys*. She wasn't sure why it came to mind. *Jeez, am I projecting?*

"Answer me," Aubrey told the girl.

Marnie blurted it out. "I'm afraid of the dark."

Celeste snickered again, and this time Aubrey allowed it. Marnie's answer was a tad childish. Bella hoped the other girls wouldn't bully her for it.

"Not, like, super scared," Marnie said, already embarrassed. "I was as a kid, but I'm better now. I just don't like not being able to see what's around me, I guess."

Turning slowly, Aubrey stood tall in the pentagon at the center of the star and lowered her arm. "And I'm afraid of being burned alive."

We get it, Bella thought. *Because you're a witch*. Again, always with the drama.

Bella hoped Aubrey would do her blind spin again to make someone else go first with the next query, but no such luck. She just went back to start.

"Question two. Bella, who do you love?"

A hollow feeling came over Bella's stomach. She could say her family, but clearly that wasn't the kind of love Aubrey was asking about.

"I don't have a boyfriend," she said. "You guys know that."

"It doesn't have to be someone you *have*, Bella. It could be someone you *want*. In fact, it's probably better that way, given the nature of the game."

Bella didn't like the implications of this. She swallowed hard, a single name at the center of her mind, one she couldn't possibly say. It didn't matter how honest Aubrey wanted her to be. Some secrets were meant to stay secret. She wracked her mind for another name, any name the girls might believe.

"Ethan Derry," she said.

Rose gave Bella a curious look, as if to say, '*Are you shitting me?*'

Bella barely knew Ethan, and he certainly wasn't goth, but he was dark and intense, an aspiring writer, and fit the mold. She hoped Rose wouldn't try to set her up with him now.

"I mean, he's not my *love*, but I have a little crush on him. That's all." Bella said this to Aubrey but intended it for Rose. "That's the best answer I've got right now."

Aubrey went around the rest of the group. Typically, Rose named her boyfriend, Tyson. Celeste insisted love was a poison, a mental illness, that she didn't feel it for any stupid man. But Aubrey wouldn't accept that, so Celeste conceded to at least feeling *lust* for Maurice James, a slim, black boy with dreadlocks and intense eyes. He was in Bella's science class and always seemed bored by everything. She had a hard time imagining Celeste with him, but she honestly had a hard time picturing Celeste with anyone. Savannah said she loved Johnny Depp, and to Bella's surprise, Aubrey allowed her to answer with a famous person. She wished she'd thought of that. Expecting Marnie to freeze up, Bella was surprised the girl jumped at the chance to name her crush.

"Ashton MacDougall!" Marnie beamed. "He's a year older than me, but I think he really likes me, ya know? I'm hoping he asks me out. He's so cute, you guys." She reached for the phone in her back pocket. "I can show you his picture."

Aubrey held up her hand like a crossing guard. "That won't be necessary."

Marnie deflated. Aubrey centered herself in the pentagon again, her feet forming an arrowhead.

"I love the dead," she said without emotion.

Bella felt suddenly cold. While Aubrey's goth dramatics could be hammy at times, something about these words struck her as dreadfully true. She hugged herself against the shiver. When Aubrey faced her again, Bella braced for what she guessed would be the most difficult question of all.

Aubrey stood ghostly in the moonlight. "Bella Whitman . . . what happens when you die?"

Bella froze. Aubrey hadn't asked what she *thought* happened, but what *did* happen. She wanted a concrete explanation to life's greatest mystery. How could she expect such a thing from her? It was a question asked since the dawn of man. There were a multitude of beliefs and theories, religions and concepts based on the foundation of the afterlife or lack thereof.

Bella steadied herself. Aubrey wanted honesty, so that's what she gave her.

"I don't know," she said.

Locking eyes, Aubrey waited for more, but Bella was finished. Not just with her answer, but with this stupid game, whatever it was. What could the point of all this possibly be? Why had Aubrey lured them out here for something so silly? Bella had thought she was cooler than that. Had yet another idol let her down?

"Rose," Aubrey said. "Same question."

Clearly Rose was even more irritated by this query. At least this was the final round.

"Nothing happens," she said. "The way things were before you were born is exactly what waits for you after you die."

This seemed to intrigue Aubrey. "So, you're an atheist?"

"I've never felt a need to put a name to it, but yeah, you could say that."

"You don't believe in the soul then either?"

"Not in the literal sense. Not as in a spirit that flies out of your body when you die."

"What other sense is there?"

Rose exhaled. "I believe in souls as just a term for what makes you who you are. Your individuality, your *heart*."

The corners of Aubrey's mouth curled, and she gave Rose a slow nod, then asked Celeste the big question.

"There's, like, a pit of the damned," Celeste said. "Not like Hell with fire and brimstone and shit, but, like, a world of darkness and blue shadows. You're hollow there. And it's so cold and lonely. No God or Devil or loved ones. Just this endless void. Forever."

She's really piling it on, Bella thought. Celeste was always trying to out-goth everyone, even Aubrey.

"I dunno about the rest of you," Savannah said, ever snarky, "but I'm gonna make a wicked ghost."

"You believe in spirits then?" Aubrey asked.

"Sounds a lot more fun than going back to being fucking unborn." Looking at Rose, she snorted a laugh, then whacked her sister's arm. "I already know what this one's answer will be. She still goes with Mommy and Daddy to church on Sundays."

Aubrey swiftly pivoted toward Marnie. The prospect of a Christian in their midst seemed to spark something within her.

"You believe in Heaven, Marnie?" she asked. "In Jesus?"

The girl stammered. "Well . . . I mean . . . yeah, I do."

"You think you'll get wings when you die and fly up to a city in the clouds?"

Even in the dark, Bella could tell Marnie blushed.

"Maybe it's not exactly all that," Marnie said, "but I will return to God."

Aubrey pursed her lips. "And what will your God do with you then?"

Marnie looked to her sister for support but received only mocking smirks. Bella felt bad for the girl. She almost stepped in, but decided it was better for Marnie to speak for herself.

"He will do what He thinks best," she said. "God makes no mistakes."

Celeste belted out a laugh and Aubrey couldn't help but snicker. Even Rose worked to suppress a giggle. Perhaps because Bella was the only one not laughing, Marnie looked at her as if for help. Bella tried to think of something to say, but Aubrey spoke before she could.

"Alright then. Babies born with no limbs aren't a mistake. The Holocaust wasn't a mistake. Thousands of years of people being tortured and executed in God's name—not a mistake."

"The Lord works in mysterious ways," Marnie said, unable to look Aubrey in the eye.

"I've heard that one before. They tell you that when people you love die. Wouldn't it be easier for God to just say 'Hey, y'all. I fucked up. My bad,' instead of insisting it was all part of a plan we're just too dumb to understand?"

Marnie fell silent. Her frown was so intense Bella thought the girl was about to cry, but then realized what she was holding in wasn't tears, but rage. Marnie didn't like someone talking about her God like this, and it showed. Aubrey picked up on it too.

"Oh," she said. "I've offended you."

Marnie crossed her arms.

"Forgive me," Aubrey said, sounding genuine. "That wasn't my intention. You gave me your honest answer. Thank you for that."

Marnie managed to meet Aubrey's gaze then, but the open door of her had closed most of the way. She gave a weak smile to show the apology was accepted, but remained guarded, silent.

"Would you like to know where you go when you die?" Aubrey asked the group, as if her answer was the only correct one. She waited for the girls to agree, then extended her arms, gesturing to the tombstones all around them. "The grave, ladies. You go to the grave."

FOUR

ROSE COULDN'T BELIEVE THIS CRAP.

Was this really what Bella was into? Candles and riddles and moonlit graveyards? Was this supposed to be edgy? Scary? If so, it was a spectacular failure. Aubrey was about as spooky as *Hotel Transylvania*, and this little game of hers was juvenile, something more appropriate to thirteen-year-olds at a slumber party, like seeing your future husband's profession in candle wax or playing "light as a feather, stiff as a board." Was this how goth girls spent their Friday nights? If so, they were even lamer than people made them out to be.

Rose tried not to be judgmental. Obviously, Bella was going through some difficult changes. Even if she wasn't, she was entitled to live her life however she chose, whether others saw the appeal of it or not. But to Rose, being goth was like giving up, something she could never do. She got depressed sometimes, like anyone, but making sure everyone knew about it seemed vain and immature. Despair was something you worked to power through, not celebrated, and life was too short to be this focused on death. But she was desperate to keep Bella in her life. She feared their friendship was thinning to a trickle. When Aubrey asked what she was afraid of, that was what had sprung to her mind first. She and Bella had been like sisters too long to let something as silly as being goth take her best friend from her. Hopefully coming along to this Wiccan ritual—or whatever the damned thing was—would show Bella just how much she still cared about her. Maybe then Bella would let her in again, and Rose could help her find a way out of this dark, mental fog.

"So . . . what now?" Celeste asked Aubrey.

The goth queen stared up at the moon. Though Rose found Aubrey a bit cheesy, she was attractive beneath all that makeup, possessing all the feminine features Rose coveted.

Sarah, Plain and Tall, she thought of herself. Too big, too flat-chested, too gangly. The teasing Rose experienced in her youth only ceased when she started fighting girls who called her a giraffe or asked "How's the weather up there?" But fighting only perpetuated her reputation as a tomboy. It was an unfair labeling. She wasn't masculine. She wasn't into "guy stuff." But ignorant people considered basketball a sport for men, as if the male sex had ownership of a game Rose played better than most men ever could. She knew people called her a lesbian and said she just wanted to be black, their prejudiced idea of insults showing just how ignorant they were. Well, she wouldn't have to deal with those cretins much longer. She was getting out of this town. Hopefully she could convince Bella to do the same.

"Let the challenge begin," Aubrey said, pulling Rose out of her thoughts.

The circle of girls waited, their eyes never leaving Aubrey.

"The game we play tonight," she said, "will reveal whether or not we've been truthful. We gave our answers, now the dead will give us theirs."

A séance, Rose thought. *I knew it.*

But she was wrong. Aubrey grabbed her little bag and started toward a chunk of concrete Rose had mistaken as a sunken tombstone.

"Come," Aubrey said.

The others followed her like a cabal. Rose joined them, looking past the group at the square concrete shoot with a frame that stuck out a foot above ground. Aubrey seemed to sink. Rose realized she was descending a small set of stairs. She looked to Bella, but her friend was watching Aubrey, equally surprised. Approaching the shoot, Rose looked down at Aubrey standing on a concrete slab littered with dead leaves and debris. The walls of the small enclave were green with mold and draped in cobwebs, and at one corner a sheet of broken plywood had been propped up. Behind Aubrey was a concrete door, partway open. A metal ring handle hung from one end, busted and corroded.

"Did you open that?" Rose asked Aubrey.

"No," Aubrey said. "We did. We all did."

"What?"

"Yeah," Bella said. "What is that supposed to mean, Aubrey?"

"By answering the questions," Aubrey said, "we accepted the invitation to the game."

Celeste went to the first step. "Cool."

"What is this thing?" Savannah asked. "An old storage shed or something?"

Aubrey shook her head. "It's a crypt."

The fine hair on Rose's arms stood up. Perhaps Aubrey was spooky after all.

"The earth has grown over the roof," Aubrey said, "so it's hard to spot unless you're right on top of it."

Marnie took a step back. "Wait . . . so there's, like, dead bodies in there?"

Aubrey opened her bag and dug inside.

"Okay," Rose said. "What is this?"

"It's a crypt," Celeste said. "Weren't you listening?"

"I mean what is this all about?"

Only Aubrey had the answer to that. She took six black rods from her bag, handing five to Celeste.

"Pass 'em around," Aubrey said.

Candles with brass holders, a ring on the side to protect their fingers from running wax. Rose looked to Bella again, and this time her friend returned her concerned gaze. The clack of an opening Zippo made Rose flinch.

"The game," Aubrey said, lighting her candle, "is unique to this crypt. It's only played here, in this cemetery, in this town. It's been played for generations by the young women of Greenwalk."

Rose looked to the others. "Has anyone else ever heard of this?"

No one spoke. They didn't have to.

"It's not common knowledge," Aubrey said. "It's this town's little secret, known only by a few. Most girls aren't brave enough to play. It takes a group of six, at least three of which must have a connection with darkness, with death."

"We have four," Celeste said, referencing the goth quartet.

"That's right. Plus, two newbies."

Rose's shoulders tightened. "Okay . . . just what is this game, huh? Spit it out already. What's this even called?"

Smile curling, Aubrey handed the Zippo to Celeste to light her candle and looked up at Rose from the doorway of the crypt, grazing it with her fingertips as if it were a lover's flesh.

"The game is called . . . The Prettiest Girl in the Grave."

Silence.

No laughter, no excitement, no teasing. Even Rose didn't have a comeback. The game's title left her feeling somehow cored. She urged to take Bella's hand but hesitated. Rose hoped her best friend would want to bow out of this too but couldn't read her blank expression.

"Here's how it goes," Aubrey said, amused by the unease she'd created. "We enter the crypt together. I'll lead and—"

"Have you been in there before?" Marnie blurted out.

Aubrey's eyes tightened. "No. None of us have. I lead because I started the game."

Marnie seemed to have more to say but couldn't get it out.

"How do we play?" Celeste asked.

Rose interrupted. "Hold it. We can't go in there."

"Why not?" Celeste asked. "I mean, after all this time it must be public property, right?"

"Not exactly, but that's not what I'm worried about. I mean . . . are you two serious? You want to go into some old, underground crypt we know nothing about?"

Celeste grinned. "You're just scared."

"Yeah, scared of scraping a knee and having it get infected, of twisting an ankle or something. Scared of black widows and rats and whatever else might be in there. It's dangerous."

Rose turned to Bella, hoping she wasn't actually considering going into this dilapidated tomb.

"What's the goal of the game?" Bella asked Aubrey.

"Simple. To become what the title says—the prettiest girl in the grave."

Rose huffed. "And what exactly does that mean?"

Holding the candle under her chin, Aubrey's face flickered between orange and black, a jack-o'-lantern made flesh. "It means you've won the game." As she continued, she looked from girl to girl. "As women, we are the givers of life, the mothers of the world. But by passing through this door, we enter the realm of the dead. Among them, we represent human life, but by facing all that is dark—by *embracing* it—the mysteries of life and death will be answered for us, a confession from beyond the grave in exchange for the confessions we all made here tonight. A secret for every secret."

The girls shared the same expression, their faces slack, mouths slightly open, eyes like fireflies in the light of their personal flames.

Savannah broke the silence, the aloof girl suddenly serious. "How do we go about winning?"

"The gameplay is random," Aubrey explained. "The only rules are those set by the crypt itself. It is said that it will offer us tests and challenges, dark things we must confront about ourselves and others. Whoever makes it to the end of the crypt and back first is the winner—The Prettiest Girl in the Grave."

"Why do they say the 'prettiest' then?" Rose asked.

"It's just the name the game was given," Aubrey said. "I don't think it's really about which one of us is physically the prettiest, but which of us is worthy of being royalty among the deceased."

"A princess of the dead," Marnie said, just above a whisper.

Aubrey smiled at Savannah. "Hey, your sister's sharp. She gets it."

Rose grimaced at this superstitious nonsense. From the look of this concrete shoot, it would be easy to run from one end of the bunker to another, and she was obviously the most athletic of the six of them. Not that she cared about winning this. She was viciously competitive, but not when the game was asinine. While she didn't like the idea of going under the cemetery, she'd told Bella she'd go along with tonight's shenanigans, and Rose didn't back out of promises. At least this game wouldn't take long.

"So," Marnie said, hands clutched together, "are there really bodies in there?"

"I've never been down here, remember?" Aubrey said. "But it's a crypt, so there must be."

"Like, in closed coffins though, right? Like in mausoleums?"

"I don't know."

Celeste came down the second step, joining Aubrey. "Only one way to find out."

Aubrey gripped the door, and it creaked like an old boat on troubled waters.

"Are we really doing this?" Marnie asked her sister.

Savannah almost looked like she was about to bail out, that she knew this was too much for Marnie and maybe even for herself. Instead, she sighed and walked to the lip of the stairway. Marnie slowly followed, looking all around, as if something in the woods was watching her.

Rose whispered to Bella. "I was gonna ask you the same thing. Are we really doing this?"

"It's just a game, right?" Bella said.

"If Aubrey's telling the truth about all this, how did she learn about it?"

"I don't know. That's just Aubrey. She's always telling us about urban legends and stuff."

"Yeah, right. She probably set this whole thing up as a prank. I'll bet she broke in there ahead of time and rigged the crypt with all sorts of things to scare us."

"I don't know . . . that doesn't seem like her."

"Why not?"

"You just don't know her. She takes things seriously. Like, to a fault."

"That doesn't mean she hasn't set up some sort of goth hazing or something."

Bella smirked. "Goth hazing? Are you being serious right now?"

"Are *you*? This whole thing is . . ."

Rose realized the others were watching them from down in the entryway. Aubrey's face glowed the fiercest, a hellfire tangerine among the huddled young girls.

"I mean," Rose whispered to Bella, "why is someone her age hanging out with high schoolers, anyway?"

Bella didn't have an answer for that. She stepped forward, motioning for Rose to join her.

"Just c'mon," Bella said. "The sooner we go in, the sooner we get out. I mean, she said it's just a game, right? Maybe it'll be fun."

Rose doubted that, but when Bella took her hand, she started walking.

"Besides," Bella said, "how bad can it be?"

FIVE

THE DOOR MADE A HORRIBLE sound as Aubrey pulled it
back, concrete scraping across concrete like nails on a chalkboard.
Over the years, the passageway must have compressed, Bella thought,
buckling as earth and gnarled roots grew over it in defiance of the
manmade structure. She and Rose brought up the rear of the group,
with Marnie in front of Bella, looking like a child lost in an amuse-
ment park's haunted house, her eyes even wider than before. They
were bug-like, almost too big for her face. Bella put her hand on the
girl's shoulder, and when Marnie turned to look at her, they shared a
nervous smile.

Bella mouthed the words, "It's okay."

The crypt creaked open in a chilling yawn. Blackness was all Bella
could see. She anticipated a foul odor but smelled nothing, the air
sterilized by winter's touch. No sounds of dripping water or scurrying
field mice—just a soft, hollow sound like a basement furnace. She
tasted something metallic upon the sepulture's air.

Aubrey raised her candle to the opening.

"Whoa," Celeste said.

But Bella couldn't see anything from where she stood. "What is it?"

"It's long."

"Long?"

Celeste looked back at her. "Come check this out."

Bella stepped between Savannah and Marnie. The sisters were frozen in place, and when Bella reached the doorway, she understood why. From the exterior, she'd expected the crypt to be a square room just big enough for the six of them to fit into. She'd imagined a dusty coffin on a pedestal, or empty slabs where caskets had once rested but had long ago been relocated to another graveyard. She expected empty beer cans and graffiti from others who'd had the bright idea to creep inside. But instead of four gray walls of concrete, what awaited them was not so much a room, but a tunnel.

Aubrey and Celeste stood side by side, their candles held high yet revealing nothing but the long black throat of the crypt. The walls were limestone packed with clay, the ground bare earth and pebbles. Though it was a cold night, the air inside the tunnel was colder. Bella frowned. This was less like a tomb and more like an abandoned mineshaft. To the end of the crypt and back wasn't going to be the cakewalk she'd imagined. Who knew how deep this hallway went or how treacherous it became?

Go back, she thought. *Rose is right. This is dangerous.*

But she couldn't run away. She couldn't humiliate herself in front of her friends, especially Aubrey, or be seen as no more mature than Marnie. If that happened, Celeste would be embarrassed by Bella and might not want to hang out anymore. Bella would find herself shunned by her fellow goths, making them yet another group she just couldn't fit in with. She couldn't take that kind of rejection, especially now that she'd finally started to feel she belonged. Regardless, she couldn't help but question the predicament.

"*This* is a crypt?" she asked.

Aubrey stared into the black abyss. "The crypt is probably at the end of this hallway."

"This looks more like a catacomb."

Celeste smiled, only half her face visible in the trembling light. "Hey, yeah. Like the ones beneath Paris. With the millions of skeletons and bones down there."

Marnie shivered. "You guys . . . I really don't think we should—"

"C'mon, Mar," Savannah said. "You said you wanted to come

27

along and I showed you how to sneak out of the house. Don't puss out on me."

"I'm not but . . . but . . ."

But you're scared of the dark, Bella thought. Under the circumstances, she could hardly blame the girl.

"Facing our fears is part of the game," Aubrey said.

With that, she took her first step inside. Her breath smoked in condensation before her and she wet her lips, her black lipstick glistening like vinyl. Celeste stepped in behind her, looking around excitedly, as if expecting stacked skulls and femurs. Savannah glanced at Marnie, a hint of doubt in her expression, then took her by the arm and gently ushered her on, whispering something Bella couldn't hear. When it was Bella's turn to follow, she turned to Rose. Her friend had been uncomfortably silent.

"Still think this might be fun?" Rose asked.

Bella didn't know what to say so she said nothing and walked through the doorway with her candle held out in front of her, as if that could save her if something went wrong. The delusion of invincibility that came with youth was absent. She felt entirely unprepared, having too little understanding of what she was in for. Hearing Rose sigh behind her, Bella followed Savannah and Marnie, the hallway just big enough for the girls to walk in pairs. The sudden sound of concrete scraping made her turn back with a start, but it was just Rose securing the broken piece of plywood in the door jamb, a precaution to keep it open. Bella hadn't thought about that. What if the door shut on them and they couldn't get it open again? What if someone came and sealed it back up with them inside?

"Rose . . ." she said.

Her best friend looked at her with a hint of disappointment.

Before they could say anything, Celeste called out. "Holy shit! This just keeps going!"

The combined light of the candles illuminated the limestone channel, revealing a descending slope. Bella swallowed hard. The tunnel wasn't a lateral passage. They were going deeper, down into the earth, down into the cemetery grounds. Into *the realm of the dead*.

"Rose . . ."

Rose came beside her, crouching to fit inside the shaft. Bella had never seen a better example of resting bitch face.

"What, Bella?" Rose said, irritated. "Either this is important to you, or it isn't. I'm only here for you, you know."

"I . . . I know. I appreciate it."

"C'mon then. We need to keep up with the others."

She took Bella by the arm just as Savannah had done with Marnie—a total big sister move, though Bella was a little older. Rose had set her mind to seeing this through, an act of stubborn headstrongness. Whenever faced with an obstacle or confrontation, another Rose Peterson emerged, a powerhouse that dominated the basketball court as well as the SATs, like a rodeo bull going into overdrive the moment the gate was unlatched. They were in this now, and Rose intended to finish it, if only to prove some sort of point.

Side by side, they followed the others as they descended the incline, watching their steps. Even in combat boots, Bella felt insecure. The slope didn't form any set of stairs, only dropped at an angle that grew steeper as they progressed. They put their hands on the walls for balance, falling hush as they focused. When one of them slowed, the others did too, the group tightknit in support of each other and keeping the combined light going strong. Even Aubrey, who prided herself on being independent, stayed close to the pack as she led the way.

The hollow sound grew louder, the white noise of the concavity like a bowling ball endlessly rolling down some faraway lane. The tunnel grew narrow, walls inching inward, the ceiling dropping closer to their heads.

"This must've been a slide," Aubrey said.

"No way," Savannah said.

"I don't mean like a playground slide. I mean a shoot for transporting bodies. Just a sled and some rope and they'd be good to go."

"Sled of the dead?" Celeste said, snickering.

"It'd be the easiest way to get them down to the crypt. Usually tombs are for whole families, so a new body would have been brought in whenever another relative died. They could bring them in easier with gravity lending a hand."

Bella expected a rebuttal from Rose, her being a living encyclopedia, but she was too preoccupied with walking in a crouch, like an adult in a child's fort. But under the surface of Rose's irritation, Bella detected a growing curiosity. Though claustrophobic, the dark tunnel offered a mystery that felt forbidden, making their passage more enthralling than the mere prospect of winning some game. The goal now was to find out where this underground channel would really take them.

Marnie suddenly shrieked as she lost her footing. She clawed at the wall but managed to hold on to her candle as Rose swooped in behind her, keeping her from hitting the ground. The commotion caused Celeste to look back, and in doing so she nearly knocked Aubrey over. The girls braced themselves, barely avoiding a domino effect on the unsteady surface.

"Thanks," Marnie told Rose, trying to hide the tremor in her voice.

Bella dusted off the back of the girl's coat, brushing away twigs and dirt and a few short, black hairs she took to be Savannah's. Marnie grasped her sister for balance and the group carried on, a pilgrimage of intruders.

"I feel like Lara Croft," Celeste said. "You know, the chick from *Tomb Raider*?"

"I feel like I'm in *Stranger Things*," Marnie said, sounding none too happy about it.

"Or *The Goonies*," Rose added. "Old school reference but my dad loves that movie. Made me watch it a hundred times when I was little. It's pretty good."

The slope leveled off and the tunnel widened, leading into a small alcove with smooth, rounded walls, as if cared for by a potter's hands. But the combined light of the candles wasn't enough to reveal what lay beyond this room. All Bella could see were dead leaves on the ground and rectangular shadows pressed like monoliths against the limestone.

Coffins, she thought with a chill. But the shadows were too tall and wide to be caskets.

There was something here she'd not felt since they'd gone underground—a draft. Her cheeks blushed against the cold, nose going damp. When she sniffed, she detected a subtle musk. Celeste entered the alcove, Aubrey just a step behind her. It almost seemed as if she were letting Celeste go first on purpose, and Bella thought of what Rose had said about this being a trick set up by Aubrey to frighten them. To Bella, it seemed more likely Aubrey was allowing Celeste to go first as a precaution, protecting herself. She was convinced Aubrey was telling the truth about not having been down here before. It showed in hesitations such as this, and besides, who would be crazy enough to come down here alone?

"Holy shit," Celeste said, her candle held high to examine what lay beyond the alcove. "Holy, holy shit."

When Aubrey joined Celeste and raised her candle, the combined light caused the large, rectangular shadows to jump and pulse, revealing they were more than crevices in the limestone. When the girls aimed the candlelight toward the black monoliths, the shapes did not reveal themselves, but instead only deepened, their darkness becoming more pronounced.

"You've gotta be fuckin' kidding," Savannah said.

The girls stood before the mouths of three more tunnels like the one they'd just emerged from, placing them at a subterraneous crossroads.

Bella gulped. "Is this part of the game?"

Everyone looked to Aubrey. She eyed the passages with cautious curiosity.

"This is where we turn back, right?" Rose asked. "We reached the end, and now we race back."

"But this isn't the end of the crypt," Celeste argued. "Look at all these different hallways."

"They must all lead back up to the graveyard," Rose replied, "just like the tunnel we came in through. More corpse slides, right, Aubrey?"

This got Aubrey's attention. She veered from the black gateways to address the others.

"This must be a starting point," she said.

Bella furrowed her brow. "What're you talking about?"

Aubrey outstretched her arms, the chains of her coat jangling as she gestured to the surrounding tunnels. "We each choose a path. Whoever makes it back to the cemetery first is The Prettiest Girl in the Grave."

A sheet of ice folded over Bella's heart. She should be at home. She and Rose should be watching a movie on the sofa with jars of edible cookie dough. They should be anywhere but down here, doing anything but this. Even a double date with Tyson and his lame buddy Colin would do.

"But there's six of us," Savannah said, "and only four tunnels."

"Right," Aubrey said. "We can choose if we want company or go it alone."

"Why would anyone want to be alone down here?" Marnie asked, hugging herself.

Aubrey's devilish grin resurfaced. "Less competition."

"Aubrey . . ." Bella said, not liking the direction this was going.

"This is a bad idea," Rose told the group. "We don't know where any of these tunnels go, except the one we came through. I say we play it safe and go back, together."

"Yeah," Marnie said. "Rose is right."

Aubrey arched her eyebrows. "You can take whatever path you choose. But one of these other tunnels may be a shorter, easier way back. The walk down this way was pretty steep. You nearly lost your balance, Marnie. Going back up that way will be even more difficult."

"At least it won't hold any surprises," Rose said.

"C'mon," Celeste said. "We haven't even seen anything good yet. This is a crypt. Bodies must be down here somewhere—the coffins, the bones, the skulls. Ain't that what we're really here to see? What the game really wants us to face—our own mortality?"

Rose shook her head, flabbergasted. "Gee, Celeste, you make it sound like so much fun, but I think I can do without it."

"We've come this far. We can't go back the way we came now like a bunch of pussies."

Rose stepped toward Celeste and Bella took her by the arm. No one else noticed the wrangling, but Rose locked eyes with Bella. Her patience had worn thin.

"I'm going back the way we came," Rose said.

Bella glanced at the others. If she chose to go with Rose, would she damage her reputation? But if she didn't, would the last remaining knot holding she and Rose's friendship together finally give?

Marnie told her sister, "I wanna go with Rose."

"Oh, of course you do," Savannah said, rolling her eyes.

"C'mon, Vanna, don't be like that."

"Well, I'm with Aubrey. I say we explore the other options." She stepped toward one of the gateways. "Like Celeste said—we haven't even seen anything cool yet. I mean, where's the tomb?"

"Well, I don't wanna see anything," Marnie said firmly, surprising everyone by taking a stand. "I wanna go home. I don't like it down here, Vanna. It's too creepy and—"

A sudden sound cut her off. Everyone fell silent as the noise rose out of the gateway the sisters stood before. It was a low groan, like a cow mooing.

"Oh shit," Rose said.

The look on her face told Bella her friend recognized the sound, but before Rose could share that information a dark shape charged out of the darkness, growling, separate from the previous animal sound. At first, Bella thought it was a large dog, like a Rottweiler or Mastiff. But it was just too big. And it was coming right at the sisters.

Savannah screamed, retreating from the gateway as the black bear bolted out of the shadows. Bella turned to run. Rose grabbed her.

"Don't run! You have to—"

If only Marnie had taken this advice. Terrified, she turned her back on the bear, legs pumping, causing it to chase her. As it leapt through the dark, Bella saw two sets of little eyes in the shadows behind it.

Cubs, she realized. *We stumbled upon their den and got too close to a Mama bear and her cubs.*

Normally, black bears were shy and secretive, steering clear of people. Unlike grizzlies, they rarely attacked humans. But like wolves, they grew agitated when their den was trespassed upon, and mother bears could go on offense if they felt their cubs were in danger.

The bear made a mock charge and Marnie cried out, further frightening it. The sow emitted a blowing sound and suddenly pounced on the girl. Outweighing her by at least seventy pounds, the sow took her down with ease. Celeste had gone pale, backing against the wall, shaking so hard she dropped her candle. It rolled into the narrow tunnel behind her. Rose opened her coat to look as large as possible and started shouting, trying to scare the bear off. Bella copied her. Aubrey backed toward one of the other gateways, keeping her eyes on the sow as she attempted a slow, subtle escape. Marnie was slammed on her stomach, shrieking as the bear bounced upon her back. Bella cringed at the sound of something breaking within the poor girl. The bear swung its paw, ripping into Marnie's thighs and buttocks. Bits of flesh glistened wet in the candlelight.

Savannah had run into one of the tunnels, but seeing her sister attacked, she turned back to help, going right at the bear with equal parts courage and stupidity. Despite their differences, Savannah instinctually tried to rescue her sibling. She kicked the sow in its side and it turned its wrath on her, swiping and ripping through Savannah's clothing, drawing blood from her leg. Savannah stumbled but did not fall, but when the bear came at her again, it bashed into her knees hard enough to drop her.

Rose jumped up and down, screeching, trying to drive the bear off. Bella threw her candle at the sow but failed to hurt it, so she took up a fistful of rocks and started chucking them at the bear's head. Celeste was frozen. Aubrey had slunk away into the camouflage of the corridor. Marnie crawled, steaming blood sousing her jeans. In a frenzy uncommon to its species, the black bear chomped down on the top of Savannah's skull. She screamed as her eyes filled with blood. The mother bear shook its head back and forth with Savannah still in its mouth, and Bella feared it may snap her neck.

"Play dead!" Rose cried.

But Savannah was in a panic, screaming. "It's killing me! It's killing me!"

Bella winced at the sound of fangs scraping skullcap. Grabbing a baseball-sized rock, she threw it at the bear as hard as she could, smacking it in the snout. It huffed and released Savannah. She hit the ground with a wet thud, sounding like a snapping twig. The sow made a mock charge, a mist of its victim's blood coming off its breath. Bella felt a hand on her arm, drawing her into the tunnel.

"Move!" Aubrey said, pulling on her.

They had no choice now. Rose gripped Celeste by the shoulders and shook her to snap her out of her trance. The four girls ran down the tunnel opposite the furious bear. It was the quickest escape, but not the tunnel they'd come in through. They charged into this black oblivion with only two candles to light their way, and Bella was grateful for the echoes of their pounding footsteps, for they drowned out the sisters' cries for help.

SIX

HOLLY SHOT UP IN BED.

Sweat stuck her flannel to her back and she gripped the covers with both hands, knuckles white as chalk. Her heart made a machine gun staccato. She gasped in deep, greedy breaths, as if she'd been suffocating in her sleep.

Bella, she thought.

Though she couldn't remember details from the nightmare, her daughter's face hovered in her mind in a disembodied phantom. She reached for the glass on the nightstand, thinking it was water, and got a mouthful of lukewarm wine. The sour shock at least helped wake her up. Flinging off the covers, she turned on the bedside lamp and got out of bed, the carpet between her toes having a calming effect, bringing her back to reality. Out of the corner of her eye, she noticed the time on the nightstand's digital clock. The red glow of the numbers seemed suddenly menacing, like demon eyes coming open in the dark.

1:47 a.m.

Bella was supposed to wake Holly up to let her know she'd gotten home safely. It was now almost an hour past her curfew. Had she forgotten to check in before going to sleep? Had she come into her mother's bedroom without Holly registering it?

Holly stepped into her slippers. She always lowered the heat at night to save on oil, and she shivered now in the chill. Putting on her robe, she came out into the hall, and an image ripped from her nightmare flashed across her consciousness. It was a painfully familiar scene—a seemingly infinite hallway of pitch-black shadow, cold and damp, with a sound like a distant tornado rising from the dead bowels of the lair. Holly winced against the mental image and walked down the hallway to her daughter's room.

She rapped on the door. "Bella?"

No response. Holly turned the knob and stepped inside. With the curtains drawn, no outside light could permeate the dark, and she thought again of the subterraneous channels that haunted her dreams.

"Bella? Are you in there?"

Her choice of words gave her goose-pimples. The simple phrase was swollen with trauma, and it surprised her she would put them together again. She was suddenly too afraid to step into her daughter's room. A foul imagining of a rotting corpse stretched out on the bed tore across Holly's mind and she flicked on the light switch. The room revealed itself, soft and void of monsters.

And without Bella.

The bed was unmade, but it always was so that didn't mean she'd recently been in it. Holly touched the pillow. Cool. She headed downstairs. Perhaps the late curfew had been a mistake. The living room was empty, the only light in the kitchen coming from the range hood above the oven. She called her daughter's name as she walked through the house, even checking the adjacent garage. Glancing up at the door to the attic above the garage, she shook her head at her own ridiculousness, knowing her daughter never went up there. Even Justin avoided it. Holly went back into the house and headed upstairs for her phone. No missed calls or texts. Surely if Bella was running late, she would have let Holly know. She knew better than to make her mother worry, for it was all too easy to do. The mental image of a maggot-riddled dead body returned to Holly, and this time it resembled Bella.

Holly cursed her own mind.

She dialed and the line rang twice before Bella picked up. She didn't greet her. All Holly could hear was a hollow thrum, like a basement furnace broiling.

Her mouth went dry. "Bella? Hello?"

There was a faint voice, indecipherable. The steady thrum returned, unrelenting as the call dropped.

"Bella!"

Holly redialed, pacing, sweating. This time the phone just rang, not even going to Bella's voicemail. Holly texted her, demanding she call as soon as she got the message. The text tried to load but failed. She moved about the house in hope of a better signal, but the messages continued to error.

"Shit!" she said, tossing the phone aside. She resisted the urge to smash the goddamned thing. It was her only lifeline to her daughter.

That sound, she thought, hands trembling. *That furnace sound. That tornado sound.*

The sound of her nightmares.

The call of the grave.

SEVEN

THE TUNNEL WASN'T A STRAIGHT shot like the one they'd come in through. It had twists and turns and the ground beneath them was treacherous with potholes, cracks, and jutting stones. Rose nearly tripped, trying to keep a slower pace with the less athletic girls. They darted by a passage branching off from the one they were in, a small corridor low to the ground supported by bowing wooden buttresses. When they reached another alcove, they were faced with three different passageways. They didn't stop for debate, only ran on, Aubrey and Rose lighting the way. Bella occasionally grabbed the tail of Rose's jacket to keep her close. Celeste was bawling.

It just doesn't make sense, Rose thought. Black bear attacks were extremely rare, and even when they did come at people, it was almost entirely a show with little to no violence. Even around their cubs, mother black bears didn't behave as viciously as grizzlies, but this sow had gone on a rampage. Rose told herself they'd done everything they could to help but wasn't sure that was true. Already guilt was chasing her like her own shadow. They'd had no choice but to run for their lives, right? Despite their numbers, they were unarmed and incapable of fighting a *bear*. How long would it battle them before retreating? Would they have had to go so far as to kill the sow before it would stop? It was unnatural, and yet it was real. Rose had seen the bear's rage firsthand. Why had it been so aggressive?

Rabies, Rose thought. But if she remembered correctly, that was another rarity when it came to black bears. What the hell was going on?

All they could hope for now was that the sow would tire of attacking the sisters and back off without mauling them to death. It was more likely than not, at least with a *normal* black bear. They had to get help, but they had no idea where they were. They were running blind, more focused on putting distance between them and the mad sow than really looking for a way out. If they weren't careful, they might become lost in a death labyrinth, running deeper beneath the earth until they were buried in this cemetery along with the corpses.

A buzzing startled her. Bella drew her vibrating phone from her pocket.

"It's my mom!" she said.

The group stopped, catching their breath as Bella picked up the call.

"Mom? Hello? Mom, are you there?"

Standing beside Bella, Rose heard waves of static on the line, roaring louder until Bella had to pull the phone away from her ear. Then the call dropped.

"Shit," Bella said with defeat.

Everyone drew their phones. Rose dialed 911 and turned on the flashlight feature. The light worked, but she couldn't get the call to go through.

"Any luck?" Rose asked the others.

They shook their heads. With the torches lit, Rose suggested they blow out the candles to conserve them. She didn't want to admit it, but they might be down here long enough to need them again. Dawn would mean nothing, for the sun doesn't shine in a crypt. Turning on their phone flashlights, Celeste's face was streaked with mascara tears and Aubrey appeared ghostly and wan, as if she'd lost ten pounds since they'd started running.

"What're we gonna do?" Celeste asked.

"We've gotta get out of here," Rose said. She explained what she hoped would happen with the sisters and the bear, but stressed they needed to get help. "We seem to have lost the mama bear now. Let's look for other doors or any signs of moonlight to point a way out."

"We need weapons," Aubrey said, her eyes vacant. "I mean, what if that wasn't the only bear down here. What if there's a bigger male one or whole families of them?"

"Don't say that," Bella said.

"All we have are rocks," Rose said, stooping to pick some up and loading them into her coat pockets. "Just don't weigh yourselves down too much."

"We need to do better than rocks," Aubrey said.

"Yeah? How?"

Aubrey looked back the way they'd come. "We passed by a little tunnel back there, low to the ground, like someone had dug it out with a shovel. I saw buttresses in there, bracing it so it wouldn't collapse. Maybe we can break some of them off, so we'll have wooden stakes."

Rose exhaled. "I don't know. That might not be so easy to do. Besides, a piece of wood won't do much in the face of another bear attack."

"But it's better than nothing, right?"

The desperation in Aubrey's eyes humbled the woman, her *daughter of darkness* routine all but obliterated by the very real danger they were in. This wasn't a goth horror show. This was true darkness, true morbidity. It stripped people of their vanities, whittling down egos in the name of survival. Rose could work with this version of Aubrey.

"I don't wanna backtrack," Celeste said. "What if that fucking bear is hunting us?"

"It's not," Rose said.

"You don't know that."

Everyone looked to Bella, waiting for her vote.

"Oh," Bella said, as if just coming awake. "Um. Okay. Let's go get the stakes. We need a way to protect ourselves. I mean, who knows what else might be down here."

The girls turned back down the tunnel, Celeste opting to stick with the group despite her objections. Now that they weren't running and had their phone flashlights, Rose was better able to inspect their surroundings. This tunnel had a taller ceiling, which made it easier for her to move around. The eroded stone walls sparkled with dew, the occasional root stretching like a river through the fractured granite— the veins of the earth.

What was this place? It wasn't like any crypt she'd ever seen—

though now that she thought about it, she'd never actually seen a crypt except in scary movies. Maybe this really was a sort of catacomb. But if so, wouldn't more people know about it? Wouldn't it be an interesting bit of local history?

"Hey, Aubrey," Rose said. "How did you know about this place?"

Bella interrupted before Aubrey could answer. "You guys, look!" She pointed at a silvery slab sticking out of the wall. Directing her flashlight upon it, Bella stepped closer, leading the others. "I almost didn't realize what these scratches were. We went right past it without noticing."

Rose squinted as she approached the slab. Words were jaggedly etched into the slick surface, as if by a knife. Aubrey read them aloud.

"'Some girls are fearful, others are brave. One girl's a princess, the next one, a slave. But all girls are equal, when they're down in this cave, until just one is left standing—The Prettiest Girl in the Grave.'"

Staring at the rhyme, a sour taste climbed Bella's throat. Beneath the crudely etched words was a darker, more finely sculpted image, as if made by a branding iron—the face of a black bear. The word "*Goldman*" was expertly engraved above it in an arched plate.

"What the fuck is this, you guys?" Celeste asked, voice trembling.

Bella turned her light away from the slab. "Just forget it. Sorry I pointed it out. I thought it might tell us a way out of here."

Aubrey whispered something under her breath. It sounded like, "Maybe it did." Bella pretended she hadn't heard it.

"What is that?" Rose asked. She drew closer to the strange shrine and shined her phone light on something small and white with blackened edges. "It looks like . . ."

"It's just a fucking pebble," Celeste said.

"No, look." Rose gingerly picked it up with two fingers and turned it over. "It's a tooth. A human tooth."

Bella's skin pimpled. Rose was right. What she held was a human incisor.

"Let's just get the wood," Bella said.

Rose dropped the tooth and the girls walked in silence. The poem had added to their trepidation. Bella found herself looking over her shoulder, suddenly worried they were being watched. Not by a black bear, but by something more intelligent and, perhaps, more dangerous. She told herself it was just nerves, but rationalizing failed to calm her. Anyone could have carved that rhyme into the slab. A screwdriver or nail file would do the trick. But the image of the bear required something more advanced, not to mention artistic skill. Had it been part of a headstone, maybe belonging to some great hunter named Goldman? Could it be a lost antique or artifact?

"That can't be a coincidence," Celeste said. "That bear plaque and the bear that attacked us have to be connected somehow, right?"

"It *is* a coincidence," Rose said. "An eerie one, but a coincidence."

"No way. Aubrey, Bella—you guys don't believe that, do you?"

Bella wasn't sure what she believed. She was still processing all that had happened—what was *still happening.*

"There it is," Aubrey said, pointing out the low tunnel carved into the base of a wall, dodging Celeste's question.

She crouched before it with Rose beside her, illuminating the shaft. It reminded Bella of a manhole, only horizontal, a dirt passage just wide enough for someone to crawl through on their belly, the tunnel supported by a flimsy frame of splintering wooden buttresses. Cobwebs stretched from side to side like curtains of cheesecloth, suggesting the passage hadn't been used in many years, at least not by humans. Mouse droppings were scattered upon the ground like burnt rice. The shed skin of a small snake was pressed against a bowing chunk of timber.

"How're we gonna get these stakes out?" Bella asked.

"We'll just have to force them," Aubrey said, reaching for the closest one. "Just yank them and—"

Rose stopped her. "Careful. Any one of these could be bearing the bulk of the load."

"We'll have to go slow and do one at a time. Make sure it doesn't fall down on us."

"One at a time?"

"Well, yeah. We'll have to get in there to get the rest."

"Are you nuts? Let's just grab the ones right here at the edge. That way, if it falls apart, we're safe out here."

"But that won't give us much. We need more than two stakes to arm four people."

Rose gaped. "You're telling me you're going to *crawl in that hole?*"

Aubrey's eyes were vacant, and yet they hardened, as if she were growing angry at a dream. She opened her mouth as if to speak, but then seemed to decide better of it. Handing her candle to Bella, she got low until she was flat on the ground and extended her phone into the tunnel for a closer look.

"It'll be like crawling through an air vent," Bella said. "Like in a movie."

"Only filled with bugs and mice and God knows what else," Rose argued. "Aubrey, it's just not worth it."

But Aubrey was undeterred. She scooted on her belly toward the opening and gave the front buttresses a nudge. When they held, she started crawling inside, her phone clutched tight in one hand to light her way, her other hand tucked into her coat sleeve as she batted away the webs and debris. Bold actions like this were what drew Bella to Aubrey. The young woman didn't cower away from things most people feared. Instead, she plunged headfirst into them—in this case, literally. The tunnel was dark and claustrophobic, a grave unto itself, and yet Aubrey slithered into it as if it were a sleeping bag.

"If something happens," Aubrey said, "just pull me out fast."

Bella had the sudden mental image of Aubrey screaming from within the tunnel, the others trying to drag her out only to come away with two bloody, amputated feet, like in some cartoonish horror film.

"C'mon, Aubrey," Bella said. "Just forget it, okay? C'mon out."

A sudden pounding made Bella flinch. Aubrey was trying to break a buttress free. The distinct crackle of snapping wood followed, and a foot and a half stake of rotted timber was tossed out of the hole. So far, the tunnel held. Bella expected Aubrey to withdraw. Instead, she went deeper, her calves vanishing into the webbed shadows of this hole in the earth. The pounding began again, more determined than before. Bits of dirt rained down from the tunnel's ceiling.

"Get out of there!" Bella said.

But the tunnel held and Aubrey continued her foraging, another two stakes pushed back to the other girls. Looking at the greenish chunks of timber, Bella thought the risk Aubrey was taking outweighed the spoils. Rose was right. Any one of these buttresses could be the primary load bearer, any one of them the trigger to burying Aubrey alive.

"Okay," Bella said. "That's plenty."

"Yeah," Rose said into the tunnel. "We'll yank these front ones out from here."

Aubrey didn't reply. She also didn't start hammering her fist at another stake. She'd gone still, silent. Her feet were slack in their boots, the only parts of her they could see anymore. Celeste came closer, the three girls huddling around the tunnel.

"Aubrey?" Celeste said, whispering for some reason. "You okay?"

No reply. Bella's stomach went tight.

"Aubrey!" Rose called out.

Bella rarely saw this look of fright on Rose's face. Her friend was too strong in mind, body, and spirit to succumb to a fear that could not be named, but in this underground crypt, the unknown was even more threatening than the very real dangers of bears and getting lost. Down here, what they didn't know was their greatest enemy. Bella had felt an ominous presence in the necropolis. Now it seemed Rose felt it too. And still Aubrey wouldn't move or make a sound.

Grabbing one ankle, Bella shook Aubrey's leg. It twitched. Rose grabbed the other leg, and together they pulled back, dragging Aubrey through the dirt and out of the tunnel. Her body trembled beneath their helping hands, and once they got her on her back Bella realized why she'd gone mute. She and Rose flinched, taking their hands off Aubrey and scooting back. Aubrey's chest rose and fell with stunted breath, her fingernails digging into the earth, eyes wide and unblinking as the spider crawled higher up her neck.

It was the size of a man's hand, with a red abdomen swollen like a water balloon. The legs were black and furry like a tarantula's, but excessively long like a Japanese crab's. Glistening like fresh drops of blood, its twelve eyes reflected the light from Bella's phone. The spider reacted to the glow, turning its wooly head toward her, its chelicerae out, flashing rows of black fangs. It elongated as it crept up Aubrey's neck, its front legs touching down upon her face. She remained silent and motionless so not to rouse the arachnid. Only her eyes communicated, telling the others: *Get it off me.*

Bella wasn't sure what type of spider it even was. She'd never seen one so large and freakish. Even if it weren't venomous, judging by the chelicerae its bite would be vicious.

"Oh shit . . ." Rose whispered at the sight of it.

The monster crawled a little higher, one leg landing just below Aubrey's right eye. She dared not even shut them for fear of startling the spider.

Celeste picked up one of the wooden stakes and raised it high over her head.

"No, wait!" Bella said in a whisper.

But Celeste had already made up her mind. She swung the stake like a golf club, and Bella forgot to breathe as the wood grazed the spider but failed to knock it off Aubrey. It went into a state of taut readiness, like a cornered cat, perching halfway over Aubrey's chin. She shut her eyes tight and suppressed a scream. Before the others could react, Celeste swung again, tilting her aim in an attempt to crush the spider rather than swat it away. The spider leapt onto Aubrey's face just as the stake came at it, its abdomen ballooning.

"No . . ." Bella said, realizing too late.

The crimson bulb of flesh burst, the top of the spider's abdomen splitting from the bottom as the stake cleaved it in two. The sack opened and a swarm of unborn infant spiders scattered in every direction, like ants on a hill hit by a mower. There were dozens of them. They scattered across Aubrey's head, going for cover in her ears and nostrils and spilling into her screaming mouth. She shot up and shucked the mother spider off her. Its legs curled inward in death. Aubrey spit and snorted out the babies that had found their way into her, frantically digging her fingernails into her ears. More babies had fallen down her neck and into her blouse, and she swatted at her chest. When Celeste went to help her, Aubrey shoved her hard against the wall.

"Don't touch me!"

Celeste backed away. "I'm sorry, Aubrey, I was just—"

Aubrey bent over. Bella went to her side with the light from her phone, and Aubrey was more willing to accept her help. Bella held the light close to Aubrey's face and helped brush away the tiny arachnids, but Aubrey had both hands at her right eye.

"Hold my hair!" she said, still bent over.

The others gathered around to give them light as Aubrey pulled back her bottom eyelid with her right hand, and deftly dug in with her left index finger. Bella winced.

"Oh my God . . ." Rose muttered.

"I can feel it in there," Aubrey said, matter-of-factly.

"If only we had some water," Bella said. She remembered the bottle in Celeste's coat. But even if they dumped out the vodka, they had no source of clean water to fill it with.

Aubrey dug her fingernail deeper under her eyelid, tears running as she dared not blink for fear of losing the spider inside her skull. A different one flitted through Aubrey's hair and Bella flicked it away, though it seemed insignificant now, as did all the others. Aubrey slowly tilted her head to one side, as if she could roll the spider free.

"I see it!" Rose said. She came in close, putting her phone's light in Aubrey's face. "Don't move."

Bella saw it too—a black dot like a second pupil near the corner of Aubrey's bloodshot eye. Rose assessed the predicament. The spider shifted and Aubrey winced, causing the other girls to wince in sympathy. She raised her hand to go digging again, but Rose took her wrist.

"Don't," she said. "You'll drive it in deeper."

"It burns . . ."

Rose handed her phone to Celeste. "Hold the light on her eye. And Aubrey, just hold still, okay?"

Rose stood directly in front of Aubrey, moved in close, and gently took her head in her hands. She tilted it slightly, so the right side of Aubrey's face was just beneath Rose's chin. Celeste and Bella lit them from both sides, casting Aubrey in a spectral glow and making Rose's blonde hair shine like hay in the summer sun, adding another layer of unreality to the situation. Rose leaned in as if to kiss Aubrey. Her mouth opened and her tongue came out, but instead of going for Aubrey's black lips, she went for the bloodshot eye. The tip of her tongue made contact, slowly licking the surface of Aubrey's eye until it felt the foreign object.

"Holy shit," Celeste whispered.

Rose withdrew and spat out the spider, still holding Aubrey's head in her hands. The intimacy surprised Bella, especially when it was reciprocated by Aubrey, who wrapped her arms around Rose and brought her in for a hug, burying her face into her shoulder.

EIGHT

HOLLY WANTED TO GO TO the police, but of course she couldn't do that. Besides, what would she possibly tell them? She could be overacting. Maybe it was just static on the line before the call dropped, the horrible thrumming just a mental fragment left over from her dream. That made the most sense, didn't it? Bella must have damaged her phone. Maybe she'd gotten it wet, like the time she'd dropped her old one in the toilet. Or maybe she was just out of range. But how likely would that be in this modern age? Cellphone towers were everywhere. The only place you might lose a signal was . . .

In the mountains.

Clenching her fist around the phone, Holly tried calling Rose. It only rang, not even going to voicemail. Holly sighed as she opened her list of contacts to the rest of the Peterson family. It'd been a long time. Would their numbers still be the same? And who should she call first, Trisha or Sawyer? What would her choice suggest? What message would it send?

You're overthinking it. This is about our daughters.

She chose to put aside what would make her the most comfortable

47

and placed a call mother to mother. Trisha's line rang three times, then abruptly went to voicemail, as if the call had been manually disregarded. The recorded greeting caused Holly to sit down. That she was hearing Trisha Peterson's voice—even just as a recording—seemed like a bad omen. If it had already come to this, what greater struggles would she have to face tonight? When the tone chimed for her to leave a message, Holly panicked and hung up. She stepped out of her sweatpants and into a pair of jeans. She wouldn't bother changing shirts but needed layers and winter socks. She knew she was getting ahead of herself. She was leaping past a step and stalling at the same time.

Holly opened her contacts again. She selected Sawyer Peterson. No photo in the icon, just his initials big and white against the gray. Her thumb hovered over the call button.

"Screw it."

She pressed and the line started ringing. Pacing, Holly clutched her hair, twirling it nervously like a teen girl calling her crush. The line stopped ringing, and she almost hung up, expecting voicemail, but then heard him clear his throat.

"Holly?" Sawyer asked, sounding just as surprised as she was that she was calling.

She had to reply, so she just went for it. "Hi, Sawyer. Hi. Yeah, it's Holly. I'm so sorry to call you this late."

"Is everything okay?" His voice went up. "Are the girls . . .?"

"That's what I was going to ask you. Bella hasn't come home yet. Has Rose?"

"Shit," he sighed.

Holly heard rustling sheets and mattress springs. A woman mumbled something—*Trisha.*

"Hold on one sec, Holly," Sawyer said.

He cupped the phone so his conversation with his wife was a muffled secret. Holly wondered why he would bother. Force of habit?

"I'm going to her room now," he said when he came back on the line. "Trish says Rose went out with Bella, but . . ."

"She did. But Bella was supposed to be home by now. Maybe they fell asleep in her room?"

Holly wanted to believe that though she knew it wasn't the case. More so, she wanted Sawyer to believe it was possible. She needed him to stay calmer than she was. She heard him knock on his daughter's door and call her name, then the sound of creaking hinges.

"They're not here," he said. "And Rose's car isn't in the driveway. Must be running late. You trying calling her?"

No, Sawyer. I called you first. Idiot.

"Of course I did. The line just goes to voicemail. So does Rose's."

She could almost hear Sawyer's expression harden. Rose was the easiest sort of daughter parents could have, but that didn't mean a father didn't worry. She'd just never given him much cause to.

"Let me try her and I'll call you back," he said.

Holly agreed, but already had her car keys in hand. Like always when she left the house, she stuffed a pocketknife into her jeans.

~

A row of red and green Christmas lights hung from the gutters of the Peterson house, blinking on and off. Holly had no doubt as to which of them decided to put the stupid things up. She got out of her car and approached the front door, hunching her shoulders against the late night cold. Trisha stepped into the front doorway in her robe and slippers. Though it was the middle of the night, she had makeup on. She'd obviously brushed her hair too. If she was trying to look good just for Holly, she'd succeeded.

"Holly," she said, flashing her Colgate grin. "How's it going?"

If it was going good, I wouldn't be here, Holly thought. "Going okay. Just need to find out where the girls are."

"Of course. Don't worry. I'm sure they're fine. They're responsible girls, and smart enough to stay out of trouble."

Holly couldn't help but feel what Trisha really meant was Rose was the responsible one, and Bella was safe as long as she was with the golden child.

"Listen," Trisha said, "I'm sorry I sent your call right to voicemail. It's a new phone, and I didn't recognize the number. Luckily, Sawyer still had you in his contacts."

Holly quickly brought them back to why she was here. "Did Rose mention where they were going tonight?"

Trisha shrugged. "Not really. Please, come inside."

Holly hesitated at the doorway, but it would be weird for her to stand out there in the cold. She came into the living room and tried not to look at the sofa. Trisha offered to take her coat.

"Thanks, but I won't be staying long."

A shadow lumbered in the kitchen doorway. He was just as tall and rugged as she remembered. Rose had taken after him when it came to height. Sawyer was like a mountain man with his shaggy, gray beard and broad shoulders. He wore sweatpants and an old flannel, similar to Holly's pajamas. His shirtsleeves were rolled up, showcasing his thick forearms and the rose tattoo he'd gotten the day his daughter was born.

"Hey, Holly."

To her surprise, he stepped in for a hug. The feeling of his body pressed into her own stirred something within her, something long lost but not forgotten. She placed her hands on his back, something she'd thought she'd never do again.

"Nice to see you," he said. "Wish it was under better circumstances."

"Nice to see you too." And, despite everything, it was. "Sorry to just show up like this but—"

"No need to apologize. We understand."

"That's right," Trisha said, a little less convincing. "I just wish we had something more to tell you."

"Did you try calling her again?" Holly asked. "Maybe from a different phone?"

Sawyer nodded. "Yeah. The girls must be out of range if both their phones can't be reached."

"But where could they be that wouldn't have service?"

"Maybe the lookout?"

It was a scenic view along Old Mill Road overlooking the valley below Black Mountain. Sawyer referencing it made Holly shift uncomfortably. Was he mentioning the place on purpose? Obviously, they shared the same memory of parking there together that first time. She recalled unbuttoning his shirt and running her fingers through his chest hair, and how the natural smell of him lured her in like a bass on a hook. His hands had pressed against her cheeks, pulling her in for that initial forbidden kiss, the first of many.

Trisha chuckled. "I doubt they went to that old lover's lane, honey."

Though Trisha remained oblivious to the affair Holly once had with her husband, hearing her talk of lovers flooded her with a nauseating dread.

"It's not just a lover's lane," Sawyer told his wife. "When I was a kid, me and the boys used to hang out there at night for lack of anything better to do."

"I know. Isn't that where you got busted with that baggie of pot?" she said, teasing. "Good thing you were seventeen and it didn't go on your permanent record."

Sawyer smirked and gave Holly a wink. "Kids today have it easy. Cops can't hassle 'em as much over a joint anymore. At least not in New England."

"Well," Holly said, breaking the small talk, "I'm going out to look for the girls. I'll check the . . . um . . ." She had trouble saying it. "You know—the lookout. Please call me if you're able to get through to Rose."

"Will do," Trisha said. "But really, I'm sure they're fine. They're big girls now. They can take care of themselves."

How could Trisha be so cavalier? Yes, the girls were eighteen, but they were still their babies. And it wasn't like them to not come home on time or leave their parents to worry. They were out in the night somewhere, unable to call for help if they needed it.

As Holly turned to go, Sawyer touched her arm—physical contact that made Holly's lonely body grow warm despite her emotional objection.

"Why don't I go with you?" he said, more statement than question. "I'm sure we'll find 'em quicker together."

Holly nearly dropped her jaw. She glanced at Trisha but saw only tired indifference.

"Oh," Holly said. "That's okay, Sawyer."

"Really. It's no trouble. Besides, you've gotten me a little stirred up too."

I'll bet, she thought.

"I won't sleep now until Rose is home," he said.

Holly thought of the bedroom she'd never been in. Sawyer had never felt right about having sex with his mistress in his marital bed, so whenever they'd had a quickie here, they ended up on the couch or living room floor.

"Um," Holly said, "well . . ."

But Sawyer had already grabbed his coat and the flashlight on the shelf. Holly looked to Trisha again, as if for permission, something she'd never asked of her before.

"I'd go with you," Trisha said, "but I have an important board meeting tomorrow. I need to get back to bed." She tightened the belt on her robe and started the hall. "Goodnight, Holly. And honey, don't stay out too late. I'm not the only one who has work in the morning."

Sawyer nodded but made a sour face once his wife's back was

turned. Holly had heard about him losing his job as forklift supervisor at Humboldt's Lumber. As one of Greenwalk's biggest employers, the massive layoffs had negatively impacted many citizens. She wondered what Sawyer was doing for work now but didn't ask. She didn't want to get personal. It was too close to being intimate. As they walked out and Sawyer locked the front door, Holly went to her car and waited to see if he'd follow her or go to his own vehicle. He passed his pickup without even glancing at it and opened her passenger door. Closeness was now unavoidable. For one awkward moment, they just sat there, staring at the house. Holly started the car just to break the silence.

"I've missed you," Sawyer blurted out unexpectedly, still staring straight ahead.

Holly gripped the wheel so hard it creaked. She didn't know how to reply, even though she knew the truth. How many diary entries had been dedicated to her feelings for Sawyer? How many times had she written poems about him like a teenager? Putting the Honda in gear, she backed out of the driveway.

"Where should we look first?" she asked, as if he'd not said what he'd said, not stuck a shovel into that long undisturbed grave.

Sawyer exhaled. "Guess they must be up on the mountain if there's no signal."

Flurries fell upon the windshield, the snow melting instantly. Holly kept her eyes on the road ahead. The streetlights cast it in a bronze that seemed somehow alien tonight. Beside her, Holly's ex-lover drew his seat belt across his lap, and she couldn't help but glance at it. He was still wearing sweatpants. He'd been the only man she'd ever been with who always wore button fly jeans instead of zippered. Popping them open had always excited her. She'd loved undressing him, even though it always preceded a shame that eventually became too much for her to stand. The only man she'd slept with since Sawyer was her husband Justin, a roll-over-and-get-it-over-with form of sex typical to a dying marriage, less fulfilling than even self-pleasure, let alone making love with someone who showed genuine passion—someone like Sawyer Peterson.

She headed toward Black Mountain. Toward a Pandora's box of memories.

NINE

"DID ANY OF THEM BITE you?" Rose asked.

Aubrey wiped away a mascara tear. "I don't think so. At least not the big one."

"Rose," Bella said, "did you recognize the species?"

Rose shook her head. "I've never seen a spider like that. It was almost as big as a goddamn lobster."

"So, we don't know if it's poisonous?" Celeste asked.

Rose didn't bother correcting her. *"Poisonous" means* you *bite* it, she remembered from Girl Scouts. *When* it *bites* you, *it's "venomous."*

"No idea," Rose said.

"I'm fine," Aubrey told them. She looked to Rose, admiring her. "Thanks."

Rose smiled. "Don't mention it."

"That tongue in the eye was pretty gnarly," Celeste said. "But cool. You may have saved her life."

Rose felt a blush coming on. "Okay, let's not overinflate this."

"It's true, Rose," Bella said. "That was fast thinking."

It was foolish thinking, Rose thought. *That spider could have bitten you.*

Still, she was glad she'd done it. Their first animal encounter here had been a horrific disaster. At least they'd escaped this one unscathed, if a little traumatized. She glanced at the curled carcass of the arachnid, almost tempted to bring it with them so she could find out what the hell it was. Instead, she started taking off her jacket.

"What're you doing?" Bella asked.

"We need cloth." Rose pulled her sweater over her head and looked to Celeste. "I need your vodka."

Celeste's cheeks turned pink, looking to her exalted leader. Aubrey's eyes tightened, but the anger Rose saw there had less to do with Aubrey's disapproval of alcohol and more to do with Celeste dumbly smushing the spider while it was still on Aubrey's face. Celeste drew the Sprite bottle from her coat and handed it to Rose with a look of betrayal. Rose ignored it and wrapped her sweater around the end of one of the stakes and tied the sleeves in a Windsor knot. She poured vodka over the cotton.

"Aubrey," she said. "Your lighter, please."

The Zippo was passed to her, and Rose noticed the butterfly engraving in the silver plate. She lit it and carefully brought the flame to the alcohol-soaked sweater, creating a torch.

"Hell of a lot better than a stake," Bella said.

The girls got to work making torches of their own, tearing sleeves and hoods and the bottoms of shirts. Aubrey used her blouse, leaving her in her black bra, a lacy piece more like lingerie than practical underwear. It seemed she was dedicated to fashion over function even where others couldn't see. She put her coat back on and closed it up.

"The flames should keep any other animals away," Rose said. "Now we just have to decide which way to—" There was a sudden buzzing, and the vibration in her back pocket startled her. "My phone!"

She dug it out, all the girls watching the screen intently. One of Rose's favorite pictures popped up, the one of she and Tyson at the beach last summer, white stripes of zinc down their noses, topped with matching rainbow sunglasses. His name glowed with promise as she accepted the call.

"Babe?" she said. "Can you hear me?"

His voice was like a lighthouse at the edge of a cruel sea. "Yeah. Can you hear me?"

"Like you're in the next room!" she said, beaming.

The other girls breathed sighs of relief. Aubrey hugged Celeste, a peace offering, and Celeste burst with tears of joy. Everything was going to be all right. They had a signal. They were saved.

"Where are you?" he asked. "You sound all echoey. And your dad's looking for you. He called and woke me up to ask if I was with you."

Rose thought of the unparalleled safety of her father's arms. She wanted him now, even more than she wanted Tyson. Though she was fully grown, a girl always needs her daddy. Nothing created a stronger feeling of security than a good father.

"Ty, listen closely, okay?" she said. "I need your help. I'm—"

"Are you okay?" he asked.

"I'm fine. But some other girls are badly hurt." Rose's heartbeat was accelerating now and she gasped for air between words. "There was a bear . . . it attacked us."

"Oh, shit. Is Bella okay? Your dad said she was with you."

"Yeah. She's all right, but two other girls were mauled."

Bella tugged Rose's sleeve. "Tell him where we are."

"Ty," Rose said, "we're up on Black Mountain in an abandoned cemetery."

"A *what?*" he asked.

"There's this old graveyard on the hill just off Old Mill Road. About two miles east of that farm with the highland bulls. You know the one, right?"

"Yeah. Those cows with the shaggy hair."

"Right. There's a dirt road that heads into the mountains. You'll see my car parked at the lot at the end. There's a trail that goes up the northbound hill. Follow it until you get to the graveyard. It's a bit of a hike, but it's there."

"Okay, got it," he said, flushing her with sweet relief. "But if that bear is still around, you really should get out of there."

"I wish we could, but you don't understand." She was embarrassed to tell him where she was, that she'd been dumb enough to come down here. "We're underground. Under the cemetery."

A pause on the line. "You're *under it?* What do you mean?"

"Look for a square concrete shoot at the end of the graveyard. It's like a little buried shed. But don't go in! The bear is not far from the entrance and it's like a maze down here."

"Jesus, Rosey, what the hell?"

"I know, I know. I'll explain later. Just get help. Don't come alone."

"I'll call the police."

Rose winced. "Oh . . . um . . . wait."

The other girls looked to her. What she said next was for them as well as her boyfriend. "Maybe not the cops. Is there anyone else you can bring?"

Bella's mouth hung open. "What're you doing?"

"No cops?" Celeste added. "We need help. *Real* help. What good is your boyfriend gonna do down here?"

"Look," Rose said. "If we're caught here by the police, we could face charges. Trespassing, vandalism, breaking and entering—something. Maybe even reckless endangerment with Marnie. If I'm arrested, I can kiss my scholarship goodbye."

She hated to say it. It sounded so selfish as it came out of her mouth, especially with Savannah and Marnie left in pools of their own blood—alive or dead, they weren't even sure.

"Fuck your scholarship!" Celeste said. "We could all die down here!"

Bella took a gentler approach. "Rose, I understand, but we need medical attention for Savannah and Marnie fast, and Aubrey too, just in case she was bit. And I really think we'll need help if we're gonna find our way out of here. We're in danger. Your scholarship won't matter if you're dead."

Rose's chest deflated, shoulders dropping. Thinking of losing everything she'd worked so hard for caused a lump to rise in her throat. Bella and Celeste were right, but she just couldn't stand it. Why should she lose everything over a stupid mistake?

"No cops," Aubrey said suddenly. Everyone looked to her. "Rose has a future to think about. I don't want to see her ruin it because of a game I roped you all into."

Bella protested. "But Savannah and—"

"Dead," Aubrey interrupted. "They're dead. They're not going to get any deader, and us getting caught up in what happened to them won't help them any, it'll only hurt us."

"Jesus, Aubrey!" Bella's eyes went wide. "What're you saying? That we just leave them here?"

"Of course not. We make an anonymous call. Say we saw a bear up here and heard girls screaming. They'll find them eventually and will probably think Savannah and her sister ran in here to try and hide from the bear."

"Are you crazy? Then if we get caught, we'll be in *really* deep shit for leaving the scene of the accident." Bella looked to Rose for support but didn't get it. "C'mon, you guys. This is too callous. We can't think just of ourselves here. We have to think of Savannah and Marnie. They might be alive and—"

"They're not," Aubrey said. "You saw what happened."

"—even if they aren't, we have to think of their family."

"With all respect to the dead, life is for the living."

"How can you be so cold? Besides, I thought you loved the dead."

"I'm just thinking about those of us that are still alive," Aubrey said. "C'mon, you're smarter than this. Instead of getting wrapped up in the death of our friends—a story that would blow up like 9/11 in this crappy town—and all of us getting dragged through the gutter, ruining our lives—instead of all that, we still do the right thing by letting the authorities know, but don't involve ourselves in it or implicate us in any wrongdoing. Deep down, you know this is the right thing to do. You don't want Rose to blow her ticket to college, do you?"

No one spoke then. Rose had to force herself to look Bella in the eyes, both girls tearing up. Their friendship had already been tested, but their differences seemed so insignificant now. Their long friendship was about to be tested more profoundly than they ever could have imagined. What they chose to do here they would carry with them forever, together or apart.

Tyson's voice came back on the line. Rose had almost forgotten he was there.

"Rosey?" he said. "What do you want me to do?"

She looked at the others. Aubrey was the only one not fraught with anxiety. It might have been a trick of light, but it almost looked as if she wore the slightest smile.

Rose took a deep breath. "Call my dad, Ty. Here's all you tell him . . ."

TEN

GETTING OFF THE PHONE WITH Rose's boyfriend, Sawyer tried calling his daughter again but couldn't get through.

"Shit," he said.

Having only heard one side of the conversation he'd had, Holly hadn't gathered the information that made Sawyer so frazzled.

"What is it?" she asked. "What's going on?"

Sawyer ran his hand through his hair. "Tyson managed to get through to Rose, but I still can't seem to. He says the girls are in trouble. They're okay, but they're in trouble."

A coldness moved across Holly. "What kind of trouble? What do you mean?"

"Bella and Rose are lost," he said. "Up on the mountain."

"Christ, I knew it. Where?"

He gave her the directions Tyson had given him.

"Tyson's gonna meet us there," Sawyer said, "but he lives on the other side of town, so let's not wait up. Hopefully he can maintain a signal to reach Rose and us."

They came around a curve, but Holly didn't slow down. She saw the sign that told them of the scenic view stop ahead, one they knew a little too well, but they were too focused on their daughters to be affected by the memory, at least on a conscious level.

"There's more," Sawyer said. "Tyson says they broke into some abandoned place."

Holly's knuckles ran white on the wheel. She tried not to think of it, tried not to remember. She could barely get the words out. "Wha . . . what place?"

"He said it was like a shed that leads underground and—"

Holly gasped so loudly it cut Sawyer off. Her mind shuddered with flashes of dark tunnels, the faint echo of the dying still lingering in her ears.

Are you there?

"Calm down," Sawyer said. "They were just pokin' around. Kids being kids. Somehow, they got lost. I don't know how that could happen, but . . ."

But I do, Holly thought.

Sawyer turned to her, putting his hand on her knee. "Look, we'll find them. Everything will be okay."

At least he believed what he was saying. Only Holly knew just how terrible of a lie he could be telling her as well as himself. She was shaking, and not because of the frigid night or even Sawyer's hand on her leg.

"I hope you understand I don't want to go to the police with this," he said.

Police. The word twisted her insides. "No. No cops."

Her curt reply raised Sawyer's eyebrows. "Oh. Good. I thought you'd want to get them involved, but I'm glad you understand. We don't want the girls getting in any trouble, especially with such bright futures ahead of them."

But Holly wasn't thinking about Bella and Rose's futures. She was thinking about a past she'd thought she'd buried, just like all those bodies in that godforsaken graveyard on the hill.

~

Holly popped the new Nirvana album out of her Walkman and flipped it over. She didn't like it as much as *Nevermind* but didn't want to admit it. Bridget and Faith would probably think she was a poser if she did, one of the herd of followers in the grunge movement. She didn't see herself that way and would be damned if she'd let anyone else. Her dad's old CB radio headphones were incredible though.

THE PRETTIEST GIRL IN THE GRAVE

When plugged into her Walkman, they were loud enough to serve as miniature speakers for her and her friends to enjoy while she wore them around her neck like an airplane pillow.

Sitting upon a boulder, Faith kicked her long legs, the striped knee-high socks reminding Holly of Pippi Longstocking, especially given Faith's strawberry hair. The billowy locks came all the way down to her waist, making Holly envious. She'd been trying to get hers that long, but her hair grew so slowly. She'd dyed it green to make it interesting enough to hold her over. Standing at the edge of the cliff overlooking Greenwalk, Bridget flicked her cigarette butt over the edge, exhaling a cloud that engulfed her bony frame. She turned around and stuffed her hands into the pockets of her shredded jeans, the flannel tied around her waist fluttering in the breeze like a kilt.

"Is this all we're gonna do today?" Bridget asked.

Faith, always true to her name, grinned in the September sunshine. Holly had always been envious of that lovely smile and its ability to melt every boy in town.

"I'm happy to just hang outside," Faith said. "I mean, before we know it, it'll be cold again. God, last winter was the worst. I *hate* the cold."

"We know," Holly said, smirking. "You've told us, like, a million times."

Faith stuck out her tongue playfully, showing off the stud she'd had put in down at the mall, having flirted with the guy at the shop enough to convince him to let her get it pierced despite being under-age. Stunningly beautiful, it was easy for Faith to flirt her way into getting whatever she wanted from the opposite sex. She insisted if she just took the stud out whenever she was at home, her parents would never know, which was vital, because if her strict old man saw she'd "mutilated" herself, she'd be grounded until she was forty. For now, she did the best she could to hide it, but made sure to put it in each day, so the hole wouldn't close. Holly worried about that. Faith was often aloof to the point of airheaded. It was only a matter of time before she slipped up. Then she'd be dead meat.

"I feel like all we ever do is just dick around in these woods," Bridget groaned.

It was a valid complaint, but what did she expect Holly and Faith to do about it?

"You got a better idea?" Holly asked. "I mean, we can go back to the mall but ain't any of us got any money."

"Screw the mall," Bridget said. "That's for preppies and douches."

Holly didn't remind her the brand-new Pixies shirt Bridget wore came from the Spencer's Gifts in the very mall she was now bashing. Bridget also liked the arcade as much as the boys but would never admit it. It seemed impossible for her to admit she enjoyed anything, as if her self-imposed image of miserable apathy and disillusionment—which she thought was so damn cool—couldn't handle being besmirched by any admission of joy, no matter how small.

As usual, Bridget was carrying a can of spray-paint in the back pocket of her baggy, hand-me-down jeans, always ready to tag street signs and underpasses and, in this case, even trees. She took it from her pocket and flicked her Zippo lighter with her other hand and sprayed, creating a quick torch flame in the air.

"Wish we had some pot," Faith said.

"Well, we know how we can get some," Holly said, teasing her friend.

Slater Mahoney was a small-time dope dealer who'd dropped out of school last year, apparently to pursue his passion for being a deadbeat. He liked to boast that he ran with an east coast chapter of The Crips, even though he was white, but word was he actually sold weed for his uncle, a Harley Davidson dirtbag who tended bar down at the poolhall. The only thing Slater seemed to like more than his Sega game console was Faith Johnson. All she had to do was bat her eyes at him and he'd throw free joints at her like a fan at Snoop Dogg.

"I'm not in the mood to tolerate that pothead today," Faith said. "Last time he got a little grabby."

Bridget furrowed her brow. "You didn't tell me that. That's it, I'm gonna kick him in the balls when I see him."

"No, don't do that. Then he might not be so generous anymore. Besides, all he did was give my butt a squeeze. I think he thought he was flirting. It was just dumb, really. He was high."

"He's *always* high," Holly said. "Jeez, how can anyone spend every day stoned and still say it's not an addiction?"

"You can't tell guys like Slater that," Bridget said. "Potheads get so defensive about their precious Mary Jane. You'd think you were saying their mother was a whore."

The girls laughed, even Bridget the Grouch.

"Still," Holly said, "I do wish we had a joint."

They laughed even harder. "Heart-Shaped Box" began to play,

which Holly considered the album's standout track. Faith swayed to the tune, still kicking her feet like a little girl on a swing. Bridget lit another Camel, then passed it to Holly for a drag.

"You know," Bridget said, gazing up at the mountainside, "I heard there's a graveyard around here."

ELEVEN

"WE CAN'T JUST SIT HERE," Rose said. "We should still try to find a way out."

Bella furrowed her brow. "But help is coming. Shouldn't we wait for them?"

"They can't come in with that psycho bear at the front. We should press on."

"And get even more lost?"

"Maybe," Aubrey said. "Or maybe not."

Bella couldn't believe this. Rose was making terrible decisions, which was so unlike her, and now Aubrey was backing up everything she said. And as always, Celeste kissed up to Aubrey, doing her bidding without even thinking for herself. Bella was outvoted and unsure what to do. None of her friends from either part of her life would back her up. They'd banded together, the last thing she'd thought they'd ever do.

"This crypt can't go on forever, right?" Rose said. "The graveyard is only so big. There's bound to be another way in and out. How else would those bears have gotten in? The doorway we came in was too sealed up."

"But maybe someone closed it after the bears were already inside," Bella said.

Rose exhaled. "Please listen to me. We can't just sit here waiting for someone else to save us. I'm glad help is coming, but what if they have trouble finding us? We have to be proactive."

"But won't they have more trouble finding us if we don't sit tight?"

"Maybe," Aubrey said. "Or maybe not."

"Stop saying that," Bella said. Normally she wouldn't snap at Aubrey. She wanted to be accepted by her. But this situation had changed her priorities.

"We don't know what'll happen," Aubrey said. "Everything is a maybe right now."

Bella huffed. There was only one other option they might go for. Though dangerous, it might be their best chance of escape.

"What if we go back the way we came?" she said.

Rose stared at her. "Toward the *bear*?"

"I know, I know. But we have torches now. That should keep it away."

"And what if it doesn't?" Celeste asked incredulously.

"Celeste's right," Rose said. "That wasn't like any normal bear. You saw how crazy aggressive it was. That thing was out for blood from the start. You want to end up like Savannah and Marnie?"

"Of course not. But that's another thing—we can check on them. Just because Aubrey says they're dead doesn't mean they are. Maybe we could help them."

"Jesus, Bella," Aubrey said, rolling her eyes.

"We're not going back," Rose said.

Bella glowered. "No one appointed you leader."

"She seems to know what she's doing better than the rest of us," Aubrey said. "I'm with you, Rose."

"Me too," Celeste said.

Bella shook her head. "No, Celeste. You're with *Aubrey*. You always do whatever she says."

Celeste flushed. "Shut up, Bella!"

Bella did. Despite the priority of staying alive, she didn't want her friendships to perish. In most cases she avoided conflict, especially when trying to fit in, as she was with the goth crowd. She had to think positive, to believe they would get out of this. That meant she had to consider what would happen once they did. She didn't want to ruin the best relationships she had going. They were too few and far between.

"Sorry, Celeste," Bella said. "I didn't mean it. I'm just scared."

Celeste cooled. "It's okay."

"We're all scared," Rose said. "But if we keep our wits about us and press on, we'll get out of here. Now c'mon. Let's see where this hallway leads."

They proceeded into new territory, the torches making their journey easier, safer. *But how long would they burn?* Bella wondered. The walls flickered orange and cast twitching, black shadows. The hollow hiss continued, maintaining a steady thrum. *What the hell is that sound?* Could there be some sort of machine or heater down here? And if so, for what purpose?

A shuffling noise behind them gave the girls a fright. They stopped and looked back, turning their torches toward the blackened hall they'd left behind. They saw nothing, but the sound continued, like sandpaper on wood.

"Is it the bear?" Celeste whispered.

Rose shushed her and they all listened, watching the darkness, waiting for whatever horror the crypt would offer next. Bella gripped her torch with both hands, holding it out in front of her like a battle sword.

At first, she thought she was looking at a mummy, a monster from an old horror movie. She gasped. Celeste shrieked. But what Bella had taken for loose wrap was actually shreds of clothing hanging off the arms of whatever approached them. It was a crimson figure with purple stripes, hair matted and stained. After that bizarre spider, Bella wasn't sure what to believe in anymore. This could be anything. The girls held their ground, needing the light to stay on the shuffling creature.

But Bella didn't want to see it.

The anthropomorphic thing was hideous. Its face was nearly nonexistent. It wasn't until it spoke that she was convinced it was human. Then she realized who it was.

"H-h-help me," Marnie said.

The girl only had one eye. The empty socket was in the center of a huge claw mark that ruined one side of her face. The remaining eye was red with busted blood vessels. Her upper lip was split, nose broken. The purple stripes were deep wounds where the bear had swatted her. She limped along. If the others hadn't stopped for the buttresses, Marnie never would have caught up with them.

"Holy shit . . ." Celeste said.

Rose went to Marnie. Bella followed. The girls looked at her helplessly.

"Oh, man," Rose said. "Marnie, you made it. You're alive. Thank God."

Marnie tried to speak but only sobbed incoherently. Despite the blood, Rose put an arm around her shoulders, gently hushing her, telling her it was okay, that she was going to be alright, even if it wasn't true. At the rate she was losing blood, Bella figured Marnie's chances of survival were slim if they didn't get help quickly. And if she lived, she would be horrifically scarred for life, mentally as well as physically.

But she was alive.

Bella looked to Aubrey, but she wouldn't meet her gaze. She'd been completely wrong about something extremely important. Bella hoped Aubrey was ashamed, but it was impossible to tell. Aubrey's face was slack and lifeless, as cold as an iceberg.

"What about Savannah?" Bella asked.

Marnie sobbed harder. It was the only answer she gave, and the only one they needed to know their friend's terrible fate.

Rose inspected Marnie, spotting a bad wound in her thigh. "We have to stop the bleeding."

Bella had taken off her sweater to use for the torch, but she wore a long-sleeved shirt under her coat. She quickly removed the coat and tore a shirtsleeve free. Rose used it as a tourniquet, tying it tight around Marnie's thigh. The gushing blood slowed to a trickle. It was the best they could do.

"Somebody help me out," Rose said, placing Marnie's arm over her shoulder.

Bella stepped forward but Aubrey was quicker. When she lifted Marnie's other arm, the young girl whimpered in pain. They braced her, careful with the torches as they helped her along. Bella had to look away. Marnie would never be the same. The poor girl had been brutally mauled and the sight of her was hair-raising. Bella swallowed back bile. She'd thought dissecting frogs in biology class was repulsive, but this was far worse. This was a human being—a child, really. Marine's stomach hadn't been opened, thank goodness, but her flayed flesh was a grotesque horror that would linger long in Bella's memory.

"What happened to the bear?" Celeste asked.

Bella winced. It seemed cruel to ask Marnie anything at all. But Celeste was right. They had to know.

Marnie struggled but managed to get words out. "I p-played . . . played dead. Like Ra-ose told us . . . it clawed me but . . . the-the-then it left me alone. I a-almost th-thought . . . thought I d-d-died."

"Help is on the way, Marnie," Rose said.

It bothered Bella that Rose didn't mention that help wasn't medics or police. It seemed misleading, like she was giving Marnie false hope. Bella had never thought of Rose as selfish before. They said tough times brought out people's true nature. Was that what she was seeing now? Rose's true colors? Bella still considered her friend a good person but was shocked by some of her decisions tonight. Rose had always been the leader in the duo, the Batman to Bella's Robin. Bella had never worshipped Rose like Celeste did Aubrey, but she'd tended to follow her lead and let her make the important decisions. That only changed when Bella went goth and found a new advisor in Aubrey. Now Aubrey was enamored with Rose. Maybe they understood something Bella hadn't realized yet. Maybe she was too frightened to think logically. The too familiar serpent of self-doubt was constricting about her now. She told herself to stay aware of its presence and not let it overpower her.

"We think there's another way out," Rose explained to Marnie.

They continued on, supporting Marnie like a wounded soldier as they explored the further reaches of the dark. Without her sweater and missing a sleeve, Bella trembled from the cold and held the torch closer for its warmth. She watched her steps on the uneven ground, not wanting to stumble and set her hair on fire. She was thinking of trying to get through to her mother again when they reached the doorway.

There was no fork at the end of the tunnel. It led only to this closed door with a rounded arch at the top. The concrete dripped with dew, queerly yellow in the firelight.

Bella gulped. Something about the door chilled her. She couldn't imagine anything good waiting behind it. At this point, it wouldn't surprise her if this was the gates of Hell.

"What is it?" Celeste asked.

Marnie whimpered. "I don't w-wanna g-g-go in there."

"It'll be okay," Rose said, sounding less than confident. "We have to try and see."

Marnie struggled against them until the girls let her go. She wobbled and Rose reached for her again, but Marnie remained on her feet. She swallowed the blood in her mouth.

"There co-could be more bears in there," Marnie said.

"I doubt it," Aubrey told her.

"Yeah," Rose said. "The door is closed."

So was the way in here, Bella thought.

But she had to agree with Rose. It didn't make sense to turn back without trying the door. Always brave—and perhaps a showoff too—Aubrey gripped the doorhandle. Everyone held their breath. The door budged but wouldn't open all the way, so Bella stepped up to help, taking Aubrey's torch so she could pull the door with both hands. It creaked loudly, echoing like a haunted house as it came open. A puff of dust struck the girls. They coughed and waved it away. Aubrey took her torch back, and she and Bella raised them through the entryway, the large room revealing itself in all its ghastliness.

Bella's mouth became a desert. Her flesh pimpled.

When Marnie had first returned to them, she'd thought she was seeing a mummy, but had been wrong. What she saw before her now was unquestionable. The fact they were under a graveyard slapped her across the face.

The room was an ossuary. Thick webs like gestation mucus ran from corner to corner, yellowed veils hanging down over decrepit coffins like canopy beds. Some of the caskets were cracked open, revealing the ashy skeletons housed within. Others featured windows where amber skulls looked upon the girls with rictus grins. Only one of the girls returned their smiles—Aubrey. Bella looked at her, but Aubrey was too mesmerized to notice the look of shock on her friend's face.

"We found it," Aubrey said.

The others approached—all but Marnie.

"Found what?" Rose asked.

"Don't you get it?" Aubrey asked, still gazing at the dead. "It's part of the game."

Rose huffed. "C'mon. We're not playing anymore."

"I don't think we have a choice."

"What the hell does that mean?"

Aubrey took a step into the ossuary. "Come and see."

Bella remembered something she'd read in Revelations when she'd skimmed the Bible out of curiosity. *And I saw the Lamb open one of the seals, and I heard, as it were, the noise of thunder, one of four beasts saying, "come and see."*

Rose entered the ossuary. Before tonight, Bella had been pretty good at predicting her best friend's actions. She'd thought she knew Rose so well. Somewhere along the line, things had changed, and it pained her to accept they'd drifted this far apart.

Marnie shrieked. "Wait f-for me! It's d-dark out here!"

She limped to Bella and clutched her arm, not wanting to be left behind without the torches to keep the darkness at bay. Either she'd been lying when she'd said she wasn't as afraid of the dark as she'd once been, or the nightmare she was going through reverted her to a childlike state. Bella couldn't blame her. Not at all.

Gingerly, they entered the ossuary, following the others with bated breath. What Bella had taken for white concrete walls she now realized were bones stacked end to end like fire logs, forming a circular wall around the room. Randomly placed skulls peeked out from within them, the faces of the dead stalking them from the shadows. Marnie clutched Bella tighter. Bella was grateful for the company.

"It really is like the Paris catacombs," Celeste said.

Dew dropped on Bella's head. She wiped it away and looked up, then instantly wished she hadn't.

"Oh my God . . ."

Rose followed her gaze and when she saw it, she covered her mouth so not to scream. Even Celeste gasped when she looked up. Aubrey remained stoic, her feline eyes like those of a deer hypnotized by headlights.

Like the walls, the ceiling was composed of bones. Femurs and ribcages and vertebrae, all roped together with thin twine, some half-embedded in the packed clay, others dangling as if they would fall at any second. Most were bare of flesh, but some still held layers of withered, mummified skin, hanging from the skeletal remains in gray ribbons. It made Bella tremble, and like some optical illusion, once she started seeing the faces, they were all she could see.

TWELVE

"THERE'S HER CAR," SAWYER SAID.

They pulled into the dirt lot, tires crunching on puddles of ice. An old black Hyundai was parked at the other end. Stickers for emo and metal bands covered the rear like graffiti.

"Recognize that car?" Holly asked.

"Nope."

"Me either."

Boys? she wondered. Rose hadn't mentioned any in her call, but who knew what they'd been up to? Holly only hoped they weren't where she thought they were. She'd believed all of that was behind her and never would have thought her daughter would make the same mistake she had when she was a teen.

Holly reached across Sawyer to the glove-box and took out her flashlight. They got out of the car and walked toward the opening of the trail. Just looking at the uphill slope made Holly's knees hurt. Bigger and stronger, Sawyer approached it without a care. She followed behind him. Joint pain was the least of her worries right now.

Holly hated being here. She'd never thought she'd have to return.

But she'd dreamed it, over and over again. The recurring nightmare was her curse, never allowing her to forget.

~

They found the graveyard at dusk.

Bridget lit cigarettes as if to celebrate, passing them around like a new father with a stack of cigars.

"Whoa," Faith said, looking upon the decrepit cemetery.

In the blue-gray gloaming, the tombstones appeared like a massive checkerboard. Black birch trees shuffled in the mountain breeze, their withering bark like a peeling sunburn, and red maples were just starting to change color at their upper tips. They shook like pompoms in the surrounding forest. The three girls were deep into the wilderness now, and with night falling, Holly couldn't help but feel uneasy.

"What is this place doing way out here?" she asked.

Bridget shrugged. "I dunno. Guess it's from frontier times or something. Maybe people who died along the Appalachian Trail."

"I don't think the trail's that old."

"Well, I said I don't know."

Faith fidgeted. "How'd you hear about it?"

"At first it was just a rumor I heard." Bridget stepped into the graveyard. "More than once, random chicks at school mentioned it. Pretty awesome, huh?"

Holly followed her into the cemetery, careful not to step on anyone's grave. Faith followed behind them, blowing smoke rings.

"We should take pictures here sometime," she said. "It'd look so creepy and cool."

Holly disagreed. She believed in being respectful in a graveyard and not using it as a prop. She'd lost her uncle the year before. It was an open casket wake, making him the first dead body she'd ever seen. Her mother kissed him goodbye, but Holly had been too freaked out to even touch him.

"*At first*, you heard a rumor?" Holly asked. "Does that mean you found out something else?"

"After I heard about it," Bridget said, "I asked my grandmother if she knew of any graveyards up here. She was born in Greenwalk and has lived here for, like, seventy years, so I figured if anyone would know, it'd be her." She took a drag, the pause dramatic. "There's a story that goes with this place."

A gust of wind. It was colder up here on the mountain, freakishly so for September. When the wind chill struck, it felt more like early winter.

"Grandma didn't know when this graveyard was built," Bridget said, "but it was before her time, so, you know, before the '20s. Anyway, she told me when she was growing up, there was a ghost story girls used to tell, one that scared her out of ever coming up here."

Faith smiled. "Ooooh, I love spooky campfire stories."

Holly didn't. She didn't like horror movies or Halloween hayrides or tall tales to tell in the dark. She couldn't understand the appeal of being scared. But she knew Bridget was going to tell them whether she wanted to hear it or not.

"There's a tomb here," Bridget said, "or at least there was."

They looked around, not seeing one.

"It was a family mausoleum," Bridget continued. "The Goldman family were upper class and could afford a large enough tomb for the parents and their children. Grandma said the first to go was Mr. Goldman, sometime in the early 1900s, I think."

"Thought you said you didn't know what this place was," Holly said.

Bridget frowned. "I don't. This is just a story—a legend. I don't know if it's true and neither does my grandmother." She flicked ash. "Anyway, Mrs. Goldman soon followed. They were both old by those days' standards, like, in their fifties. They had a lot of daughters—like seven or eight—and a coffin for each of them was placed in the tomb for when the time came. Soon after they died, their youngest, Madeline, was found dead in her bed. She was just nineteen. No one knew why she'd died and her sister—Janis, the oldest of the sisters—didn't want an autopsy, for religious reasons. Something about the body being intact when Madeline went to God. So, she was put in a coffin, then placed inside the tomb.

"Some folks say Madeline was poisoned by her big sister, that Janis really didn't want an autopsy or embalming 'cause she worried traces of poison would be discovered. They say she killed off Madeline 'cause she stood to inherit a fortune she felt was rightfully hers, being the oldest and there being no male heir to carry on the family name. But no one could prove Janis had done it, and she was the next to die anyway, several years later, of something called consumption."

"Oh yeah," Holly said. "I remember from history class that consumption was a big problem in the old days. Pretty awful way to go."

"Not as awful as what happened next." Bridget paused and took a drag, setting a mood. "See, the place had been sealed up for years now, and when the family went in to put their eldest sister to rest, they found the body of their youngest sister on the floor of the mausoleum."

Faith gasped. "Oh shit . . ."

"Madeline's coffin was wide open, with claw marks on the inside of the lid. The door to the tomb was clawed too and stained with dried blood from her desperate efforts to escape. Seems she was never really dead, only thought to be, and was in some sort of coma when she was buried. She'd been sealed inside the tomb—*buried alive*."

The hairs on Holly's neck stood up. "Jesus, Bridget . . ."

"That's not even the worst of it. See, Madeline was put in there not long after her parents were. She was trapped in the tomb with their bodies. So, she did the only thing she could do."

Holly put her hand over her mouth. Faith's eyes went wide.

"Madeline's coffin wasn't the only one open when the others went in there to bury Janis," Bridget said. "Not wanting to starve to death, Madeline ate her parents."

"Oh my God," Holly said.

"Their bones were picked clean. Of course, poor Maddy still starved to death."

Faith's shocked expression became a smile. "No way . . ."

"Yeah. Pretty gnarly." Bridget flicked her cigarette butt into the gathering darkness. "I wonder where the tomb is, or if they destroyed it after that."

"We should totally look for it," Faith said.

She frolicked through the graveyard, staring down at the tombstones that lay flat on the ground.

"Guys," Holly said, "there's obviously no tomb around here. We'd have noticed it. That story must be an urban legend."

"Maybe they demolished it and buried the Goldmans in the ground," Bridget said.

"Hey, yeah," Faith said.

She crouched, getting a closer look at the names that were still legible on the slabs. Holly couldn't help but look too, curious if there was any validity to Bridget's story. She hoped not. But reaching the far end of the graveyard, she spotted something unusual.

"What the heck is that?" she asked.

Bridget and Faith joined her, and the three girls stared at the concrete hole in the ground, partially hidden by fallen branches and vines. A short staircase led into the pit. There was a door. Holly stepped back, already wishing she hadn't pointed it out.

"Guys," Bridget said. "Maybe that's it."

Faith scratched her head. "Why would it be underground?"

"I dunno. Maybe the Goldmans just wanted it that way."

"It looks like a bomb shelter from the '50s."

"Yeah. It's pure *Twilight Zone.*"

Holly shivered. She'd seen the *Twilight Zone* movie as a kid, and it disturbed her enough to turn her off horror movies for good. Later, she heard about the film's curse, how one of the actors and two children had been accidentally torn in half by a helicopter. She'd thought it was just tall tales, but it turned out to be true.

Some scary legends were based in fact.

"I wonder if we can get inside," Bridget said.

~

The ground finally leveled out. Holly put her hands on her thighs and bent over to catch her breath. She was sweating despite the freezing nighttime temperature. Sawyer waited anxiously, wanting to move on and rightly so, but Holly needed a moment to ease the pinch in her ribs.

"You okay?" he asked.

She nodded but said nothing. He came to her, placing one hand on her back. She stood up straight and his hand stayed there. Looking up at him in the dark, his eyes twinkled in the moonlight like the nearest stars. He looked good. He smelled good. She told herself to step back but found she couldn't. Warmth was spreading through her abdomen, old feelings stirring at the worst possible time.

"We should keep moving," she said, unable to step away from him.

Sawyer started walking along the trail. As they pressed on, Holly tried calling Bella again but got the same result. Up here, her phone barely had half a bar for a signal.

This place does everything it can to keep you here, she thought.

She shut her eyes against the memory of Faith screaming. Even three decades later, she recalled the sound as clearly as her own daughter's voice.

"Say," Sawyer said. "I heard there's some old artifacts up around here. Did you ever hear about that?"

Holly's jaw tightened. Sawyer wasn't a Greenwalk native, nor was he a woman. How could he know about the graveyard or the twisted secrets it held? It was a curse reserved for the fairer sex, a terrible game played by a select few, one the participants rarely spoke of again. Even the legend of The Lady in the Tomb was passed on from female to female. Sometimes a man would hear something about it, but when he tried to retell it, he couldn't get any of the details straight, just like how Sawyer was off right now.

"Artifacts?" Holly asked.

"Yeah," he said, "like the remnants of an older version of Greenwalk. Back when I lived in Illinois, my hometown had a place like that, with the remains of an old carousel and a church and a well, all in a nature preserve."

"I see."

Her cold reply caused Sawyer to stop. "Listen, Holly. I'm sorry, okay? About everything. I know I put you in a tough spot and—"

"You didn't force me to do anything," she said. "I knew you were married."

"But I never—"

She cut him short. "Not now. Okay?"

"Then when? When are we gonna talk about this?"

"I dunno, all right? Maybe never." She turned her flashlight toward the trail. "C'mon. Let's find our girls."

~

"You really think we'll find her?" Faith asked.

The girls stood atop the first step, looking down at the awaiting concrete pit, a gateway to the macabre. Holly wet her lips. Curiosity had risen to combat her dread. Her itch to go inside surprised her. She wasn't a coward but tended to avoid unnecessary risks. What made this hole in the earth different? What was behind its undeniable draw? Surely it wasn't just the story of Madeline Goldman's tragic demise. Something else was calling to her with subliminal whispers, sinking its teeth in.

"I say we go down there," Bridget said. "See if the door's locked."

Still, the girls stood at the top of the stairs, no one taking that first step.

Faith giggled, a nervous tick. "Maybe we should all go at the same time."

With a deep breath, Holly stepped forward and took Bridget by the hand. Faith took Bridget's other hand, and they went down the steps in a human train formation, separating only when they reached the bottom. Holly stood closest to the door. It was sealed with a rusted iron bolt above the handle that could be slid back from the outside. She reached out slowly, as if the bolt was a dog that might bite her. When she gripped it, flakes of rust fell away, and when she tried to slide it, the ancient thing broke apart like a clump of dirt. The door opened slightly. Holly flinched. They all did.

"Oh shit," Faith whispered.

"Open it, Holly," Bridget said.

She almost expected the handle to fall away like ash too, but it held firm as she slowly drew the door back. None of them could breathe. Faith and Bridget hovered behind Holly, their faces on her shoulders, half hidden behind her green hair. The door opened, and even in the darkness they could make out the claw marks on the inside of the door.

Faith screamed. She stumbled backward, landing on her butt upon the steps.

"Holy fucking shit!" Bridget said. "It's true!"

The claw marks dug deep—into *concrete*. If Madeline Goldman had made the marks instead of just some prankster, she must have scratched until her fingers were bloody nubs. Holly gazed into the tomb, but before them was only darkness. The ghostly smell of dust and decay rose in an invisible plume. Standing at the threshold, Holly's breathing echoed back at her like some phantom mimic.

"This is too freaky," Faith said, no longer amused. "We should get away from this place."

"Screw that," Bridget said. "We got it open. Let's have a look."

"You guys . . ." Faith whined. "No . . . c'mon . . ."

Bridget drew her Zippo from her pocket, flicking a flame to light their way as Holly stepped into the blackness.

THIRTEEN

"WE HAVE TO GET OUT of here," Bella said.

Rose heard her but didn't register the words. It was as if the boneyard ceiling had hypnotized her. She stood with her head back, eyes wide, staring into the hollowed eye sockets of the dead. The corpses were as confusing as they were chilling. The bodies wore a variety of different clothing articles, all rotted, but some of which she could tell had been too casual for someone to be buried in.

"This is messed up," Celeste said.

"I'll say," Bella agreed. "Why would anyone set bodies up like this? I mean, this is like . . . like . . ."

"Like Jeffery Dahmer's apartment," Celeste said with a snicker.

"I don't know how you can laugh right now."

Aubrey shushed them. "Show some respect for the dead."

Rose came out of her deep thoughts and rubbed her eyes, spots fading before her vision. The ossuary seemed to turn. The other girls appeared only as spindly, humanoid forms, but when she blinked, they returned to normal. She'd never taken hallucinogens but imagined the effects might be like what she was feeling now. What had brought on this sudden spell?

"You okay?" Aubrey asked.

Rose approached her. "What did you mean when you said this was 'part of the game'?"

Aubrey didn't flinch. "Just what I said. We wrote invitations to this dance, and the crypt responded in kind. It—"

"Stop speaking in fucking riddles," Rose snapped. "I want simple, honest answers."

"I am being honest. I've no reason to lie to any of you. I told you this place would test us based on our answers to the questions I asked when we started. Remember? *What are you afraid of? Who do you love? What happens when you die?* The game started the moment we answered those questions. Now the dead are answering back. They're testing us. That's why we're down here."

Rose ran her hand over her face, exhausted by this nonsense. "Jesus, Aubrey, I thought you'd put this hocus pocus aside. I thought you'd realized the seriousness of the situation."

"I do realize it, but the hocus pocus is *real*. Just look around you. Look at this place. Our true fears are being unearthed—fear of dying, fear of what waits beyond death's door. Marnie's fear of the dark and—"

"Have you forgotten about the bear? What has that to do with your ridiculous game?"

Aubrey took a deep breath. "I wasn't totally truthful in my answer when I said I was afraid of being burned. I mean, I am afraid of that, but I'm also really afraid of bears. Bears and spiders."

Rose nearly laughed at the absurdity. "Are you shitting me? You're trying to tell me this crypt is *challenging* us, that it's somehow *conscious*?"

"Rose—"

"We don't have time for this bullshit."

"Listen to me, please! I think the only way we stand a chance of getting out of here is to prepare ourselves for the rest of the game, because it's happening whether you want to believe in it or not. Remember what you said you were afraid of? *Losing*. Well, what have you been doing since we've been down here, huh? You've taken on the role of leader. You've turned this into another contest, another sport. But at every turn, things have gotten worse. You're losing and it terrifies you."

Rose didn't think, only acted. She dropped her torch. Grabbing Aubrey by the collar of her stupid coat, she spun the woman and flung her against a standing casket, making the old wood crack. Aubrey's torch rolled away.

"Rose!" Bella said, running to her, trying to hold her back.

Celeste kicked Rose in the shin. "Leave her alone, you bitch!"

Rose broke free of Bella's grip and shoved Celeste. She fell on her ass—*her fat ass*, Rose thought. Celeste at least managed to hold on to her torch.

"Stop!" Marnie cried.

Her voice seized everything. Looking at the mutilated girl, Rose felt suddenly sick with herself. *What the hell am I doing?* She didn't start fights anymore. She wouldn't back down from one, but never threw the first punch. Why had Aubrey's comment stung so deeply? Was she really that afraid of losing, or was she just terrified of losing *this*? If she was leading them all astray, there'd be much direr consequences than not receiving a trophy. There was no greater defeat than death.

"I'm sorry," she said, holding out her hand to help Aubrey up.

Aubrey looked at her suspiciously.

"Really," Rose said. "I'm sorry. I shouldn't have done that. That's not the kind of person I am. I'm just scared, like all of us."

Aubrey let Rose help her up. Rose brushed the woman off, clearing the dust, and they gathered their torches. Rose couldn't believe she'd dropped it so carelessly. They were lucky it hadn't gone out.

"All right," Rose said. "Real talk. Aubrey, I need you tell me how you knew about this place and this game. I need you to tell all of us. *Now*."

Rose was surprised to see Aubrey's eyes grow wet. She looked up, trying to hold the tears in, but they fell anyway. She took shallow breaths, bracing herself for confession.

"My mom wrote about it," she said. "In her diary."

They all fell silent, the only sound the persistent white noise of the thrum. Rose watched Aubrey, studying her for any sign of lying. No more games or spooky stories or goth bullshit. She wanted the truth. Whatever Aubrey had been keeping to herself had to come out.

"My mother died a long time ago," Aubrey said. "I was raised by my aunt and uncle. Never knew my dad. When my aunt thought I was old enough, she gave me boxes of my mother's things she'd saved. One of the boxes was filled with diaries. I only skimmed them at first. It felt a little too intrusive. But eventually I decided it wasn't really an invasion of privacy if the person is dead. I was her daughter and had so few memories of her, so I figured the journals were the best way to get to know my mom. But there were so many. I didn't know where to start."

Rose itched to tell her to *get to the point* so they could keep moving, but it was best to let Aubrey finish. The whole story might contain some clue Aubrey wasn't even aware of, something that could get them out of here.

"I read them at random," Aubrey said. "Not in chronological order. It gave me snapshots of my mother through different periods in her life." Her eyes misted again. "My mom wasn't well—I mean mentally and emotionally. She had a lot of dark thoughts. She wrote about using drugs and alcohol to try and escape them. It's why I hate dope and booze. There was trauma from something she was never really clear about. It wasn't until I read a diary from when she was younger that I came to what seemed like a turning point for her.

"I only read it recently. In it, she talked about a cemetery—*this* cemetery. It haunted her dreams but was more than a nightmare. She wrote about it as if it were both real and imagined . . . I'm not sure how to explain it, but that's how it read. She said it existed in our world, in our town, but was also part of some other place."

"What place?" Bella asked.

"Another world. Like an alternate dimension. She said she'd discovered a portal between the land of the living and the land of the dead."

Despite her skepticism, a chill crept over every inch of Rose. She'd never believed in the supernatural, but standing in this underground ossuary, inside its walls and ceiling comprised of dead bodies, the realm of the dead seemed not only possible, but glaringly real. She told herself it was just her nerves getting the better of her but knew that wasn't the only culprit. There was something strange about this crypt and everything in it, from the overly aggressive bear to the demonic spider to the blood-curdling rhyme she couldn't get out of her head.

Some girls are fearful, others are brave. One girl's a princess, the next one, a slave. But all girls are equal, when they're down in this cave, until just one is left standing—the prettiest girl in the grave.

One left standing, she thought, *and I don't like to lose.*

The thought made her stomach go cold and hollow. There was an evil energy about it, the same alien force that had filled her with rage a moment ago.

"So, your mom knew this place was here?" Bella asked Aubrey.

Aubrey nodded. "Yeah. She'd been here before . . . and seen terrible things."

FOURTEEN

THE TOMB WAS ROUGHLY THE same size as Holly's parents' living room. Though dusty, it was well-preserved, no graffiti on the walls or discarded garbage on the floor. Was it possible that she, Bridget, and Faith were the first ones to ever break into it? The coffins were atop stone slabs, lining the tomb like beds in army barracks— nine in all. The walls were blank stone, the door they'd come in through the only way in and out.

"This is so freakin' creepy," Faith said, sticking close to Holly.

Holly ran her hand over one of the coffins, clearing the dust to reveal a name engraved in the wood—*Janis*.

"It's them," she said. "It's the Goldmans."

Bridget grinned. "This is unreal. Totally unreal."

"It's real all right."

"I can't believe this place has been here all these years! It looks like it hasn't been touched in eons. When do you think the last time a living person was in here?"

"I dunno," Holly said. "Definitely a while."

Bridget rubbed her hands together, looking from casket to casket as if she were playing blackjack with them. "We've gotta find her."

Faith raised her eyebrows. "Whoa, whoa, whoa. No freakin' way!"

"What? Why not? Don't you wanna see Madeline?"

"We can't break into *coffins*! Jesus, Bridget, what're you? A ghoul?"

Bridget smirked. "I can be. C'mon, we'll be like Indiana Jones."

"No, we'll be like serial killers. Remember that old guy we saw that documentary about? He dug up bodies and made leggings out of corpse skin. Gross!"

"Jeez, Faith. We're not gonna go *that* far."

She crossed her arms. "Well, I don't wanna be a graverobber either."

"Who said anything about robbing? I'm not gonna steal her jewelry, I just wanna take a look-see."

They turned to Holly, who'd been silent.

"What do you say, girl?" Bridget asked. "We've come this far, right? What's it gonna hurt to go one step further?"

Faith looked at Holly in desperation. "I say we get out of here. I'll go ask Slater for some weed, okay? I don't care anymore. I just wanna leave."

Holly said, "No one is stopping you."

Faith's expression fell slack. Then the hurt began to show. She walked toward the door but didn't leave. It was dark out now and she was too chicken to be alone in the woods at night, so she just pouted like a kid sent to the corner.

Bridget joined Holly, clearing the dust from the coffins' name plates, and on their fourth try they found her.

Madeline Goldman's casket was short. She must have been small even for a teenage girl.

Holding the lighter over the coffin, Bridget looked at Holly, asking her to do the honors without saying a word. Holly placed her hands on the edge of the coffin lid, her fingertips tingling. Was she really doing this? She felt as if she were observing herself from a distance, watching a movie instead of participating in real life. She was a puppet controlled by another part of herself, something dormant rising anew.

The lid came up.

"Holy shit," Bridget said, stepping back.

On the underside of the lid, claw marks were gouged into the wood. Old blood stains decorated it like tie-dye. Inside the coffin was a darkness that seemed endless. Holly pulled on Bridget's flannel, bringing her closer to give her more light. The orange glow trembled as the Zippo's flame danced above the open casket.

It was empty.

~

She still knew the way.

Even after all this time, Holly hadn't forgotten the spot where a thin path branched off the main trail. The cemetery waited just over the next hill. Long ago, she'd told herself she'd never come back this way, but now this cursed earth had her daughter, and Holly knew, in the darkest shadows of her heart, that Bella was vying for the title, whether she realized it or not.

"This way," she told Sawyer.

"But the trail goes on a ways."

"Trust me. We've got to branch off and take this little path here. There's no place for the girls to have broken into on the main trail, but there's a place where this smaller trail ends."

He gave her a curious look. "You saying you know where they are?"

"I've an idea."

"Why didn't you say so before?"

"Because I didn't want to believe it."

He cocked his head. "Wait . . . what?"

"Look. There's no antique playground or whatever the hell you were talking about before. What's up here is a cemetery, an old one— a dangerous one."

"Dangerous? How?"

"It's . . ."

How could she tell him? How could she expect him to understand, to *believe*? She had to try. It might be the only way to rescue the girls . . . if they weren't gone already.

Don't think like that!

"It's . . ." she said. "Okay, so . . . below the graveyard is a tomb. But there's a trick to it. When you go in there, *you'll* just see four walls and some coffins. That's because you're *you*. But there's another place *within* that tomb, behind it and yet part of it. Sometimes it's all you can see. It's kind of like tracing an image on a piece of paper, only you get a totally different image than the one you tried to copy. Does that make sense?"

He blinked. "No. Christ, of course it doesn't. What're you talking about?"

"All right." She threw up her hands. *Fuck it.* "I know it sounds crazy, okay? But there's one door that leads to two totally different places. One is a just a tomb. The other is a labyrinth. When *you* walk through that door—a *guy* who hasn't been issued an invite—you won't be able to see or get to the labyrinth. At least, I don't think so."

Sawyer gave her the exact look she expected. His mouth hung open, his brow furrowing like he'd just smelled a fart.

"What in the hell are you talking about?" he asked. "A maze only women can see?"

"Not women. *Girls.* You have to be young. You must have the beauty of youth. That's what it wants."

Sawyer rubbed the bridge of his nose. "Are you high on something? I mean, really, *what is this?*"

"Please, listen to me—"

"Wait . . . does this have something to do with *us?* Are you trying to tell me something with this male-female stuff?"

"No. That's not—"

"God damn it. Haven't you messed with my head enough?"

She flushed. "*Excuse me?*"

"You break things off when things were going so good. After everything we had together, you suddenly give me the cold shoulder and won't return my calls or text me back. You didn't even give me an explanation, you just kicked me to the curb and ghosted me."

"An *explanation?* Are you kidding me? You're fucking *married.* So am I. You think I messed with your head? How do you think I felt—screwing you in secret and then going home to a husband I didn't love half as much as I loved you. You knew how I felt about you, but you were never going to leave Trisha. You were just stringing me along." She smacked her forehead. "Jesus, why are we even talking about this now? C'mon! This way."

Sawyer took her arm. "Damn it. That's not fair."

"Life's not fair," she said. "And neither is death."

Sawyer let her go. "My God. What's going on with you? Do you hear yourself?"

"Okay, look. I know this all sounds nuts to you, and I can understand why. But if you ever cared about me, you'll try to believe what I'm saying. You might think I'm batshit crazy, but you know I love those girls—*both* of them. If we're going to save them, we must get to the right place, and there's only one way to do that."

"And what's that?" he asked with a sigh.

Holly looked to the trail ahead. "We've got to play."

~

"Where's her body?" Bridget asked.

They stared into the empty casket. Holly's throat was too dry to gulp.

"Oh my God . . ." Faith said, watching from afar. "Oh my God, did someone freakin' take it?"

"Maybe they moved her," Holly said. "I mean, after what happened."

"You mean after she *ate her parents*?" Bridget said, snarkily. "I guess that's one way to get booted out of the family tomb."

Faith was less amused. "This isn't funny, you guys!"

"Oh, calm down, princess. A minute ago, you wanted to take pictures in the graveyard just to look cool."

"Yeah, well, I changed my mind." She fingered her ankh necklace. "This place gives me bad vibes. Can we please go?"

"Hold up," Holly said, looking closer at the underside of the coffin's lid.

Bridget leaned in too, bringing the flame closer to the blood-stained wood. Among the claw marks were deliberate etchings. They were crooked and jagged, as if engraved with a knife, but the words formed three sentences.

What do you fear?
Who do you love?
What happens when you die?

FIFTEEN

THE COFFIN HAD SHIFTED WHEN Rose tossed Aubrey against it. Now it slid from its propped position, falling to the floor just as Aubrey said her mother had seen terrible things down here. It gave the girls a start. Bella leapt backward, her hands covering her mouth. Standing close, Rose and Aubrey practically jumped into each other's arms.

"Jesus!" Celeste said, hand to her chest. "I nearly pissed my pants."

Though it had fallen on its side, the casket remained sealed until Celeste took a step toward it. The lid popped open suddenly, startling them again, and the girls huddled close together, watching the cloud of dust thin, revealing the skeleton inside. It was about five foot three, Bella estimated, probably the remains of someone who'd died young.

"I think we need to keep moving," she said.

"Me too," Celeste said. "Screw this place."

Rose looked to Aubrey. "Anything else you want to tell us about your mom's diary?"

Aubrey shrugged one shoulder. "That's pretty much it."

"She didn't elaborate on what terrible things she'd seen?"

Looking at the floor, Aubrey crossed her arms, as if creating a barricade. Bella noticed it but said nothing.

"No," Aubrey said. "She just said it was a bad place."

Rose glowered. "Well, then why the hell did you bring us here?"

"I just thought it'd be cool," she said. "Like visiting a haunted house or something. I didn't know all of this would happen. How could I?"

"What about all that séance crap back in the graveyard? Why did you need six of us?"

Aubrey sighed. "I just made that part up, okay? I only did that 'cause I wanted to have a pentagram. Witchcraft, you know?"

"Sure. Typical goth bullshit."

"Fine, if that's what you wanna call it."

"There's no other way to put it."

Bella stepped in. "C'mon, guys. Let's just go."

"All right," Rose said, throwing up her hands. "What's the use? None of this is ever going to make any sense."

The path ahead went directly past the fallen casket. Rose led the way and Bella helped Marnie along. The girl had grown quiet, sinking into herself. Bella worried shock was setting in but didn't know what to do about it. As they passed by, Aubrey stopped at the cracked coffin and stared.

"What is that?" she said. She squatted beside the casket.

Bella exhaled in frustration. "Aubrey . . ."

"I'm serious. Come look at this."

Rose was the first to investigate, with Celeste following behind.

"Holy shit," Celeste said. "Is that . . .?"

They gathered their torches around the open casket. On the underside of the lid, claw marks were ripped into the wood, as if someone had been trapped inside. But there was more than that. An artistic etching had been made on the inside of the lid, and the scratches ran over it. But with the light of the flames, Bella could make out the image of a young woman in the wood. What struck her was the clothing the female image wore. They didn't look like they were from the nineteenth century. They looked modern yet frayed. The claw marks had raked across the image's body, one digging so deep it put a hole where one eye would have been. Dried blood had sunk into the wood, creating a splatter pattern like a gory wound. It all made it look like the woman in the image had been mauled by a wild animal.

"Is that . . . *Marnie*?" Celeste asked.

Bella went cold. There was no denying the resemblance. At the sound of her name, Marnie stirred but could barely open her remaining eye. Bella wasn't sure if the girl was even registering what was happening.

"What the fuck?" Celeste said, her voice trembling.

"Let's just go," Bella said. "Let's just go, let's just go!"

"Look at these scratch marks," Aubrey said. "It looks like this person was still alive when they were put in here."

Celeste shook her head. "Fuck this."

She backed away from the casket, toward the tunnel that awaited them. Bella joined her, shuffling Marnie along. Rose and Aubrey called for them but didn't leave the coffin yet. They were still investigating. Bella didn't want to stay in the ossuary another second, but she also didn't want to lose sight of anyone.

"Hey," she called out to Celeste. "Hold up."

But Celeste didn't listen. She was picking up her pace. Bella followed her into a smaller, tighter passage through the crypt. Here the walls were made of rocks stacked like bricks, the ceiling so low she had to carry the torch in front of her. Marnie moaned, aching in keeping up with her.

"Celeste, wait!" Bella said. "Marnie can't go this fast!"

Celeste stopped but didn't turn around. Her shoulders shuddered as she cried into her hands. The three girls drew close, and Bella put her arm around her friend, holding two girls at once.

"It's okay," she told them. "We're gonna make it out of here. Help is on the way."

"I'm just so scared," Celeste said. "Why're we down here? What did we do to deserve this?"

"Nothing. There's no, like, karma involved. It just happened."

"You really think we're gonna get out?"

"Yeah," she said, wanting to believe herself. "We'll get out of here just fine."

"All of us?"

The question sent a quiver up Bella's spine. It nestled in her head, feeding her fear, and she fell mute, but knew she had to say something. "Of course." She patted Celeste on the back. "C'mon. Let's get the others to move their butts."

Celeste nodded, wiping her tears, and the girls turned around to fetch Aubrey and Rose from the ossuary. The gateway they'd come in through was now void of the glow of their friends' torches. Bella squinted. They hadn't come that far. They should be able to see the light of the flames. She moved on, counting her steps as they entered the tens, then the twenties. The darkness ahead did not give way to light. It didn't even lead them to the ossuary. The tunnel just went on and on, an endless channel of darkness.

"*Where the fuck is it?*" Celeste asked, nearly choking on her words.

"Did we make a turn somewhere?" Bella asked.

"No! It's just a straight shot tunnel! *What is going on?*"

She ran ahead with her torch held out, waving it side to side, searching the walls for any sort of door or crawlspace. But there were only the rows of smoothed, stacked rock.

Celeste called out for Aubrey, even called for Rose. The only answer she received was the echo of her own cries, rising out of the sepulture like chamber music.

"We're lost," Celeste said.

She dropped to her knees and sobbed, and this time, a dropped torch went out.

~

"Bella!" Rose shouted again. She stood before the passage where the other girls had gone, seeing only darkness, getting no reply. "Bella? Celeste? Marnie?"

Aubrey came beside her, surprising Rose by taking her hand. Rose allowed it. It was comforting to have physical contact, but more importantly it secured Aubrey by her side. She didn't want to lose sight of her too and be left totally alone in this nightmare world.

"We have to go after them," Rose said.

"But what if something happened?"

"Exactly. They'll need our help."

"No, I mean what if what happened to them will happen to us too? What if they fell in a pit or something? What if . . . if . . ."

"If what?" Rose asked, flustered.

"What if something *got them?*"

Rose thought of the crazed bear mangling the sisters and the spider creature that had crawled up Aubrey's face. Another monster seemed entirely possible.

The game's terrible question ran through her head again—*what are you afraid of?*

"We'll be extra careful," Rose said.

"I . . . I don't want to go in there."

"It's the only passage out of here, except the door we came in through. And we're not turning back without them." The thought was too upsetting. It made Rose angry to even have to say it. "We're not leaving them behind."

Aubrey's face fell. "I wasn't saying that."

Rose gripped her hand harder and guided her toward the tunnel's entrance. It gaped like a hungry mouth, making Rose think of starving babies in third world countries and soldiers screaming as they died in battle. The dark thoughts swirled, and Rose winced against them. Where were they coming from? She never thought like this. She always tried to avoid the true-life horrors on the news. Being down here had brought out a morbid energy in her. She wondered if it was truly her own, or if the crypt was infecting her somehow. It was a strange theory, but she'd seen a lot of strange things tonight, and as they entered the passageway, something told her she was about to see things even stranger.

They called out for the girls as they journeyed into the tunnel.

No answer.

Aubrey's hand grew moist in Rose's, but they dared not let go. The walls seemed to dance from the unsteady light of the torches, casting shadowy illusions. In the corner of her eye, Rose could see the shadow of a person, but it vanished the moment she looked at it head-on. But for some reason, her fear started to ebb. Her heartbeat decelerated and a sudden sense of well-being waved over her like a drug. She felt certain they were going to get out of here alive, even Marnie. They would find the other girls just ahead, probably only a few feet away from an exit that would take them up into the woods. The positive feeling made her feel warm and tingly, and though it was odd, she welcomed its peace.

"I feel funny," Aubrey said.

"Me too."

Aubrey smiled at Rose, and she smiled back. They giggled and stopped walking, their torches casting them in a golden glow. Aubrey's face was intimately close. Despite her goth makeup, she seemed angelic and somehow younger, like an innocent cherub.

"I'm really sorry I pushed you," Rose said.

"It's okay. You also saved me from that spider." Aubrey reached up and caressed Rose's chin, then ran her fingertip along her bottom lip. "You're so beautiful."

Warmth spread through Rose then, her blood rushing to her

erogenous zones. She'd never felt this way with anyone other than Tyson. And she'd never lusted after another girl . . . had she? But Aubrey wasn't like other girls. She was special. *They* were special.

Aubrey let her torch fall to the ground so she could take Rose's head in both hands. Her fingers went into her hair, sending vibrations through Rose's entire body. She let her torch fall too, the light on the ground still going, cocooning the two girls in a private, tangerine orb, alone at last.

Aubrey kissed Rose, and she opened her mouth to accept her.

A whisper fluttered out of the darkness beyond.

"Who do you love?" it asked.

~

Bella's mind wandered as they continued through the crypt. A mental fog made her uncertain as to which way they were even going. Were they still heading back toward the ossuary or were they back to searching for a way out?

"Where're we g-going?" Marnie asked.

Bella couldn't lie to the girl. "I don't know. Can you stand on your own?"

"I . . . think so."

Bella reached into her pocket for her phone. She was going for her compass app when she noticed the time.

Midnight.

It had to be a mistake. It was midnight when they'd started the séance at the cemetery. It had to be closer to two in the morning by now. Could the lack of a signal affect the clock? She opened her compass app and the needle spun like a dreidel, never settling.

"Shit. Celeste, what time does your phone have?"

Celeste had stopped bawling, but her dread remained. She already had her phone out to use its flashlight. They'd tried to ignite the torch after it had gone out, but it only offered a weak, blue flame before dying, and there was no more vodka to make it flammable. With only one torch to light their way, the girls walked close together, Celeste helping to brace Marnie.

"What the hell?" Celeste said. "It says twelve midnight."

Bella had her try the compass. Though they had different model phones, both had the same results. At least the flashlights worked.

As they carried on, Bella's mind drifted to matters less pressing, the thoughts she'd been having in the outside world taking precedent over the dire situation at hand. She worried about school and if she'd be able to make it into a good college. She wondered if she wanted to go to college at all, or if she should take some time off to explore, maybe backpack through Europe. Her deadbeat dad and quietly depressed mother ran circles through her mind, all the stresses that had slowly pushed her into the arms of emo culture, making her relate to the lyrics of goth bands and securing her decision to wear only black from now on.

All this led her back to her deteriorating relationship with Rose. Bella blamed herself for losing her best friend. Rose was still in her life, but it was only a matter of time before they drifted apart completely. Bella's change in lifestyle had put too much of a burden on the back of their friendship. She'd just kept on piling luggage until it was impossible for them to make it up life's many hills together. But while Bella blamed herself, she felt she wasn't the only one who'd contributed to this downfall.

She'd never confronted Mom about what she'd seen.

On that summer day, Bella had planned to spend the afternoon at the lake with friends, but after taking a few hits on a joint she started feeling too anxious being around people and rode her bike home, cutting across her neighbor's yard to the back of her house. It was a Saturday, so Mom was off work, meaning the kitchen's side door would be open so air could get in. The hydraulic brace had broken off the screen door, and if you let it go it slammed behind you, so Bella had gotten into the habit of supporting it so it would close gently. She started toward the fridge for some orange juice, but a noise drew her attention.

It came from the hallway, a muffled voice—a *man's* voice.

Her dad was spending more and more time at her grandmother's house as the bickering between Bella's parents had grown worse. She hadn't expected him to be here and frankly wasn't interested in speaking to him. If she had to pick a side in this war, she was going with Mom. Dad made it an easy choice.

Bella tiptoed toward her room, hoping not to be noticed. She didn't want to get between her parents arguing, even if she didn't hear any yelling. But as she drew close to her parent's bedroom, she heard her mother moan. The male voice returned, louder and clearer.

"Yeah, baby," he said. "That's it. Just like that."

It wasn't her dad's voice, but it was familiar. The door to the bedroom was open a crack. Bella held her breath as she approached, putting one eye to the gap.

She instantly wished she hadn't.

Rose's dad stood beside her parents' bed with his jeans around his ankles. Mom was only half dressed, down on her knees in front of Mr. Peterson, pleasuring him with her mouth. A shiver went through Bella, and she looked away, backing out of the hallway as quickly and quietly as she could. She left the house and rode down the driveway, passing by Mr. Peterson's truck. Having gone in the back way, she hadn't seen it earlier. Numbness struck her as she headed to the park. She thought she should cry but didn't feel the need.

How long had this been going on? Did Rose know? Wouldn't she have told Bella? Maybe not. Bella didn't think she could bear to break this news to Rose, and so, she never had. She kept what she'd seen a secret, too afraid to even write about it in her journal. It would make it all too real.

But soon she started having the fantasies. In them, Mr. Peterson would divorce his wife and marry Mom, after she divorced Bella's father. Then she and Rose would be sisters, and Bella would have the happy home-life she'd been robbed of. After the initial shock of finding them having sex wore off, she quickly warmed up to the idea of Mom and Mr. Peterson being a couple, so much so that she'd almost confronted her mother about it to encourage her but chickened out. If she busted her, Mom might be too ashamed of the affair to continue it, and that was the last thing Bella wanted.

The only thing that ruined the fantasy was realizing Rose would be crushed by her parents' separation. They had what appeared to be a good marriage, and were wonderful, caring parents. And if they did get a divorce, didn't the mother usually get custody? Rose wouldn't move in with Bella and Mom; only Mr. Peterson would. Life could be so unfair. Just when Bella had started to believe something could work out in her favor, reality came crashing in like the wrecking ball it was. And knowing Rose would be devastated by her parents separating made Bella resent her. Though it was only an imagined scenario, Rose destroying what could have been a new, happy family for them both planted a seed of contempt in Bella's heart. It was another nail in the coffin that would soon seal her up in the goth lifestyle.

Coffin, she thought, walking through the crypt. What they'd seen was so bizarre. How could a picture of Marnie be in the casket? And had the person inside really been buried alive? Maybe it was just a trick of the light that made the artwork look like Marnie. Maybe it was just because the claw marks weirdly matched the ones on her body. Perhaps without those scratches, the girl in the picture wouldn't look like her at all.

She was still contemplating this when a voice called out of the darkness ahead.

"Hello?"

The girls froze.

"Hello?" the voice called again.

It wasn't Rose or Aubrey. It was the voice of a man.

"Who the hell is that?" Celeste whispered.

Bella flushed, a smile stretching across her face. "It's them! They found us!"

"Rose's dad?"

"No," she said, her heart fluttering. "It's her boyfriend." She called out to him. "Tyson! We're in here!"

"I'm coming!" he said from the blackness. "I'm coming!"

She tingled. She'd heard Tyson say this before, under more intimate circumstances. It'd only been once, when they were both a little drunk, but it intensified the crush she'd had on her best friend's boyfriend all these years.

Tanya Griffith's parents had gone out of town, and she'd invited nearly half the people in her grade for a party, getting the older boys next door to buy a keg of beer and a few bottles of the stronger stuff. Rose was planning to go but came down with a stomach bug so bad she actually missed school—unheard of for the academically obsessed teen—so she stayed in bed, missing the party of the year. Though they'd not come together, Bella and Tyson found each other among the crowd, and after a few shots and red solo cups, they ended up in Tanya's parents' bedroom, then hid in the master bathroom for a quickie. Tyson was only the second boy Bella had ever had sex with, and though it was only once it meant so much more to her because she was in love with him.

She'd initiated things, luring Tyson in, preying upon his boozed-up, teenage libido. It was easy to blame the alcohol, but Bella's anger toward Rose for getting in the way of her imaginary perfect family made it easier to act upon urges she'd repressed for years. Tyson was tall, funny, and handsome. Not a meathead jock like some of his friends, but more masculine than the sensitive boys Bella often dated. And yet, he was very romantic with Rose. Even though they'd been together a long time, he still brought her flowers sometimes when he picked her up for date nights and surprised her with random gifts. He loved Rose in the way Bella had always wanted someone to love her, and that envy had become corrosive, sinister. Mom hadn't let a man being taken stand in her way, so why should Bella? She didn't want to steal Tyson from Rose exactly; she just wanted a little taste of the good life her friend got to enjoy every day. As she'd expected, Tyson flooded with regret almost as soon as it was over. He seemed to avoid Bella as much as he could after that but was always nice to her when she was around, probably wanting to stay on her good side so she wouldn't tell Rose what they'd done. Bella had no intention to tell. Tyson could hate himself all he wanted, as long as he kept their secret.

His voice echoed through the chamber. "Bella! I'm coming!"

"I'm here!" she said.

Heat spread through her. The memory of his hands on her body sent a shiver across her flesh. She let go of Marnie, letting Celeste hold her, and started toward Tyson's voice.

"Hey," Celeste said. "Hold on."

Bella handed her their only torch so she wouldn't have anything to complain about. What did Bella need it for now? They were saved. The man she adored had come to her rescue. She charged into the shadows, ignoring Celeste as she called out for her, not even registering the words. Her mind was too preoccupied with something she'd been asked earlier that night.

Who do you love?

She'd lied, naming a random boy, but her heart knew the truth and now, so did the crypt. Here in the black bowels of the earth, the rules of the world above did not apply. Aching for Tyson, Bella began to sweat, she twisted out of her jacket and tossed it to the ground. She started unbuttoning her blouse, wetting her lips in anticipation of a kiss, knowing it was madness but unable to control the urge.

Who do you love?

"Tyson!" she called out. "Come to me. I want you."

Her skin went to goose flesh as her blouse fell away, and she was just reaching back to undo her bra when a figure took shape before her.

Bella gasped. Her feet locked in place and the warmth that had been spreading through her turned to stabbing icicles. The shadowy figure was just a little more than five feet tall—much shorter than Tyson. It moved forward, light on its feet like a ballroom dancer, and though there was only the faintest trace of light from the torch Bella had left behind, she could see the outline of scraggily, long hair, and the rotted gown that clung to the emaciated body. The face remained in shadow, but when the arms came up Bella could see the hands in detail. The fingers were worn down past the first knuckle, leaving bloody stumps with jagged bone jutting through the gangrenous flesh.

Bella opened her mouth to scream but couldn't make a sound. Her lungs swelled as if filled with smoke. Though she didn't want to see any more, she couldn't even blink. Horror had struck her like a fist.

A gravelly female voice surrounded her. "Ladies and gentlemen. Let's meet our next contestant."

SIXTEEN

"LET'S MAKE A GAME OF it," Holly said.

Bridget and Faith gave her the same confused look. Holly pointed at the three questions etched into the underside of the coffin's lid.

"Let's answer them," she said, smirking. She wasn't sure why, but she was enjoying this. Bridget had been right. It was creepy, but cool. "Who wants to go first?"

Bridget slowly shook her head. "This is messed up. Who carved that in there?"

"Probably just vandalism," Faith said, unconvincingly. "We can't be the first ones to break in here, right?"

Bridget perked up. "Hey, yeah. We need to tag this place. Let 'em know we were here."

She handed Holly the lighter, drew her spray-paint from her back pocket, and approached the wall, decorating it with her name.

"Maybe Madeline made her mark too," Holly said. "I think she carved these questions in her coffin."

"Why would she do that?" Faith asked.

"Think about it. She was trapped in here, eating her parents. She must have gone mad. Maybe she was asking herself these questions because she knew she was going to die. 'What are you afraid of? Who do you love? What happens when you die?' These sound like death bed questions to me."

Faith shuddered. "Please don't say that."

"She had to sleep somewhere, so I'll bet she spent her nights in this coffin. Not that she had much light to know if it was day or night. Time had no meaning down here."

"Holly, stop!"

Faith glared at her, so Holly quit talking about poor Madeline Goldman and backed away from the casket. Bridget finished spraying and handed her the can, but Holly turned her down. It didn't seem right to ugly a sacred place, even one with such a history of horror.

"All right," Bridget said, sounding bored. "I'll go first. Which one's the first question again?"

Holly grinned. "Madeline wants to know what you're afraid of."

"Oh, please," Bridget said, scoffing. "I'm not scared of anything."

The door to the tomb slammed shut.

~

Just looking at the entrance made Holly tremble, and she shoved her hands in her pockets to try to hide it from Sawyer. She felt the pocketknife tucked away in there, giving her a small sense of security. The steps leading down to the tomb—to the labyrinth—were more cracked and chipped than they'd been thirty years ago, but they still held, an open invitation for visitors. In the pit, a broken slate of wood was wedged in the doorway so it was slightly open.

"What the hell is this?" Sawyer asked.

"The tomb. The gateway to the maze."

He ran his hand over his head. "Shit, Holly."

"Look, I don't blame you for doubting me. But I'm asking you to trust me."

"Okay. So, what do we do?"

Holly bit her bottom lip. Now that Sawyer asked, she wasn't sure she had the answer. All she had to go on were distant memories she'd spent her whole life trying to suppress. She looked at the open door— a red carpet to Hell, welcoming her home.

"We have to go in," she said.

"I thought you said a man couldn't."

"You can go in the tomb," she said, "but I doubt you'll be allowed into the labyrinth."

"*Allowed?* What does that mean? Is there a bouncer at the door?"

"I'm being serious. There's a game that goes with this place that only girls can play. Once you start the game, it lets you in. But men try to get in the labyrinth and fail. I've heard of boys coming here to see if the legends were true, but they never see anything more than the tomb. The gateway never appears for them. She doesn't want them."

He raised an eyebrow. "Who is *she?*"

And so, Holly told him. Told him everything.

Well, almost everything.

~

Faith wasn't the only one scared now. The girls pulled on the door to the tomb, combining their strength. It was like trying to pry open a safe. The door refused to move.

"Oh fuck!" Bridget said.

"Don't panic," Holly told her, though she couldn't even take her own advice.

Faith covered her face and wept. Holly was too frazzled to console her. With the door shut, the darkness in the tomb was absolute. The Zippo's flame gave them only a small pocket of light, an illusion of safety in an unknown sea of black.

"It closed so quickly," Bridget said. "I think somebody shut us in."

She screamed and pounded on the door, demanding to be released, but if someone were on the other side, Holly doubted they'd be able to hear anything. Bridget turned around, putting her back to the door.

"We're so fucked," she said.

"Don't say that," Holly told her. "We can't think that way."

Faith uncovered her face. "But what're we gonna do? I'm scared."

The hairs on Holly's neck stood up as a breeze hit her from behind. It was a gentle gust coming from the back of the tomb, something that should have been impossible. She turned with the lighter, expecting to find a small hole in the wall, maybe something they could chip away at to try to escape. Instead, there was a tunnel that hadn't been there a moment ago. It was tall and wide, like a hall in a subway, and its black shadows were punctuated by dim spots of blue light like moonbeams in a dense thicket. The girls stared at it in shocked silence, Holly's hand shaking so much she nearly dropped the lighter.

Holly's CB headphones crackled with sound, startling them. At first, she thought she'd accidentally hit the play button, but it wasn't Nirvana that came through the speakers. It was a high and fluttery female voice, making clear announcements.

"Ladies," the woman said, "welcome to the pageant."

The girls froze. Holly looked around the tomb. Were there hidden cameras? One-way mirrors? Optical illusions? Was someone watching them? She gazed into the tunnel of darkness. *What was it they said about staring too long into the abyss?*

"Oh, God . . ." Faith whimpered.

"Who are you?" Holly demanded of the disembodied voice. "What do you want?"

The voice crackled through the headphones. "I'm so glad you're here. We welcome new contestants. You're all so young, so lovely . . . especially the redhead."

Faith gasped.

"I'd say she has an advantage in that regard," said the mystery woman. "But the games have just begun."

"Let us out," Holly said.

"You can't step down once you've entered. It's going to be a wonderful contest."

"What contest?"

"Why, the beauty pageant, of course," the voice said with a giggle. "Sisters always have a friendly competition. As a former winner, I'll be one of the judges. Me, Mum, and Dad."

Bridget shook her head. "No . . . no fucking way . . . this can't be real."

"We'll decide the winner," the voice said. "It's time, ladies and gentlemen, to choose The Prettiest Girl in the Grave!"

The clamor of applause filled the headphones. The audience sounded large, as if they were attending a Broadway play.

"Let us out!" Holly said. She tried to think practically. Someone had found a way to feed sound into her headphones; she just didn't know how. "I don't know who you are, but this isn't funny. We're minors and you're holding us against our will."

Faith and Bridget pulled on the door to no avail. The applause grew louder around Holly's neck. She unplugged the headphones from her Walkman, but the cheers continued.

"We've had one answer to our first question," said the voice. "Thank you, Bridget. Now we move on to Faith."

Faith spun around, wanting a solution Holly just couldn't give.

Should they play along? Would the woman set them free if they did?

"So, Red," the voice said, "what are you afraid of?"

Faith sniffled. "I'm afraid of being here. Please, let us out."

The audience clapped for her.

"Very good," said the voice. "Now we come to Holly. You seem to have a strong constitution. Tell us . . . what are you afraid of?"

Holly swallowed hard. If she told the woman her fears, would she try to make them come true? She'd locked them in here. She was toying with them, messing with their minds. Well, Holly wasn't going to make it any easier for the bitch.

"I'll tell you what I'm *not* afraid of," she said. "*Confrontation.* How about you? Why don't you show yourself?"

Bridget grabbed her arm. "Don't."

But Holly's answer was already out there.

The floor began to vibrate. Holly tensed as the walls shuddered. This was more than a prankster should be capable of. A terrible word went through her mind—*earthquake.* They were extremely rare in the northeast but not unheard of. The girls huddled as dust fell from the ceiling and the room filled with the blue glow coming from the hallway, illuminating the casket before them as a spindly figure sat up within it.

They all screamed.

The coffin had been empty. Now a woman was climbing out of it.

Blood dripped from her mangled hands and there were haunted circles around her eyes. She was young and pretty, but too thin to be healthy. Her gown had once been beautiful, but was now covered in filth—dust, dirt, dried blood. She came out of the coffin in her bare feet, so small and dainty. She looked at the girls, chilling them, but seemed not to see them, as if she were looking through them, staring off into space. The woman walked to another one of the coffins and opened it, then raised the arm of whoever lay inside.

Holly cringed. It was a man's arm, terribly mutilated, the flesh stripped away almost to the elbow, leaving only bone and dried sinew. The young woman bent over and sank her teeth into the man. The girls watched in horror as she peeled away a sliver of meat. Though the corpse didn't bleed, the red of its muscle tissue gleamed purple in the azure light of the tomb. After devouring the flesh, the woman opened the other coffin. The older woman inside was slightly decomposed, her eyes stitched shut.

The ghostly young woman raised her arms and smiled with bits of human gore stuck between her teeth.

"Now it is time for the dance competition," she said to the corpses. She began to twirl, spinning light on her feet, clearly skilled. She smiled lovingly at the dead. "Don't be biased just because I'm the youngest, okay? I want your vote to be honest."

Bridget broke away from the group, walking backwards toward the nebulous hall. She was shaking her head and muttering through clenched teeth.

"It's true," she said. "Jesus, it's all true."

"Bridget, wait!" Holly said.

But her friend turned and ran. Faith pulled on Holly's arm, guiding her toward the hallway, anything to get away from the cannibal ghost. As the headphones filled with ballet music, the woman danced on her tiptoes, twirling closer. The girls ran, following Bridget into the unknown. The further they got down the tunnel, the fainter the music became, so Holly ran until they couldn't hear it anymore. Eventually, they had to stop to catch their breath.

"What the fuck is going on?" Holly asked. She looked to Bridget. "What were you saying back there? What's 'all true'?"

Bridget leaned back against the wall, breathing heavy. "The story. The one my grandma told me. There's more to it. I didn't think all the details were important when I told you but . . ."

Holly came closer with the Zippo to better see Bridget's face. "What is it?"

Bridget stared into space and drew a cigarette from her pack. She leaned into the flame to light it, taking a long drag, her hands still shaking.

"Madeline Goldman was a beauty queen," she said. "Grandma told me the Goldman daughters did pageants. They even competed with each other sometimes, and it created a wicked rivalry. She said it was well known the sisters hated each other, especially Madeline, because she was the prettiest. Even when they were little, they would put on shows at home for their parents. Madeline was the youngest, so she got the most attention from their mom and dad, making the others hate her from an early age."

"Holy freakin' shit," Faith said. "Is that what . . . what she was doing back there? Putting on a pageant?"

Bridget exhaled a cloud of smoke. "Maybe when she was trapped in the tomb, she went crazy and, like, started her own beauty contest in her head."

A chill went through Holly. "The Prettiest Girl in the Grave."

"Oh, God," Faith said. "So . . . so she wants us to play?"

"I think so," Bridget said. "Maybe her spirit can't rest without it."

Holly handed Bridget her lighter back and hugged herself. She felt cold and small, a dust speck in space. "A ghost. It's just not possible."

"Well, I believe in the paranormal," Faith said.

"Yeah," Bridget said. "After all that, how can you not?"

"If we go along with this game, will she let us go?"

Bridget was stoic. "I don't know."

"If . . ."

Faith stopped short, but Holly knew what she was thinking, what they all were thinking.

If only one of us can win, what happens to the losers?

SEVENTEEN

WHAT AM I DOING? **ROSE** suddenly wondered.

They lay on the ground of the tunnel, beset by the light of the torches. Beneath her, Aubrey's eyes were closed, her lips still wet from Rose's kisses. A hickey was forming on her neck and her coat was open, the lacy bra the only thing covering her upper body. Her hands were under Rose's clothes, caressing her back, her nails softly grazing the skin.

What had felt so right a moment ago now seemed alien. This wasn't like her at all. Rose would never cheat on Tyson. And she wasn't a lesbian or bisexual. Getting to her knees, she pulled her letterman jacket tight around her. Aubrey opened her eyes. They were full of hunger.

"Come back to me," she said, panting.

"Wait . . ."

Aubrey tugged on Rose, trying to draw her back into the soft embrace she'd broken. Rose pulled herself free.

"Something's going on," Rose said. "Snap out of it."

Aubrey sat up. "I want you."

"No, you don't. It's this place." Rose grabbed her torch and got to her feet. She extended her hand to Aubrey. "C'mon, we have to get out of here."

"You know you want me too." Aubrey scooted toward her. "Deep down, you know it."

"Aubrey, stop."

But she didn't. Aubrey stood and came closer. She reached out to stroke Rose's cheek, the same motion that started all this in the first place, and Rose grabbed her wrist and held it, hard. Aubrey's face fell with surprised disappointment.

"But . . . don't you love me?"

Though she'd rejected many boys in her life, Rose had always tried to let them down gently. She hated breaking hearts. It made her feel like a thief or traitor. Once during their relationship, Tyson had suggested they take a break and see other people. It crushed Rose, the pain so deep and true she had trouble forgiving him when he came crawling back two weeks later. Even now, she feared her love for him. It was the only thing that made her feel weak and vulnerable. She didn't want to put such a curse on someone else, but she had to put a stop to this strange, sudden romance with Aubrey.

"I'm sorry," Rose told her. "But I'm taken, and I'm not gay."

"That's okay,' Aubrey said with a smile. "I'm not gay either."

Rose blinked, stunned. "Then what are we doing?"

Aubrey started to reply but had no answer. Her brow furrowed, the first sign she was returning to her senses.

"It's this place," Rose said. "It's testing us, just like you said it would. It wants to challenge our answers to the second question."

"*Who do you love?*" Aubrey said.

"Right. I said Tyson, my boyfriend. The crypt is trying to tempt me. With you."

Aubrey looked into Rose's eyes, and for a brief moment Rose felt the urge to pull her in for another passionate kiss. She shook the feeling loose.

"I started to like you," Aubrey confessed, "after you saved me from the spider. I admire how strong you are, how smart you are. I always wanted to be someone like you." Her eyes misted. "I was just never able to fit in. Sometimes I feel like I don't even know who I am."

Rose smiled. "Hey. It's okay. We all feel like that sometimes."

"No. It's more than that. You wouldn't understand."

Rose wanted to say something encouraging, but Aubrey went to her dwindling torch to pick it up and Rose chose to stay silent.

"I'm not really gay," Aubrey said. "I do like men. But sometimes, I kind of like women too. I've never made out with one before, though. I guess I'm just bi-curious. And seeing you and Bella together . . . well, you know."

"Wait, what?" Rose squinted. "What about me and Bella?"

"C'mon. You say you're not gay, but it's obvious you two have something going on."

Rose's jaw fell. "You think Bella's my *girlfriend?*"

"You're saying she's not?"

"*No.* She's just my best friend."

"But you're so different. I thought it was an *opposites attract* sort of thing."

"Yeah, well, we didn't used to be so different. Hanging out with you people changed her."

Aubrey glowered. "*Us people?*"

"Don't get offended. You know what I mean. Once she started hanging out with goths, she changed. That's all I'm saying. Now let's go."

She started walking and Aubrey kept up with her, calling out for the others. It seemed the conversation had ended for now. With the tunnel's love potion wearing off, Rose felt irritable again, frustrated.

"This was a bad idea, you know," she said.

"Yeah," Aubrey said. "I know. I'm sorry, okay?"

"We should've never come here. I knew this night was a mistake."

"Yeah, well, nobody forced you."

The urge to push Aubrey again was intense, but Rose stifled it. Instead, she pushed using her words. "If there's anything else you haven't told us, I think you owe it to me to spill it."

"I told you, that's pretty much it."

Rose stopped. Aubrey did too.

"Well, 'pretty much' is a little too vague for me," Rose said. "Considering what's happening here, I don't think any detail from your mom's diary is too small to mention. You said she came here and saw terrible things."

"I also said she wasn't specific."

"But how did she get away from those terrible things? If she got trapped down here too, how did she get out?"

Aubrey started walking again. Rose grabbed her and Aubrey

resisted, shoving her, but Rose didn't let go.

"Answer me, damn it!" Rose said.

"Stop it."

"Our lives depend on this!"

Aubrey shoved Rose off her, and Rose reared back and slapped her across the face. Aubrey stumbled. Minutes ago, they'd been making out; now they were on the verge of a fistfight. But Aubrey wasn't foolish enough to challenge the taller, stronger Rose. Instead, she held her torch out in front of her with both hands to defend herself.

"Fine, you bitch," Aubrey said with a snarl. "You wanna know how we get out of here? We play the fucking game! I've been telling you this from the beginning. The Prettiest Girl in the Grave is a competition. My mother played it here with her friends thirty years ago. I thought it was just a spooky story she wrote in her diary, like a half truth." Her eyes grew wet again. "But this shit is one hundred percent real. You know it, I know it, and the others know it too."

"I don't know anything," Rose said. "That's the problem."

"Well, you know as much as I do."

But Rose didn't believe her. If Aubrey's mother lived to tell the tale, she would have explained how she escaped. If this really was a contest, maybe Aubrey was keeping secrets for a reason.

It gives her an edge over the competition.

A scream came out of the darkness, and despite their quarreling, Rose and Aubrey went to each other, facing the horror as one.

~

Bella ran.

The shadows were so thick she could hardly see. She thought of using her phone for light but didn't want to stop. Bolting down the cold corridor, she nearly tripped on the coat she'd tossed off. She grabbed it quickly and ran on, screaming. She couldn't see the torch, couldn't see Celeste and Marnie. The crypt had swallowed them too. She was all alone now. Alone with the undead thing that reached out of the ether with mangled fingers. The ghost woman's words ran through Bella's mind.

Ladies and gentlemen. Let's meet our next contestant.

She screamed again, hoping to rid her thoughts from it.

"Bella?" someone called from ahead.

Bella halted, looking in every direction, though the corridor offered only blackness. She dug for her phone and turned on the flashlight.

"Bella?" the voice called again. "Is that you?"

Tears of relief wetted her eyes. "Rose?"

"Stay where you are. We're coming."

Every muscle tightened. Was this just another trick? The ghost had used Tyson's voice to draw her into a trap, using the same words. Was the ghost mimicking Rose now too? Bella backed up, but that was the direction the ghost had come from. She couldn't go back that way. Not alone. Rose called for her, and a golden glow appeared around the curve ahead. Aubrey and Rose soon followed, their torches breaking the darkness, a small mercy.

Bella ran to her friends. It had to be them. It just had to.

"Are you okay?" Rose asked.

Bella put her arms around her best friend and held her tight, clinging to the reality of her in the insanity of the crypt.

"Why are you only in your bra?" Rose asked. She took the coat from Bella and put it over her back like a shawl. "Jesus, you're ice cold. Put your hands in my armpits."

Bella did as she was told. It was good to have someone else tell her what to do, someone she trusted. When Aubrey helped her into her sleeves, Bella noticed the hickey on Aubrey's neck. Had it been there before? It didn't matter. All that mattered to Bella now was she wasn't alone anymore. But where were Celeste and Marnie? Aubrey and Rose should have passed them before getting to her.

Rose asked before Bella could. "Where are the others?"

"I . . . I don't know . . ."

She explained what happened, leaving out the lust she'd felt for Tyson. It all sounded like madness when she heard herself say it, but she told them of the ghost and how it had tricked her, making her lose sight of the other girls. She looked to her friends for support. Aubrey seemed to believe her, but there was doubt on Rose's face.

"You heard Tyson?" she asked. "So, he's here?"

"No. It wasn't him. It was her. She said I was a contestant."

"We all are," Aubrey said.

"But what does it want?" Rose asked. "What does *she* want?"

"We need to go on to the next round," Aubrey said, pale in the firelight. "The final question."

The girls fell silent, remembering. *What happens when you die?*

The sound of shuffling feet turned their heads. Bella couldn't help but hide behind Rose as they watched, the sound growing louder, something drawing near. They didn't ask who was there. They only waited. And when Celeste shuffled out of the shadows, Bella felt a rush of relief, but it didn't last long. Celeste had a dazed look about her, her brown eyes looking black in the firelight—black and lost. Her clothes were bloody. Her hands were bloodier.

"Celeste," Bella said. "Where's Marnie?"

EIGHTEEN

"JESUS," SAWYER SAID.

Her story shocked him, as she knew it would. It had shocked the police when they'd questioned Holly thirty years ago about what happened down in the tomb. She'd given them most of the story, but twisted the truth about how she'd gotten out, a lie she'd stuck with all this time. She put the same spin on things when telling Sawyer.

She, Bridget, and Faith had been trapped down there for days. Bridget wore a digital watch, but it had suddenly stopped working, and with no natural light they had no way to track the time. They searched the halls for another way out, but the tunnels seemed endless, and when Holly etched markings on the wall with a penny, they ended up seeing them again, confirming they were going in circles. They slept in shifts, so someone was always on guard. They grew hungry enough that they ate the rest of Bridget's cigarettes, which made them nauseated. Dehydration began to set in, and Holly suggested they drink their urine, but having nothing to catch it in, they would have to cup their hands under themselves when they peed. The girls decided it would be a last resort. Bridget said, "At least it's sterile," and Holly didn't have the heart to tell her that was a myth, that they would be drinking bacteria.

"What does she want from us?" Faith asked. "How do we play her stupid game?"

They'd not heard or seen the ghost woman since the tomb. They'd tried dancing the way she had and announced each other like they were in a beauty pageant. When they tried to return to the tomb, they could no longer find it. It wasn't until they came across the ossuary that it occurred to Holly.

In their travels through the crypt, they'd faced many forks in the halls, but hadn't chosen the path leading to the ossuary until now. Blue skeletons lurked in the shadows like night terrors and moldy coffins were haphazardly strewn about. Some of the caskets had names carved into them and engravings of bear heads like a crest, and when Holly saw this, she remembered the questions etched into Madeline's coffin back in the tomb.

"Hey," she said to her friends. "I think I've got it."

Bridget and Faith were huddled close around the Zippo's flame, as if it could protect them. Holly was increasingly worried about what they'd do when the lighter fluid ran out.

"The questions," Holly said. "The ones in her coffin. Maybe they weren't just to scare us. Maybe they're part of the game. I mean, in beauty pageants, don't they ask the women things, like what their goals are and what they believe in?"

"I don't know," Bridget said. "I don't watch that shit."

"Me neither, but I know enough about them to know that."

"You're right," Faith said. "They do that. I used to watch those contests on TV when I was little. Back then, I wanted to be a beauty queen, but I grew out of it before I was old enough."

"Okay. So maybe that's why she pressed us on what we're afraid of. What if it's part of the game, right? I never answered. Maybe the game's on pause because she's still waiting for me to tell her."

The girls looked at each other as the notion sank in.

"I didn't want to give her another way to mess with our heads," Holly said. "I figured if we told her what scared us, she'd just use it against us. But—"

"But what if we have no choice," Faith said, finishing Holly's sentence. "What if that's the whole game?"

Holly took the deepest breath of her life and looked around the ossuary, half expecting their poltergeist tormentor to appear. Even in the dense shadows, the ceiling looked white here, but she couldn't quite see why. She considered lying about what she was afraid of but sensed anything other than the truth would backfire. She thought of her parents and imagined them in distress, wondering where their daughter had disappeared to, fearing she'd been abducted by some murderous drifter. She thought of her older brother and her other friends at school, and everyone else she loved having in her life. The truth struck her in the heart.

"I'm scared of being alone," she told the crypt. "Did you hear me? I'm scared of being *alone*."

Applause crackled in her headphones, causing the girls to jump. The haunting voice returned, and strangely, it was a relief to hear. It meant the ghost woman was communicating again. Only she could tell them the way out.

"Strong-willed and smart," the ghost said. "Holly must make her parents very proud. We're so glad you lovely ladies returned to the pageant. Step right up, step right up!"

Holly stared up at the ceiling, still expecting the spectral woman to appear out of oblivion.

"What happens now?" Faith asked, more to Holly than the ghost.

"We have two more questions," the ghost said, sounding like a carnival barker or the host of an old radio show. "Then we move on to the more exciting part of our pageant—the test."

Holly didn't like the sound of that but had to play along. They all did.

"Fine," she said. "The next question."

She remembered what was written inside the coffin but figured it best to let the ghost tell them in case she was wrong. She didn't want another long silence from the late Madeline Goldman.

"Who do you love, ladies?" the ghost said to a round of applause. "Who do you love?"

At the time, Holly had just dumped her boyfriend, Jack, and had a crush on a blond skater named Ryan, who didn't even know she was alive. Bridget was the most promiscuous of the group but wasn't the type of girl who enjoyed romance and relationships, only hedonistic flings when the mood hit her. Though Faith drew the most male attention, many guys seemed too intimidated by her beauty to ask her out. And she was so worried about being taken advantage of by guys who only wanted one thing that she shied away from anyone who showed a strong interest in her. She'd confessed to Holly that she'd fooled around with boys but had yet to go all the way because she wanted her first time to be special. They'd kept that secret from Bridget, who they knew would only laugh.

"I love Ryan Ellis," Holly said, hoping a crush would suffice. She had a spiral notebook at home full of love poems about him. She'd always had a knack for rhyming verse but kept her writing to herself for this very reason.

Faith spoke up next. "I love my mom."

They waited for Bridget. Holly had no idea what her friend would say. Bridget showed no passion for boys that wasn't merely physical. She also came from a dysfunctional home and rarely had anything good to say about her parents or siblings.

"Fine," Bridget said. "I love my cat, Fuzzy."

The headphones filled with clapping and a few whistles.

"Final question, ladies," the woman said, a macabre game show host. "What happens when you die?"

The audience murmured in a hush.

"I know, folks, I know," the ghost said. "I certainly asked myself that many times down here."

The audience's uncomfortable laughter echoed through the headphones. Bridget and Faith looked to Holly, waiting for her to go first.

She shrugged. "I'm not really sure. Maybe you go to an afterlife? I don't know."

Holly braced for applause or booing, but the audience seemed to be waiting for their host to decide for them. A tense silence hung in the air.

"Not the best answer we've ever heard," the ghost said, "but it is acceptable."

Light applause.

Bridget shouted, "I don't know either!"

The audience jeered, making Holly's skin pimple. Would Bridget be punished?

"I'm sorry, Bridget," the ghost said, "but you can't give the same answer as Holly. Each contestant must have their own."

"But I don't—"

Holly touched her friend's shoulder, silently encouraging her to try something else.

"Okay," Bridget said. "When you die . . . you go to Hell!"

Holly cringed. *Why would she say that?* Obviously, she was trying to insult the ghost, which was foolish enough, but by mentioning Hell was she inviting something hellish to be unleashed upon them? The audience applauded Bridget's answer, though, and the ghost asked the final contestant the same question. Faith fingered her ankh necklace and bit her bottom lip, more uneasy with this question than the others.

"I guess . . . you become a ghost. Like you, Madeline."

She said it almost affectionately, like she was trying to get the ghost to open up to her by showing she understood. Again, the audience fell hush. Sweat beaded in Holly's hair as she waited for the judgment to come down upon her friend. She feared by using the ghost's name, she may have invited more harm than Bridget had with her reference to the devil's playground.

"So," the ghost said. "Red has more than just good looks. She's got a real head on her shoulders."

The audience applauded louder than before, and Faith even smiled at the praise. She looked hopeful now, and it gave Holly a sense of unease, though she wasn't sure why.

"All right, ladies," the ghost of Madeline Goldman announced. "The time has come. Who is The Prettiest Girl in the Grave?"

It began raining bones.

~

Faith had been afraid of being down there, and thinking back on it, Holly believed that was why the spirit let the girls see the ceiling for the fragments of skeletons it was. The bodies were not so much tacked to the ceiling but comprised it, a roof constructed of the dead. The girls ducked and covered their heads as the bones sprinkled down, fragments of the necropolis falling in a gray sleet. In the fog of ash, Holly lost sight of her friends. Now she was alone in an ossuary beneath a graveyard. Fear crept through her until she couldn't hold back the screams. She tripped over something, and as she fell into the dust her hand landed on a yellowed piece of paper. Even in the dimness, she could make out the single word scrawled upon it in what looked like blood.

Sacrifice.

She scurried away from it, as if it might strike her like a rattlesnake. The blue illumination, which she still couldn't find the source of, gave her just enough light to make out the tunnel ahead, but when she entered it, the darkness was thick as molasses. The limestone dripped with insidious condensation, and Holly cried for her friends, but the only reply she received was the mocking crackle in her headphones.

"So, you were telling the truth," the ghost said. "You are afraid of being alone. Honesty is very becoming of a lady. Congratulations, Holly."

The hallway suddenly burst with orange light. Holly shrieked as airborne fire filled the dead space like a flamethrower. There was a quick flash, then the flame fell to the size of a walnut.

"Holly!" Faith said. "Over here!"

Now Holly could see her friends in the gloom, and the spray-paint can Bridget held, having made a blowtorch out of it to get Holly's attention. As they huddled together, new voices filled the corridor, and they didn't stem from the headphones, but the crypt itself. The voices chittered and hissed without words, sounding both animal and human at once. The audience returned to the headphones then, but instead of applauding they were laughing—the guttural, demonic laughter of the damned.

"No," Holly said, afraid she knew what was coming.

The tunnel grew hot and filled with a pulsing red light. Between the cracks in the stone walls, a smoldering, yellow substance burned like lava. The vestibule began to flood with acrid smoke, and the girls choked upon it until Holly told them to run.

Like a bat out of Hell, she thought.

~

Sawyer shook his head. "I'm trying to believe you. But you're telling me this tomb leads to Hell?"

"No. Not exactly."

He started to say something, but Holly shushed him. She'd told him enough. There was no time to waste. She took the first step, staring down at the doorway that had haunted her dreams since her escape.

You're going to die down here, she thought.

But it didn't matter as long as Bella survived.

Sawyer stepped down behind her. Holly doubted he believed her—at least not completely—but he believed enough to follow her into the tomb. She hadn't wanted to tell him. As far as the town was concerned, it was all ancient history, just a tragic accident involving three teenage girls in the woods. The '90s were just long enough ago for Greenwalk to forget. No one talked about it anymore, and that's the way Holly liked it. And with Bridget and Faith gone, there was no one to contradict her story, no one to tell the whole truth.

She and Sawyer entered the tomb.

"Make sure to keep that door wedged open with the wood," she said.

Looking around the tomb's cold insides, a chill rippled through Holly, and she took her ex-lover's hand. So warm and strong. It soothed her . . . a little.

Sawyer ran the beam of his flashlight around the four walls. "I don't see any hallway. And I don't see the girls. They must be somewhere else."

"No. They're here."

"Holly—"

"I'm back!" she called out, knowing the ghost would be listening. "A former winner has returned."

Sawyer let go of her hand. "Enough of this! I'm getting out of here."

As he turned to go, Holly grabbed Sawyer and drew him near, but he protested and freed himself from her clutches. She knew it was coming now. He was going to call her crazy. Holly had told her husband Justin only vague pieces of what happened to her here, but she lived to regret it when he threw it all back in her face whenever they had an argument, using her trauma to gaslight her. If Sawyer called her crazy too, she might slap him or break down crying. Maybe both.

But before he could say anything, the earth tremored, the ground rolling beneath their feet. Sawyer tried to pull Holly toward the door, but it was too late to turn back. The wood in the jamb snapped, sealing them in, and the concrete wall behind the family's coffins cracked, crumbled, and opened like stage curtains.

The queen of 1993 would have her homecoming.

NINETEEN

CELESTE WAS IN A DAZE, still as a mannequin in clothes soused with blood. The torch Bella had given her was gone. She wouldn't look at the others, only stared into the vast hopelessness of the crypt.

"Are you okay?" Bella asked.

Celeste sniffled and when she wiped her nose it left a wet, red streak.

"Celeste?" Rose said, approaching her with caution. "Where's Marnie?"

A tear ran down Celeste's cheek, cutting through the thumbprint of blood. "She's dead."

Bella curled inward from the hurt. This couldn't be real.

"What happened?" Rose asked, stern.

"She just collapsed. I think she finally just bled to death."

"Bled all over you, it looks like."

Bella tensed at Rose's tone. Was she suspicious of something? Should they be?

"I was carrying her," Celeste said. "Of course I got bloody. You saw how she was."

"It's true," Bella said. "She was bleeding on me too."

She held out her sleeves to show the blood on her coat, but it was hard to see against the black leather. It only showed on Celeste's dark clothing because it was still wet.

"You sure she was dead?" Aubrey asked.

"I checked," Celeste said. "She had no pulse and wasn't breathing. I tried to help her, but . . . I just couldn't. She just fucking died."

"Okay," Rose said. "Where is she?"

Celeste looked away again. Bella saw something she didn't like in her friend's expression. She looked like a child being scolded. Normally, Celeste was gruff and sarcastic. Puppy dog eyes were unlike her. They seemed alien upon her face.

"She's back this way," Celeste said.

Bella's muscles tightened. Celeste was pointing toward where the ghost had tried to grab Bella with its mutilated fingers. She'd already *heard* someone who wasn't really there. Was it possible she was *seeing* people who weren't really here? Was Celeste a figment just as Tyson's voice had been, something to lure them all into a specter's clutches?

"Where's the torch?" she asked Celeste.

"It died," Celeste said, a cryptic choice of words.

Rose and Aubrey followed her into the void.

"Wait!" Bella said. "That's where it was. That's where *she* was."

"We have to keep moving," Rose said.

"But—"

"I know you saw something. I believe you. But we can't go backwards. If we're gonna find a way out, we have to face our fears, remember? That's part of the game."

"Screw the game!" Bella began to cry, the weight of it all crashing in. "I don't want to play anymore. I never did!"

Aubrey put her arm around Bella. "It's okay."

"No, it's not." She moved out of her friend's embrace. "This is all your fault, Aubrey."

Aubrey's face fell. "Don't. Don't do this."

"We all know it. Might as well say it. You brought us here. You started the game."

"I didn't mean to. Not for real."

Bella looked to the others. "Am I wrong? It's her fault, isn't it?"

Rose said nothing, which said it all. Celeste's sad eyes showed sympathy for Aubrey, but she found no other way to express it.

Aubrey teared up and backed away from the others. Bella hadn't intended to scare Aubrey, but the ability to gave her a rush of power.

"I looked up to you," Bella said. "I wanted to be like you. What a joke."

"I'm sorry," Aubrey said.

Celeste came between them. "That's enough."

"Hey," Rose said. "Why are you always defending Aubrey?"

"Because she's my friend!"

"You worship her," Bella said. "She led us down here, but you led me to her."

Rose pointed at Bella. "And you led me to them."

The words shot into Bella's heart like arrows. It was an accurate accusation, but she hadn't expected Rose to strike her with it.

"That's the problem with the blame game," Aubrey said. "Everyone's guilty of something."

"Not me," Rose said. "I'm not guilty of a damn thing. You three are the reason we're stuck here. You and your goth bullshit. Now two people are dead. And who knows how long the rest of us are gonna last."

Bella wept. "Rose! How can you say that?"

Her best friend looked at her with arctic eyes, and it was in that moment Bella realized their friendship was truly over. And what hurt worst was she couldn't blame Rose at all.

"Enough," Rose said, looking away. "Celeste, show us where Marnie is."

The girls journeyed on through the stone chamber, the furnace sound the only thing breaking the silence. It seemed to be growing louder, hungrier. Bella couldn't help but imagine a red bull snorting fire, patrolling the maze like a centaur sentry, ready to drag trespassers into the rotted innards of the necropolis. The longer they were down there, the more claustrophobic it became. Was it possible they were going deeper underground by following these tunnels? Was this truly a bottomless pit?

They weren't walking long before the girls came to a thick puddle of blood on the gound, and a wet trail mark where the bleeder had been dragged into the darkness beyond.

~

The spread gore made Rose gag. It wasn't just the ghastly sight of it, but the smell. Fresh blood filled the stale air with the odor of greened pennies. There was another smell beneath it—something fouler, meatier. Tiny shreds of flesh on the ground suggested more than she wanted to know.

"Where the fuck is she, Celeste?" Rose asked.

Celeste blubbered. "She was right there, you guys, I swear to God!"

"Something dragged the body away," Aubrey said, pointing at the long smear of blood. "Maybe the bear came back?"

"How would it get here without us seeing it first?" Rose snapped.

"I don't know! Maybe there are shortcuts we haven't found."

They fell silent then, all eyes on the blood trail. Rose doubted the bear managed to find a way to beat them to this spot. This sepulture could be the hibernation spot for multiple bear families though. It was a disturbing thought. The girls could be on the verge of waking more beasts from their slumber. Every entrance and exit could be blocked off by packs of black bears who considered these tunnels their home. She thought of the poem on the plaque again, and the image of the sculpted bear head. Who'd put it there and why? Was it some kind of warning or omen? There were so many questions—too many to make this game fair.

These goths were hiding something. Even Bella couldn't be trusted anymore. She'd changed so much Rose didn't even know her. She probably held as many secrets as these caverns. Rose was being left out, given just enough information to placate her without telling her the whole truth. Instead, she was fed stories about old diaries and ghost women with her boyfriend's voice. Something unnatural was happening here—Rose knew that for sure—but that didn't mean she believed everything the other girls were telling her. She was more focused on what they decided *not* to tell her.

Rose was the outsider, and with trust dwindling, she'd started thinking of leaving the others behind. She'd tried to lead them and still wanted them to escape, but she had to prioritize. She wasn't one of these mopey losers. She was a winner. But a team is only as strong as its weakest player, and these teammates were pathetically fragile. They *celebrated* weakness, making despair part of their personality, painting their faces like sad clowns and dressing like extras in an old Tim Burton movie. They didn't have her drive. They didn't have her survival skills. They didn't love life—they loved *death*. Aubrey had said so herself. So, maybe these crazies wanted to be here. Maybe they wanted to die.

Aubrey said she only made up the part about needing six people for her little ritual, but Rose wasn't so sure about that. She and Marnie weren't part of the group, so why would the goths bring them here? With Marnie now missing—and dead, according to Celeste—paranoia festered within Rose. She'd never thought Bella would hurt her, but she'd never thought her friend would join up with weirdos like Aubrey and Celeste either. Anything, no matter how terrible, was possible.

"What do we do now?" Bella asked.

Rose rolled her shoulders. "We follow the blood."

"Fuck . . ." Aubrey whispered.

"You got something to say?"

Aubrey's eyes tightened but she shook her head. Looking at her now, Rose was baffled by her previous desire for the woman. The strangeness of it was one of the main things convincing her something supernatural was at play, and as she stepped into the darkness she suddenly stopped, a new thought hitting her like a smack across the face.

What if Aubrey really is a witch?

Before tonight, Rose would have considered the idea ludicrous. Witches were from storybooks. No intelligent person would believe in spells and sorcery in the twenty-first century. But considering all Rose had experienced tonight, her mind had to remain open if she were to figure out what was really going on. Something had to be responsible for all of this, and Aubrey had initiated *everything*—from the opening ritual, to coming down here, to controlling the narrative with her mother's diary confessions. She was like a dungeon master in a live action role playing game, coloring the world around them. But what if she was more than that? What if her witchcraft was real? What if she'd put some sort of love spell on Rose, but it hadn't been strong enough to last? Maybe she'd put the same spell on all the girls. It would explain why they seemed to worship her. And what if Aubrey had some power over animals and made the bear attack? Maybe she wanted all this blood to be spilled, offering up human sacrifices in exchange for more Satanic powers.

"What is it?" Bella asked when Rose stopped walking.

Part of Rose wanted to confide in Bella, to pull her aside and make a sisterly pact. But the bond she'd once counted on had been neglected too long, like a bicycle left out in the rain, and when Rose had tried to pick it up it fell apart. She needed her best friend, but the girl standing before her now was a stranger.

"Nothing," Rose said, and walked on.

~

The tunnel grew wider. Bella stayed close to the others, using Rose and Aubrey like human shields, cowering behind them for fear of crossing paths with the ghost woman again. Those decayed fingers and rotted dress, the face hidden in impenetrable blackness. The memory raked across Bella's mind with every step she took, and as the furnace sound intensified it began to change, another sound layering over it.

"Do you guys hear that?" she asked.

"Yeah," Aubrey said. "It sounds like burning. Like fire."

Someone echoed through the cold corridor. At first Bella thought it was Celeste—it was definitely her voice—but Celeste wasn't talking. She only stood there in pale shock, hearing herself.

"Not like Hell with fire and brimstone and shit," her disembodied voice said, "but like a world of darkness and blue shadows." A soft glow appeared like a beam of moonlight, revealing a large room ahead. "You're hollow there. And it's so cold and lonely. No God or Devil or loved ones. Just this endless void. Forever."

"That was your answer, Celeste," Bella said. "When Aubrey asked what happens when you die, that's what you said."

"But who's saying it now?" Aubrey asked.

"Must be a recording," Rose said.

"Stop trying to make logic out of this," Bella said.

"I'm not. I think we can all agree something supernatural is going on. But that's Celeste's voice, right?"

Celeste nodded, her eyes growing wet. The girls stared at the strange illumination ahead. It was an unnatural moonglow, like a bug zapper's on a porch in summer. The tunnel ended with it, leading to a wide-open space around the corner.

"What is it?" Bella asked.

"It's Hell," Rose said. "It's Celeste's vision of Hell."

"No," Celeste whimpered. "No . . . it's not my fault."

"Why would it be her answer and not someone else's?" Bella asked.

"Maybe it belongs to all of us," Aubrey said. "Better remember what you all said would happen when you die. It might await you around that corner."

"I said I didn't know," Bella said. "Rose, you said it was like . . ." She couldn't say it. It was too awful a thought.

"Like being unborn," Rose said for her. "Yeah. I know."

"That can't happen, though."

Rose remained stoic. "Let's hope not."

"Marnie said we go to Heaven," Celeste said softly. "I hope she was right."

"You think that's where she went?" Rose asked, a little too cynically. "You think she was dragged to paradise? Somehow, I doubt it."

"It's better than your fucking answer."

"No argument there."

Bella wished they wouldn't bicker. Every time she thought they'd all banded together to get through this, something else divided them. She wanted to patch things up, but fear dominated her every thought, making it hard to concentrate on anything else.

"Okay," Rose said, approaching the blueness, "might as well face it, whatever it is. There's no turning back now. No other way out."

The others stood still, watching Rose go, waiting to see what happened to her. Bella cursed herself for her cowardice. No matter what was going on between her and Rose, she couldn't let her do this by herself.

"Wait for me," she said, catching up.

They looked into each other's eyes. Bella liked to believe there was something still there, some shred of their long-time bond, but all she saw in Rose's eyes was tough determination. Her game face was on. Bella doubted she could ever look as strong as Rose did, let alone be as strong. She'd never had that sort of confidence, not even in things she knew she was good at. She hoped her old friend would continue to guide her through this. She trusted Rose's judgment more than her own. This whole thing was a twisted game, and Rose was here to play.

They rounded the corner, entering a theater of the dead.

Broken pieces of caskets and buttresses had been used to build makeshift chairs. There were twenty of them lined up haphazardly in two crooked rows. Skeletons were propped up in them, wearing the Sunday best clothes they'd been buried in, looking as dapper and elegant as dead bodies could. The women's dresses were mildewed, the men's suits moth-eaten, and cobwebs stretched from their skulls to their shoulders. This audience of corpses all faced the same direction, their empty eye sockets staring at the stage before them.

Braced by columns of human spines, the bulk of the stage was comprised of grayed, mummified flesh and broken bones. Tissue that had dried and hardened was packed like cabin logs among petrified severed heads and body parts. It was a mass grave compacted into a rectangular mold, like a giant cardboard bale. Hanging above the stage was a pair of curtains made of dried human flesh, faces and bellies and buttocks all fused together as if by invisible stitches.

The blue glow centered where the curtains met.

They began to open.

TWENTY

"THE HOMECOMING QUEEN," THE GHOST of Madeline Goldman announced as Holly and Sawyer stared into the labyrinth. "She has returned with her king."

So that's why he was allowed in, Holly thought. A winner returned with privileges. Madeline always loved any semblance of tradition, be it pageants, ballroom dances, or in this case, some sort of reunion. Holly was allowed to bring her beau so she'd have someone on her arm, a man to show off like a trophy. Though she and Sawyer were hardly romantic partners, Madeline didn't need to know that.

The ghost also didn't ask the three questions before opening the gateway. Holly had already given her answers long ago, and Sawyer was a man, making him ineligible for Madeline's twisted contest, just like the policemen who'd investigated the graveyard after Holly's escape all those years ago, finding nothing and gaining no entry to the labyrinth. But if Holly and Sawyer weren't here to play the game, why had Madeline allowed them passage? Was it her desire for company or love for traditional celebrations? Was she impressed one of the former champions had dared to return? Holly doubted any other survivors would have been foolish enough to come back to this pit of horrors.

Sawyer looked around for the source of the voice, but Madeline wasn't making an appearance. At least, not yet. Holly led him into the first corridor. The place was exactly as she remembered—just as dark, just as chilling.

Sawyer gaped at it, waving the beam of his flashlight. "This is insane. How is this possible? And who was that talking to us?"

Holly kept moving. "I can tell you a long story or we can save our daughters."

She shined her flashlight into the crypt. Last time she'd been here, Holly and her friends had only a Zippo to guide their way. Things would be much better this time. It was hard to imagine anything worse than what happened to her, Bridget, and Faith.

~

The hall became a circle of Hell.

Bridget had invited it by saying this was where they would go after death, and Holly could have killed her for it. They ran through the tunnel, leaping over cracks in the ground that burned red hot with magma. The walls transformed into brimstone. Volcanic ash whirled through the corridor in a black tornado, threatening to choke the girls. They took each other's hands so not to lose sight of one another and cried and screamed through the searing heat as demons cackled, laughing at their terror. When Holly dared look back, she saw a wall of flame following them, rising in a tsunami. Sweat soaked her and she ached from dehydration. She felt she may vomit or collapse. The urge to give up was the hardest thing to fight.

"Look!" Faith shouted.

While Hell followed behind them, ahead was a clearing of pale blue stone, void of all the dangers of the molten tunnel. The girls ran faster, the ground crumbling beneath them, steam rising through the cracks. Holly's lungs swelled, her heart pounding, and with one final lunge the girls leapt out of the smoldering shaft and into the cold shadows of the alcove. They lay on the freezing ground, soothing the blisters that had begun to bubble upon their skin. Holly coughed, expelling the final traces of smoke, and when at last she sat up she felt a single dew drop fall upon her head. She gasped and looked up, hopeful, and another drop fell, landing on her nose.

"Water!"

She opened her mouth and stuck out her tongue. Her friends did the same. A drop landed upon Holly's dry, cracked lips, and she nearly cried from relief, but the bitter taste made her wince. Still, it was wet. She opened her mouth for more and several drops rained down from the darkness. The girls drank what little moisture they could, necks craned like baby birds awaiting their mother's meal. The strange blueness increased, bringing the room into view, and when the shadows were pushed away from the ceiling, Holly gagged at what she saw.

Above them was an arch of dirt and sod. Tree roots ran through the underbelly of the earth, cradling it like a net, but the bottoms of coffins poked through the entanglement. Fungus and mold covered everything in a haze. The wooden caskets were worn, holes torn into them by burrowing critters and worms. Some were big enough to see the skeletal remains of those buried inside, and it was from these cracked coffins that the drops of water rained down.

The girls were underneath the cemetery plot, drinking the dew of the dead.

Faith screamed. Bridget retched. Holly stared at the densely packed earth above, searching for even the smallest speck of daylight, seeing none. Her friends retreated to a corner where no dew fell and held one another close. Holly went to them, and they welcomed her in, the girls banding together like sisters. Despite everything, Holly felt they could make it through this as long as they had each other. Holding them gave her strength. Touching them gave her what she needed to carry on through all this horror and death.

"You're my best friends," she told them. "I love you."

They told her they loved her too, and the girls pressed their heads together and clutched hands tightly. The cold of the chamber gave way to comforting body heat. Hunger and thirst disappeared. Even fear ebbed until it was gone completely.

Holly smiled. Why had she been so afraid? There was nothing to be scared of. Everything was going to be all right. Everything was wonderful.

Euphoria rippled through her then. It was beyond any high she'd experienced when smoking weed or taking ecstasy. This was a unique bliss, brewed in the belly of pure love. It swelled within her, stirring desire, and her hands wandered as she closed her eyes, feeling the soft bodies pressed against her own. Her mind shuddered with images of her crush, Ryan Ellis. His blond hair covered one of his eyes as he smiled at Holly and leaned in for a kiss. Their mouths linked as his hands explored her. Another mouth found her earlobe, her lover mutating but never losing his beauty. Holly panted as she was snaked by multiple arms. Fingers entered her hair and the waistband of her jeans. She moaned, and someone else moaned in reply, but it wasn't Ryan. It was a softer voice, high and feminine, and when Holly opened her eyes, she saw Bridget. They were both pressed against Faith, whose face was pinched tight, her buttocks in Holly's hands.

"Let me go, Slater," Faith said, eyes still shut. "Please . . . don't . . ."

Her friend's beauty struck Holly hard. Those eyes, that long red hair, and that incredible smile. Holly ached as if punched in the stomach and squeezed Faith's backside harder, putting anger into it. Faith squirmed and protested, and Holly reveled in her friend's discomfort. Faith deserved it. It wasn't fair that she was so much prettier than Holly and Bridget. She could have any boy she wanted but pushed them all away, including ones Holly would give anything for the chance to date. What an entitled snob. What a manipulator, using her looks to get whatever she wanted, and not just from men. Girls wanted to be Faith as much as guys wanted to be with her. People flocked to the gorgeous redhead, fawning over her, always eager to please her just for the chance to have her smile upon them. And now, even the ghost of the crypt favored her.

"Slater, stop!" Faith said, seeming to believe the drug-dealing groper was upon her instead of her female friends. "Get off me!"

Bridget now had her hands up Faith's shirt, and Holly was sliding one hand down into her jeans. The little virgin girl was about to be taught a valuable lesson. Bridget snickered as Faith tried to wiggle free but was overpowered. Suddenly Faith's eyes snapped open.

"Holly!" she said, seeing her now. "Bridget! What're you doing? Stop!"

The fog of angry lust receded, and Holly snapped back to her senses, the euphoria and resentment ending abruptly, like lights coming up at closing time. Bridget blinked rapidly and withdrew from Faith with a look of disgust.

"What the fuck?" Bridget asked herself.

"What just happened?" Holly asked, stunned.

Faith looked around the crypt. "Where is he?"

"Who?"

"Slater," she shook her head as if to rattle something loose. "Wait . . . no, that's not right. He can't be here, right?"

"No," Holly said. "I don't think so. Not the real him anyway. I saw Ryan Ellis. At least, I did at first."

"Yeah . . . I saw a few different guys . . . some I liked, some I really didn't."

Bridget realized her fly was undone and she zipped it back up. "Let's just get out of here. Like, right now. Before anything else happens."

"Was it the water?" Holly wondered aloud. "Maybe it's hallucinogenic?"

"Why try to make sense of it?" Bridget said. "Nothing makes sense down here. We ran through a hallway in Hell and then started making out. I mean, what kind of sense are we ever gonna make of that?"

She had a point.

"It's all part of this fucked up game," Holly told them. "We just have to keep playing, whatever that means." She held out her hand to Bridget, asking for the can of spray-paint. She handed it over and Holly made an X on the wall behind her. "We need to keep marking everywhere we've been. I have a bad feeling we're just getting more lost."

~

Normally Holly was terrible with remembering directions—she always relied on her GPS to get her around—but the passageways of this labyrinth had been burned into her memory. Spending several days within it all those years ago imprinted a vague but permanent map in her head.

She also remembered how important it was to keep moving.

"Okay," she told Sawyer as they reached the door. "Brace yourself for this."

He helped her pull the door open. When the flashlight beams fell upon the skeletons within, Sawyer gasped and stepped away.

"We have to go through here," Holly said.

"What is this?" he asked, eyes wide as silver dollars.

"It's an ossuary."

"A *what?*"

"It's a place that houses the dead."

Sawyer swallowed so hard she could hear it. "Jesus. This is all too much."

"It'll be okay," she told him, though she wasn't so sure. "Just follow me and keep your eyes on the floor."

Holly said it as if the floor was unsteady or dangerous, but really she just didn't want him to see the ceiling. She took Sawyer's hand like a child and guided him into the awaiting ossuary, moving slowly but ready to run if it started raining bones. She hoped such horrors were behind her since she'd already proved herself to Madeline, but the ghost was anything but predictable. The sour stench of death hung in the air like fumes.

A bright beam of light suddenly surrounded them. Small, white particles fell, and Holly tensed before realizing it was confetti. She didn't want to know what it was made of. The light formed a circle on the ground around her and Sawyer, putting them in an intimate cone of blue.

Madeline's voice rose out of the open caskets just as it had through the headphones of Holly's Walkman. "The queen has returned to have a spotlight dance with her king."

Dots of light spun about the ossuary like white fireflies and the spotlight grew wider, giving Holly and Sawyer room to move while staying inside it. His face twitched with confusion. Holly stepped into him and raised one hand. He took it. She grabbed his other arm and put it around her waist, then pressed her free hand against his back. Ethereal music echoed through the crypt, a morbid love song.

"You lead," she told him.

Sawyer moved his feet. He wasn't the most graceful dancer, especially under these circumstances, but it would do. They glided back and forth, swaying to the instrumental ballad. Holly clenched her teeth. There wasn't time for this, but they had to keep Madeline's ghost appeased, otherwise she might initiate a whole new game instead of being a gracious host.

"Um . . . Holly?" Sawyer asked, baffled.

"Just go with it."

But as the confetti continued to fall, Sawyer looked up, and his mouth opened as if to scream.

Holly pulled him in close and whispered. "Don't! Please, don't scream."

"Jesus Christ," he said under his breath.

"Don't look at them."

She took his chin and forced him to look at her. He was trembling. Sawyer had always been the traditionally masculine type, a man's man with broad shoulders and a strong jawline. He was outdoorsy and built furniture from scratch. But no matter how tough and rugged, no man is totally fearless. The blood had left Sawyer's face as he'd stared into a ceiling forged of skeletal remains. Holly looked into his eyes now, trying to ground him.

"It's okay," she said. "Stay with me."

"I'm trying . . . I . . ."

But he was slipping. Who could blame him? Holly had dragged Sawyer into a world of phantoms, where rooms were built of corpses, then asked him to have this dance. She petted his cheek, feeling the stubble that had once scratched against her naked thighs, and shushed him softly, the same way she had with Bella when she was a baby. Sawyer leaned into her as if trying to hide in her embrace. He was offering up all his trust. Holly understood this place—something Sawyer never could—and because of that he was following her lead. He needed her now more than ever before.

Holly kissed him as they swayed under the spotlight, and the confetti gave way to gentle flurries of ash—the bone fragments of the cremated. Looking down on them from above, the skeletons of all the girls who'd lost the game watched the champion dance with her tall, handsome sweetheart.

She was their better.

She was their idol.

Holly, Queen of the Dead.

TWENTY-ONE

ROSE STARED UP AT THE parting curtains of flesh.

Beside her, Bella whimpered, holding in a scream as the blue gave way to a brilliant white, illuminating the stage.

Propped up centerstage, the bodies of Marnie and Savannah were mannequins of raw meat.

Savannah was particularly decimated, her torso shredded to dripping ribbons, her belly open and robbed of its insides. One side of her face was gone, and she was missing an arm and half of one foot. Her neck was snapped, and a shard of bone had burst through the flesh, jutting out of her throat like a spearhead.

Marnie was drenched in blood. There wasn't an inch of her that wasn't crimson. Her one eye stared straight at Rose—through her. From the puddle of blood at her feet, a smeared trail led to the side of the stage, then down to the floor. There were no footprints. She'd been hauled here by someone else—some*thing* else.

Looking at the slack bodies, Rose couldn't understand how they were even standing up. Nothing seemed to be bracing them, and yet the dead girls were upright at centerstage. The spotlight highlighted them in grotesque detail. What remained of their mouths almost seemed to be smiling.

Contestants, Rose thought with a shudder.

Bella appeared beside her. Aubrey and Celeste had joined them, and the four girls banded together within the macabre auditorium, staring up at the mangled carcasses of their friends.

A woman's voice emanated from somewhere behind the dead skin curtains.

"Congratulations, Aubrey! You gave the right answer. As you can all see, you come *here* when you die. You come to *the grave.*"

Applause filled the room like thunder. The girls looked all about for the source of it. Rose almost expected the gallery of skeletons to be the ones clapping, but they were still as stone in their twisted chairs. The applause seemed to come from nowhere and everywhere.

"Is that it?" Rose asked the darkness. "Is that what's happened? *We're dead?*"

The audience laughed like something out of a sitcom.

"Who are you?" Rose demanded. "Why are you doing this?"

The voice returned, as joyful as a commercial. "I'd like to take this moment to point out some very special people."

The spotlight swirled, landing on the front row of decrepit skeletons. One wore a withered suit, the others dressed in gowns so frayed they looked like flies wrapped in spiderwebs.

"Ladies and gentlemen," the voice said. "Please give a round of applause for my family—The Goldmans." Applause shook the theater. "My parents and all my sisters are here tonight—even Janis."

"Tell us what you want!" Rose shouted over the commotion. "How do we finish this fucking game?"

The audience fell silent. A sudden gust of wind blew out the girls' torches. Bella gasped. The furnace thrum intensified with a sound like logs crackling on an open fire.

A shape took form in the darkness at the back of the stage. It was small and ethereal, a humanoid specter of shadow and moonbeam, but as it drew closer to centerstage Rose could make out the gown rotted to black and the decayed veil that hung before an obscured face. Bella gripped Rose's arm with both hands, trembling.

"It's her," Bella said.

The female form seemed to glide into the spotlight, her arms raised in welcome, her mangled fingers spasming. Brittle hair hung over her chest and shoulders like seaweed, and even in the spotlight her face was but an oval shadow. Rose had to remind herself to breathe.

Keep your head in the game, she told herself.

"We've heard your answers, ladies," the ghost woman said. "And we've also *seen* your answers. Some of you are more truthful than others." The audience murmured, amused as their host went on. "Now we come to the final round, girls. It's time to show us what you're really made of. Show us what you have to offer."

"What do you mean?" Rose asked.

"An offering from you to us. From the living to the dead."

The girls looked at one another for answers none of them could give. A drop of blood left Marnie's corpse and hit the puddle beneath her, sounding like a rock skipped across a pond.

An offering, Rose thought, staring at the corpses.

"My sisters all wanted to be beauty queens," the ghost woman said, gesturing to the row of dead women. "We were always challenging each other, but they were never a match for me. Yes, they all entered, but I was the only Goldman daughter to win pageants. I was better than my sisters—more talented, more beautiful. That's why they poisoned me."

Hushed whispers fluttered through the audience.

"Janis was the one to put the drops in my tea," the woman said, "but all my sisters devised the plot. It's the only time they ever worked together—to kill their little Maddy. Sisters do love to quarrel, but we all know that now, don't we?"

Rose and Bella glanced at each other.

"Remember, ladies," the woman said. "There can only be one winner."

~

Bella shrieked as Rose grabbed Celeste by the collar.

The blue glow of the theater pulsed. The furnace sang.

"You killed her!" Rose shouted.

Celeste cried out. "No! Let me go!"

Rose backhanded Celeste. "You killed Marnie, you bitch!" She whacked her again. "She didn't just drop dead. You murdered her. She was your *offering!*"

"I didn't kill her . . . I just . . . I just . . ."

Celeste struggled against her attacker. Bella looked to Aubrey, wondering what they should do, but Aubrey was just as shocked as she was, and they didn't move fast enough to keep Rose from punching Celeste in the stomach.

"Rose!" Bella shouted. "Stop it!"

But Rose didn't listen.

As Celeste bent over in pain, Rose brought up her knee, bashing Celeste in the face. Blood burst from her nose and she collapsed, her skull cracking on the concrete. Aubrey and Bella had to intervene now, no matter how intimidated they were. They pulled Rose away from Celeste, and Rose spun against them, knocking Bella off. Bella crawled to Celeste to see if she was all right. She wasn't moving. Aubrey held on to Rose and they struggled briefly before Rose slammed her to the floor. Aubrey scurried to get away from her.

"I knew it!" Rose said. "You're all in this together. All this goth witchcraft! You made an offering out of Marnie, but you're not gonna make one out of me!"

Bella gazed up at her. "No . . . that's not—"

"Don't!" Her eyes filled with tears. "You're the worst one of all. You brought me here . . . brought me here to die."

"No! I didn't! I swear I—"

Bella started to get up, but Rose kicked her in the chest. She fell into Celeste, who still didn't move or make a sound. Blood was pooling around the girl's head and Bella's hand slipped in it as she tried to brace herself. Her breasts ached and she struggled to get her wind back. Rose hadn't just given her a nudge. She'd punted her like a football.

Now Rose was receding into the gathering shadows.

"You wanna play?" Rose asked. "Fine. Game on."

She vanished to great applause, slinking backward toward the mouth of the tunnel. The last thing Bella saw was Rose's eyes, the tears reflecting what little blue light remained within the crypt. Then she was gone.

The theater fell dark and silent. Bella looked to the stage, but the ghostly woman had disappeared, leaving only Marnie and Savannah to stare down at her with their dead eyes.

Aubrey touched Bella. "You okay?"

"Yeah . . . but Celeste."

They went to her. Aubrey drew her Zippo and tried to reignite a torch, but it wouldn't take. She held the lighter's flame close to Celeste's busted face, the butterfly engraving on the Zippo seeming to flap its wings in the flicker. Bella shook Celeste and called her name, but the girl was unresponsive.

"Oh, Jesus," Bella said.

She took Celeste's head in her hands and turned it slowly so they could get a better look at the wound. The movement seemed to unplug something, and the wound gushed. Panicking, she shook Celeste, but the girl's eyes had rolled back and her mouth hung slack. Aubrey took Celeste's wrist and pressed her fingertips to a vein. Bella watched, waiting, begging.

Aubrey quivered. "I . . . I can't find a . . ."

Bella's stomach hollowed out, dread making her feel weightless.

"No," she said, tapping Celeste's bloody cheeks. "No, no, no. Wake up, Celeste. You can't be . . . you can't."

Aubrey stood. "We have to get out of here."

"But Celeste . . ."

"She'd dead. Oh my God . . . Rose fucking *killed* her. Oh my God."

"No. No, no, please—"

Aubrey tugged on her again. "We have to run. Before she comes back."

"This can't be happening."

"It *is* happening! Now c'mon." She pulled Bella up and hugged her. "You okay?"

"No," she whimpered.

"But you're not hurt."

She shook her head, weeping into Aubrey's shoulder. Aubrey patted her back like a mother, and Bella wished she could just close her eyes and bury herself into the embrace. Maybe she could drift off to sleep and would awake to find this was all just a horrible dream, the worst nightmare she'd ever had.

"We're okay," Aubrey said, shushing her softly. "But we have to get moving. Rose thinks we're out to get her. I think she intends to hurt us."

"She couldn't have meant to kill Celeste. Rose would never . . ."

"Never say never. Rose has snapped. We have to protect ourselves and stick together, right?"

Bella nodded. Keeping one arm around her, Aubrey guided her toward the rows of propped skeletons, searching for another way out. Bella clung to her as they crept along. She felt like a scuba diver on the ocean floor, lost in an unforgiving netherworld where strange monsters lurked. They stepped into the row dividing the two groups of carcasses, having just enough room to hold on to each other as they passed through. Bella shivered as her thigh grazed against a sitting corpse. The dead woman smiled at her with a frozen rictus, and when a cockroach darted out of her eye socket, Bella jumped, and Aubrey had to soothe her again.

A voice startled them. "I knew it."

Rising from the shadows, Celeste was silhouetted by the remnant of the blue glow, and when she turned around her face was in clear view, the blood from her broken nose appearing black in the gloom, covering her mouth like a wet beard.

"I fucking knew it," she said as she shuffled forward.

"Celeste?" Bella said. "Oh, thank goodness, you—"

"You stole her from me."

Bella paused. "What?"

"You were just gonna leave me to die, weren't you?" Celeste hissed, coming closer.

"No . . ."

Aubrey shook her head. "We thought you were already dead. We're sorry."

"*Sorry?*" Celeste said. "You're not sorry. I see you two hugging. I saw that new hickey on your neck, Aubrey. I get it. Bella's prettier than me. She isn't a fat loser like me, right?"

Bella and Aubrey glanced at each other, baffled.

"What're you talking about?" Bella asked Celeste.

"You hit your head," Aubrey told her. "You're confused. C'mon, we need to get out of here."

"No!" Celeste shouted, close enough now that they could see her in the light of the flame. Her eyes were huge and black, and she carried her extinguished torch. "You know *exactly* what I'm talking about, Bella. You were never really my friend, were you? You were just using me to get close to Aubrey."

"What?" Bella said. "That's not true!"

Or was it? Bella suddenly thought, further confusing herself.

"Aubrey," Celeste said, tears of blood falling from her eyes. "You want to know who I love? I love *you*. I do everything I can to show you that, but you never even notice me."

Aubrey's mouth hung open. "I didn't know . . ."

"You knew. You just didn't care. Even when I was bleeding on the ground you didn't care!"

"That's not—"

"You left me to die. You knew I was alive but were leaving me here as an offering to this fucking witch or whatever she is. She gets a human sacrifice, and you and Bella get rid of the third wheel that's been holding you back. Two birds with one stone, right?"

Aubrey and Bella stepped back.

"Celeste," Aubrey said, "Please, listen to me. That's not what's happening here. No one is offering anybody to anything. We thought you were dead."

"Well, you don't seem too happy I'm alive."

Celeste snorted blood and shoved one of the corpses out of her way, entering the row of seated skeletons. She made no effort to avoid touching them as she staggered forward, leaning on their brittle bones as she closed in on Aubrey and Bella, holding the burnt piece of wood like a club.

"You're being irrational," Aubrey told her. "Just calm down and we can talk this through."

But Bella knew it was too late for that, and when Celeste bared her teeth in a jealous rage, Aubrey knew it too.

TWENTY-TWO

THEY WALKED DOWN THE FRIGID corridor, flashlights
swirling in the dark. Holly held Sawyer's hand, afraid they'd lose each
other if she didn't. Besides, she didn't want to let go of him once the
dance had ended. She'd pushed him away too much already. Breaking
off their relationship had hurt her as much as it had him, and Holly
couldn't understand how she'd not seen the error of this until now.
She could have danced with him forever, even in the grotesque ballroom of the ossuary where the dust of the dead drifted like fog and
decayed faces gawked at them with an eternal envy of the living. But
they had to keep moving, keep playing the game.

The deeper they went into the tunnel, the warmer it got. Holly
could still see her breath, but a pleasant heat was coasting through
her now. It made her smile. She brought up her flashlight to see if
Sawyer was smiling too. He squinted against the light and snickered.

"Was I speeding, officer?" he joked.

Holly loved a sense of a humor in a man. She also loved large
hands like the one clutching hers right now. She pressed into Sawyer,
putting her flashlight under her chin like she was telling a campfire

story.

"I might just have to pat you down," she said, putting her palm on his broad chest.

Sawyer smirked and snaked his arm around Holly's waist. Somewhere in the back of her mind was a nagging thought, something she couldn't quite grasp. There was a sense of urgency there, but it was too nebulous to act upon. What she could act upon was desire. She forgot why she was down here. She forgot her daughter. All she could think of now was Sawyer, and how she could get him closer, deeper.

Standing on her tiptoes, Holly kissed him. Their mouths opened. The warmth spread through them like fire. She went under Sawyer's shirt and twirled her fingers in his chest hair. He grabbed her by the belt and drew her in, his hands exploring her tender places, making her shudder.

How she needed him. How she loved him.

Unable to delay their passions, they undid their jeans just enough and Holly pressed against the wall of the crypt with Sawyer behind her, making love to her in a fever, pleasuring her in a way her husband never could. And even when they heard footsteps nearby, they didn't stop. In this moment, Holly wouldn't have stopped for anything.

~

Rose covered her mouth but couldn't avert her gaze. The beam of one of their flashlights was up, revealing the faces of her father and Bella's mom as they moaned and panted. They were having sex, right here in the crypt.

Everything seemed to spin. When she'd first seen them, Rose swelled with relief, thinking she was going home, that her father had come to save her. But just as she was about to call out to him, Rose realized what he was doing with Mrs. Whitman. She stumbled back in shock, the hurt swelling her heart. She wanted it to be an illusion, some hallucinatory projection crafted by the witchcraft, but knew what she was seeing was real.

Another betrayal.

First Bella led her down into this hellscape, turning on Rose in favor of her new friends. Now Bella's mother had seduced Dad, making him a cheater, something that was bound to destroy Rose's family. She'd always thought of Mrs. Whitman like an aunt, never realizing what a treacherous whore she really was. Now Rose understood where Bella must get it from. She'd seen the way her so-called best friend looked at her boyfriend, Tyson. She'd never called Bella out on it, but it was obvious she had a crush on him. Given the chance, would she seduce him like her mother seduced married men?

The Whitman women were vicious, conniving serpents hiding in plain sight. But now the masks were off. Rose knew what she was dealing with and what she had to do.

No one could rescue her. She had to save herself the same way she always did—by *winning*. Bella and her stupid goth friends would never be The Prettiest Girl in the Grave; not while Rose was still playing. This was the final round, and she would do whatever it took to defeat them.

There had to be an offering.

Slinking into the shadows, Rose turned and ran back the way she'd come.

~

"What the hell did we just do?" Holly asked.

Their passions spent, she and Sawyer pulled up their jeans and stared at each other. The shock on his face matched her own. He'd been swept away too. Holly thought she'd been ready for all the trickery of Madeline's maze, but even though she'd known what was coming, she'd been unable to stop herself. It wasn't like when she, Bridget, and Faith had sexually caressed one another down here. This time the *who do you love* portion of the game was stronger, for she and Sawyer already desired one another, and though she'd been trying to get over him, her feelings for him remained, and he longed for her as well. They'd been easy targets. Madeline must have wanted the king and queen to be together, to live out some fantasy vicariously.

"I don't know what came over me," Sawyer said. "What came over both of us."

"This place has a way of messing with your mind. We have to be careful." Holly buckled her belt. "Let's forget this happened. At least for now. We can deal with it later."

Sawyer nodded, his eyes heavy with shame. He'd wanted what they'd just done, but not here, and certainly not when his daughter was in danger. Collecting themselves, they walked on, Holly determined to see them through this tunnel of love without relapsing into another heated tryst.

"Did you hear something?" she asked. "While we were . . . you know."

"Yeah. Like footsteps."

"Right. I wasn't sure, but that's what it sounded like."

They called out for their children, their echoes a sad haunt in the obsidian chambers. Holly wondered if the girls were still getting along or if Madeline's twisted competition had turned them against one another by now. Bella and Rose were best friends. But Holly had been best friends with Bridget and Faith too.

So much for friendship.

"She's going to win," Holly said.

Faith had gone off to pee in a corner, giving Holly the moment alone with Bridget she'd been waiting for. Bridget crossed her arms and looked away.

"You know it's true," Holly said. "That ghost bitch said it herself—Faith is beautiful. Much more gorgeous than we are. She'll beat us for Prettiest Girl in the Grave, easy."

Bridget stirred. "Holly . . ."

"You know it's true."

"Okay, maybe it is."

"Maybe my ass. Faith wins this thing and then what? She gets to go home while we rot down here?"

"That's not gonna happen," Bridget said unconvincingly.

"Yeah? Then why'd the ghost ask us what happens when you die? We just came out of a hallway in Hell."

Bridget didn't have a reply to that.

"She's torturing us but praising Faith at every turn, saying she's so pretty and has a good head on her shoulders." Holly huffed. "I mean, seriously? *Faith*? She's a *moron*. Why would this Madeline woman think she's the smart one? Ugh. It's the same old crap. Everyone just loves Faith. Even the dead love her."

The sound of Faith's shuffling footsteps made the girls stiffen.

Bridget whispered, "So, what are you saying?"

Holly's insides felt hard as granite. The warmth she'd felt while caressing her friends had escalated to a mean heat, making her sweat. Something dark turned over inside her. She was scared. She was angry.

"I say we even the playing field," Holly said.

She hated herself for even thinking this, but the danger was increasing. She was dehydrated and starving, cold and lost. Only one way out seemed clear to her, and that was playing the game.

And every game has its losers.

"Give me your lighter," she said.

Bridget stared at her, wild-eyed, but handed over the Zippo. The flame put the girls in a small orb of light as Faith returned, and Holly put the lighter closer to Faith to better see her. Her lovely face was like an oil painting in the golden firelight, soft with symmetrical perfection. The plump lips. The freckles smattered across her nose and cheeks. The hopeful, blue eyes, slightly larger than average.

"Well," Faith said. "Now what?"

Holly slid the spray-paint can from her back pocket.

"I'm sorry," she said.

She brough the nozzle to the Zippo and pressed the trigger. The red paint burst into a jet of flames that engulfed Faith's face. She shrieked as her flesh cooked and her hair caught fire. Holly held the trigger down, continuing the torch effect, and when Faith tried to get away Holly moved upon her again in an unrelenting assault. Bridget screamed her name, but Holly ignored her. Faith covered her face with her arms and Holly ignited them too, Faith's clothes burning, her flesh blistering. She tried to pat the flames out as they swallowed her head, but Holly just kept spraying more, feeding the fire. Though Holly didn't want her friend to suffer, she had to make sure the job was done right. A sunburn wouldn't be enough to disqualify Faith for the title. Her beauty had to be peeled away like a carrot stick.

Just as Holly sprayed one last burst of fire, Faith screamed, and the spiraling flame entered her mouth and shot down her throat. Her singed hands went to her neck, and she dropped to the ground, convulsing as her lungs were scorched from the inside.

"Faith!" Holly cried.

This was too much—*way* too much. The fire crackled and surged, growing louder. The smell of seared human flesh filled the air. What she had done came to Holly in a terrible rush. She got low beside her friend and tried to bat out the flames. She turned to Bridget, who stood shaking in the entrance to the tunnel, tears rolling down her cheeks.

"Help me!" Holly yelled.

But fear had paralyzed Bridget. Holly removed her flannel and dropped it over Faith, patting it down to smother the remaining flames.

"I didn't mean to," she whimpered. "I didn't . . ."

Faith stopped twitching, her arms dropping to her sides. The singed flannel hid her face. Holly didn't know if she would ever be able to draw it back. She hoped she wouldn't have to, that Faith could do it herself.

"Faith . . ." she said, tears in her eyes. "I'm sorry . . ." She looked to Bridget. "I just wanted to make her less pretty. I didn't mean for it to go this far, I swear."

Bridget hugged herself and cried, offering no consolation. She didn't tell Holly she'd only done what had to be done, didn't tell her she understood and that it was just an accident. She only wept, useless and judgmental.

Smoke seeped through the flannel on Faith's face and shoulders, carrying an acrid stench. Holly's coughing became sobs. Faith still wasn't moving.

"You fucking killed her," Bridget said.

Holly paled. "No . . ."

"Yeah, you did."

"I didn't mean for it to be this bad."

"*This bad?* You set Faith *on fire.*"

Holly stared down at her friend still cloaked under the shirt. She had to know.

Pinching the material, she drew the flannel back, revealing what was left of Faith Johnson. Her face was yellow and bubbling. Crisp tissue pocked her skin like fish scales, blood having cooked the instant it poured, caking onto her cheeks in burgundy stains. The girl's eyebrows were singed away, eyelashes gone. Even her teeth had been blackened by smoke.

Bridget whimpered from the tunnel entrance. Holly placed the flannel over Faith's head and shoulders, a doctor drawing a sheet when calling the time of death. She stood slowly, then turned to Bridget, her only friend.

"I just didn't want to die down here," she said. "I didn't want that for either of us."

Bridget shook her head, her nose scrunched up like an angry dog. "Bullshit. You killed Faith in cold blood."

A pang of resentment rippled through Holly. "You handed me the lighter. Let's not forget that."

Holly threw the Zippo at Bridget and she caught it.

"I didn't know what you were gonna do!" Bridget said.

"Yes, you did, and you made no effort to stop me. You wanted to keep Faith from winning, same as I did. You just didn't have the guts to do anything about it."

Bridget started backing into the tunnel. "You're crazy. Are you gonna come after me next? You are, aren't you?"

Holly hadn't thought about that. She didn't want to. Shaking her head, she put up her hands up in a passive manner. "It's honestly not like that."

But there was no honesty anymore. Not down here.

In this dungeon, secrets were a girl's best friend. Secrets were protective. They concealed what shouldn't be seen and silenced what others weren't meant to hear. Deception was part of all games—faking out your opponent, making them second guess their every move. And in these catacombs, there were only opponents. Holly was sure of that now. Friendship was a liability, a weakness. She was bonded to nothing but her own survival. It had to be that way if she ever wanted to see the sun again.

She moved toward Bridget, not really knowing what she intended to do. She did regret killing Faith, even though it had been—to an extent—an accident. She hadn't wanted her friend to die, only lose. Perhaps losing this game was a death sentence in and of itself. In that scenario, it would be the ghost of Madeline Goldman that took Faith, or perhaps the crypt itself would open like the mouth of a whale and swallow her into its haunted, black depths. But Holly had taken Faith out of the game *permanently*. She'd taken her out of life, adding another corpse to the necropolis.

"I didn't want to hurt anybody," Holly said. "But what choice did I have? She was going to beat us."

Bridget took another step back. "Just stay away from me, you bitch."

But Holly kept walking. She'd never felt so spontaneous before and the feeling frightened her. She felt out of her own control, like a drunk unable to walk in a straight line.

"I said stay back!" Bridget shouted.

Then she ran, and without thinking about it, Holly chased after her.

The teens hurtled through the tunnel. The flaming Hell was gone, leaving them in darkness as Holly followed the sound of her friend's heaving breaths. Blood pounded at her temples. She ignored the exhaustion, denying her fear, hunger, and thirst. So many times she'd accepted defeat. Sometimes it was in the form of boys turning her down. Sometimes it came after struggling with her school studies. She'd never been much of a jock, and usually found her way onto the losing team in P.E. But none of those failures mattered anymore.

What had seemed so important was now revealed to her as trivialities. There was only one true test in life, only a single challenge.

Can you make it through the game?

An ethereal, turquoise radiance swelled ahead, silhouetting Bridget. Draped in blue-black shadows, the ossuary's earthly remains seemed to welcome the return of the girls, skeletal arms reaching out of the walls for an embrace. The ceiling writhed with bodies.

Bridget cried out, "Leave me alone!"

She might have been talking to Holly or the crypt itself. Maybe both. It didn't matter to Holly now. All that mattered was catching Bridget, stopping her from finding some easy way to win, some little cheat or code.

Sacrifice, Holly thought, remembering the cryptic piece of paper.

She reached for her friend's hair but couldn't get close enough. Holly's side ached from running, but Bridget showed no sign of slowing down. Holly had to do something fast, before her prey escaped.

Holly lunged onto Bridget's back. The girls fell forward. Bridget's knees hit the edge of an open coffin and she crashed into it, landing face-first on top of the skeleton inside. Its bones splintered and Bridget sank into the body's cavity, screaming as the dust of decomposition wafted up around her in a gray plume. She knocked her forehead on the upper ledge of the casket. Holly fell on top of Bridget, and something stabbed Holly in the abdomen. She winced and rose from the casket, and whatever had jabbed her pulled free from her body. Blood dribbled from the wound, but the cut wasn't deep. She waved away the cloud of dust and peered down at Bridget, and as the haze cleared Holly saw the bone that had snapped off the dead body below and impaled Bridget through the stomach and out her back.

"Oh, fuck . . ." Holly said.

There was a red smear on Bridget's forehead, and a lump was already forming where she'd hit it on the casket. Her eyes were closed, the lashes sprinkled with blood.

"Bridget?" Holly asked, trembling. "Are you dead?"

Bridget didn't answer. The crypt did instead.

A round of applause surged through the ossuary as it filled with white light. Celebratory big band music whirled about Holly, dizzying her, and confetti fluttered through the air like it was New Year's Eve. She looked up to see the bodies of young women in various stages of decay. Unlike the other corpses in the crypt, they weren't dressed in formal clothes. Instead, they wore bellbottom jeans, band t-shirts, poodle skirts, and modern blouses, with various popular hairstyles from the twentieth century. Some were little more than skeletons, others were bloated and purple. Some were locked in rigor mortis while others twitched with burrowing insects. It was not confetti that fell, but dried flakes of skin and maggots. Though many of the bodies were swollen and decayed, their size and attire suggested they'd died young.

"Ladies and gentlemen," the ghost voice announced, "we have a winner!"

Holly screamed as the corpses above her came alive.

They crawled over one another, linking arms and hooking legs, forming a stalactite of living dead bodies. The mass angled downward in the shape of a funnel, coming toward her, the deceased girls moving like a chain of acrobats. Holly scurried away, but skeletal hands rose from the earth below and snatched her ankles. Every coffin opened, their inhabitants lurching forth and grabbing her so she couldn't get away.

The ghost shouted over the roaring crowd. "And now Holly Whitman will receive her prize!"

The rotting girls descended from the ceiling in a swarming hive, their dead eyes showing no emotion as they surrounded Holly. She cried out, but there was no one left to ask for help. She could only watch in horror as the dead girls snapped parts of their bodies free. A finger was broken off. A cheekbone shattered. One girl took to ripping off her toes, the gray tissue tearing like an old bedsheet. A braid of brittle hair was pulled from a skull. Holly bawled and closed her eyes, and when she finally dared to open them, she nearly passed out from the sight.

Faith stood before her. Her charred face flaked as her grin widened, the ocular fluid of her melted eyes dribbling down her burnt cheeks. Her hands were cupped in front of her, and she raised them higher so Holly could see what she cradled.

The tiara was made of bones and dried strips of human carrion. The cartilage, fingernails, teeth, and black chunks of festering flesh had been bound together using hair from the braid of the girl who'd scalped herself. The dead had forged a crown for their queen.

Faith smiled, half her teeth smoked black, the rest having been ripped from the gums—her contribution to the tiara. The smile Holly had always envied now belonged to her.

Faith placed the tiara upon Holly's head.

"Congratulations," she said. "You're The Prettiest Girl in the Grave."

TWENTY-THREE

CELESTE CAME FOR BELLA. CAUGHT between her and Aubrey, and flanked by rows of skeletons, Bella had nowhere to run. Having never been in a fight before, she wasn't sure what to do, so she just cowered away and covered her face as Celeste madly swung the piece of wood. Aubrey tried to grab Celeste, creating a domino effect that sent them all tumbling into the laps of dead theater patrons. The makeshift chairs tilted. Parts broke under the weight and the girls spilled onto the floor. Bella scrambled to get up within a bed of scattered bone as Celeste rose above them in a menacing shadow, raising the wooden plank over her head.

"No!" Bella cried.

She kicked out one leg and caught Celeste behind the knee, tripping her. Bella rushed to Aubrey to help her up and even though she had caused Celeste to stumble, she didn't drop, and when she came at them again, she cracked the plank across the back of Bella's head. When she fell, Celeste continued her attack, bashing Bella at the base of her spine. Her vision spun with stars. She was hit a few more times before Celeste was pulled away from her. At first, all Bella could see were shadows struggling in the shrapnel of broken bones, but as her vision cleared, she saw one of the girls was now straddling the other who lay prone upon the floor. Their silhouettes were too obscured to identify who was who.

Bella gasped as the one on top raised the plank with both hands, not holding it as a club, but as a wooden stake. All the girls screamed as the stake came down hard and fast, followed by a wet popping sound.

"No!" Bella cried.

The girl on top of the other one rose to her feet, revealing her tall, slender form against the azure glow.

Aubrey, Bella realized.

While she was relieved Celeste's rampage had been stopped, how it happened made her sick inside. As Aubrey backed away from Celeste's splayed body, Bella gingerly stepped forward. She hesitated to look, and yet she had to.

The plank was driven straight through the soft area just below Celeste's sternum. Blood was already pooling. It bubbled at the corners of her mouth as she lay there like a slain vampire, staked to death.

Aubrey whispered, "She was gonna kill us."

The pain in Bella's head and back assured this was possible. If Aubrey hadn't stopped Celeste, her wrath may have proved fatal. Bella might owe her life to Aubrey, but she was still mortified by the brutality of what she'd done. It left her cold and mute.

"I had to do it," Aubrey said, a tremor in her voice. "I had no choice . . ."

Celeste's dead eyes stared into the oblivion Aubrey had sent her to. They'd been huge, black saucers moments ago; now they were shrunken and soulless, extinguished forever. Bella wanted to shut the eyelids but was too afraid to do so. If only there was a blanket or something they could drape over the body. Whatever madness had transpired here couldn't change the fact that Celeste had been a friend before the girls entered this horrible crypt.

"What's happening to us?" Bella asked.

"It's this place," Aubrey said, taking a deep breath. "C'mon. I have to tell you something. But first I want out of this theater, okay?"

They moved to the other side of the room, finding the entrance to yet another corridor. Bella despaired. Their Hell was an endless pilgrimage, and just as cold and lonely and blue as Celeste predicted. The crackling furnace sound intensified, and Aubrey flicked the

Zippo, it's slowly ebbing flame offering little assistance as they entered the winding passage.

Aubrey's shoulders hunched as she began to cry. "Jesus . . . I killed Celeste."

The adrenaline rush over, the guilt of the murder slammed Aubrey like a hammer on an anvil.

"Couldn't I have stopped her without killing her?" Aubrey cried. "It all happened so fast, I don't . . . don't . . ."

She nearly collapsed into Bella, so they simply held each other, their rush to escape put on hold so to grieve. When she was all cried out, Aubrey offered a startling confession.

"I haven't told you everything about my mother. Everything I said was true, except she wasn't as vague in her journals as I said she was about the terrible things she'd experienced here. I didn't give the details earlier because I was worried it would just make everyone freak out even more, but now that all of this has happened, I feel like you should know." She sniffed and wiped her eyes. "My mother's name was Bridget. And she nearly died down here."

Bella's mouth hung open. "What happened?"

"About thirty years ago. She and her friends came to this place and were haunted by the ghost who lives here."

She told Bella of the nightmarish adventure Bridget had documented in her diaries, a tale shockingly similar to what Bella and her friends were experiencing tonight.

A beauty pageant poltergeist named Madeline Goldman. Illusions and hallucinations. Sudden, uncontrollable sexual desires. Violence erupting between friends.

They'd endured the same contests, the same horrors.

"After falling into a coffin," Aubrey said, "a bone went through my mother's stomach. When she came to, her friend who'd been chasing her was gone. She must've figured my mom was dead, because she just left her there in the ossuary. So, my mother limped her way back to where they'd come in, and the ghost must've been finished with them, because the door to the graveyard was open."

Bella's eyes went wide. "You mean they got out the same way we came in?"

Aubrey nodded.

"Why didn't you say so before? We've been getting nowhere!"

"We couldn't backtrack because of the bear, remember? Besides, I wasn't convinced yet that everything my mother had written about was real."

"We've gotta go back. It might be the only way out of here."

Aubrey sighed. "I just thought we might find another way out. A better one. My mother claimed she and her friends were down here for days. When she finally got back to the surface, a search party was already looking for them."

A tingle went through Bella. There was something too familiar about this story. Hearing it was like moving puzzle pieces into the beginnings of a clear picture.

"She was found at the base of the mountain," Aubrey said. "She'd managed to make it to the dirt road, then passed out from blood loss. Spent weeks in the hospital. For the longest time, she couldn't remember what happened. All she knew was she and her friends had gone to the woods to hang out and got lost and separated from one another."

Bella's throat went dry. Aubrey couldn't be talking about . . .

"The other girl who got out gave the same story," Aubrey said. "That they just got lost in the woods. They never found the body of the third girl, the one that evil bitch burned to death. By the time my mother's memories started coming back, she'd been having terrible nightmares, and wasn't sure what had been real or imagined. She was institutionalized. When she tried to tell what little she remembered, of course it came out as spooky stories about ghosts and a crypt in a parallel world. No one took her seriously. Even her grandmother— who'd first told her about the graveyard and the Goldman curse— thought my mom was crazy, that she'd somehow taken an urban legend and made it real in her mind."

"And the other girl who got out . . . did her story ever change?"

"No. Why would she change it? Apparently, she'd gotten away with murder. She'd won."

Bella mustered the nerve to ask a question she feared she already knew the answer to. "Who was she?"

"Her name was Holly," Aubrey said. "Holly Clark."

Hearing her mother's maiden name, Bella's heart fell into her stomach. The world began to spin again, and she had to lean against the wall. The story Aubrey told was vastly different from the one Bella's mom told her about the time she went missing as a teenager. She'd never mentioned a surreal underworld or even a graveyard. She and her friends were simply walking through the woods, went off the trail, and got lost after dark. The next morning they'd argued about which way to go and split up. After days in the wilderness, Mom made it back and was rescued by a search party. One of her friends had been hurt in a fall but turned up later. The third girl was never found. Mom and the other survivor were cleared of any foul play, and in time the town of Greenwalk forgot about the tragedy that had befallen the poor teenage girls.

But Aubrey had more to say.

"My mother was in and out of mental health centers and drug rehabs the rest of her life. She became obsessed with this underground world and the ghost of Madeline. Did as much research as she could about the Goldman family."

She explained about the sisters, how they were all beauty pageant contestants but only Madeline ever won titles. Her popularity and success made her daddy's favorite, and with no male heir, the patriarch left the family fortune to Madeline, which made her sisters furious enough to kill her, but she was accidentally buried alive.

"My mom studied the supernatural," Aubrey said. "I think she wanted to come to terms with what happened to her here. I think she wanted to prove to herself that it was all real, that she wasn't crazy. But she carried a lot of demons with her and, well . . ."

Aubrey's eyes grew wet.

"What happened to her?" Bella asked.

Aubrey sighed. "My mother killed herself."

There was a silent pause between them then. Aubrey wiped her eyes with her sleeve.

"It was shortly after she had me," she said. "She wasn't even sure who the father was. Apparently, she was promiscuous as well as a drug addict, doing everything she could to chase the pain away until she couldn't run from it any longer. Like I said, I was raised by my aunt. All my mother left me were her weird diaries and some junk, including this Zippo." She took a deep breath. "I guess my interest in the occult all stems from some need to better understand her. It seems crazy now but . . . I just thought if I came to the cemetery and played out this ritual shit . . ."

"Jesus, Aubrey."

"I know, but I didn't really think it was *real*. I thought it was all in my mother's head, you know? I just figured going to the cemetery with what I knew would give me some perspective or maybe even some kind of answers. I didn't expect there to really be tunnels down here, for there to be a real ghost. And I swear, I didn't think anyone would get hurt." Aubrey's chin dimpled, her face going hard. "But now I know everything in my mother's diaries is real. And what's worse—that bitch Holly Clark must've known it was real all this time. She really did set that other girl on fire. She really did try to kill my mother by stabbing her with a fucking bone. All to be The Prettiest Girl in the Grave."

Bella hugged herself.

How much more did Aubrey know about Holly Clark?

TWENTY-FOUR

ADORNED IN THE CROWN OF the dead, Holly shuffled through the darkness, leaving the ossuary and her friends behind. She hadn't meant to kill Faith and Bridget, but in doing so, she'd become their successor, and her reward was release. It had to be. If she just returned to the Goldman tomb, she would find the door open. She knew this just as surely as she knew the piece of paper she'd discovered in the ossuary must have been placed there deliberately.

Sacrifice, it had read.

That's what the ghost of Madeline Goldman had wanted all along—a sacrifice. Her sisters had taken her life; now she wanted the lives of others in a twisted form of fairness. But it didn't seem right that Madeline would be the one to leave the note. There was no reason for her to favor Holly enough to give her the solution, especially after favoring Faith so prominently.

Holly thought of Faith's animated corpse bestowing her with the tiara, and how she'd merged with the other dead girls as they receded into the ceiling. Faith was one of them now. Bridget's grandmother had been right. Now and then, young girls came to this place for one reason or another, but few ever left. It seemed only the winners lived to tell the tale, but who would ever believe them? The only ones who could understand were those who'd experienced it for themselves.

One of them left the note, Holly realized.

Instructions from one winner to the next, left behind as a clue to whoever was sharp or lucky enough to spot it. Perhaps that was one of the responsibilities of holding the title. Maybe Holly was supposed to leave a note of her own, something that would warn newcomers what they were in for. But it couldn't be too clear, could it? Madeline would destroy anything that might spoil her wicked game. But Holly had to do better than a simple word slathered on scrap paper. As an amateur poet, she felt she could say much more.

As she drew closer to the tomb, she passed by the mounted sculpture of a bear's face inside a circle on the wall—the Goldman family crest. Taking the tiara from her head, Holly inspected the human remains and dug out a blackened tooth, a remnant of Faith's once lovely smile. Putting the incisor to the wall, Holly dragged it along and it pierced the concrete more effectively than she'd expected, like a knife etching into a tree. She took her time relaying the message in the form of an ominous riddle, one she hoped would make sense to whatever poor souls came down here next.

Some girls are fearful, others are brave. One girl's a princess, the next one, a slave. But all girls are equal, when they're down in this cave, until just one is left standing—the prettiest girl in the grave.

When finished, she started toward the opening of the tomb, but an echoing voice carried down the hallway behind Holly, chilling her. She dropped the tooth and turned back, listening as the voice grew clearer. It sounded like it was coming from the ossuary.

"Holly?" Bridget called. "Are you there?"

Holly closed her eyes tight. It couldn't be Bridget. Holly had already won, so Bridget had to be dead, didn't she? Maybe it was some sort of test. Perhaps Madeline was verifying Holly's inner strength, seeing if she was truly worthy of release. She had to prove she wouldn't let anything stand between her and victory. Bridget's plea for help had to be a trick. But even if it wasn't, if Holly's own survival meant leaving her friend to die, so be it.

"Are you there?" Bridget called out again.

No, Holly thought as she walked into the tomb.

The light of a new dawn shone through the open door leading up to the cemetery.

THE PRETTIEST GIRL IN THE GRAVE

No, I'm not here. Not anymore.

~

Holly spent years trying to understand the crypt. But because of what she'd done down there, she couldn't confide in anyone with the truth. Besides, if she had, she'd only have ended up like poor Bridget, a walking disaster who self-medicated her madness with drugs, alcohol, and strange men. It had stunned and terrified Holly when her friend was found barely alive on the side of Old Mill Road. It was as if she'd come back from the dead. Holly thought for sure Bridget was going to turn her over to the police for what she'd done, but the girl was an amnesiac and remained a basket case until the day she died, never revealing their secret in any effective way. And though Faith Johnson was never found, rumors circulated. Some said her body was at the precipice of the mountain, with a few young bullshitters claiming to have seen it. Many believed the popular teen had run away with a boyfriend or gone off to Hollywood to become a star. Others said she was still alive and lived a feral existence in the woods, eating cottontails and insects. It was an unsolved missing persons case, but no other young girls disappeared in Greenwalk after that—until now.

That was what kept the crypt a secret. It seemed Madeline only allowed one Prettiest Girl in the Grave competition per generation, so there was never a steady problem of teen girls going missing, and no cause for alarm. The vanishings were spaced out over decades, never leading people to connect the separate events.

You should have warned Bella, Holly thought now. *You should have told her the truth.*

But how could she? How could she possibly get her daughter to understand, to believe in the unbelievable? How could she look her baby girl in the eye and tell her she'd killed someone? Holly always thought it was best to stick with her story. She'd thought it was all over, that Madeline Goldman's sick game had come to an end, but after three decades of silence, the horror beneath the cemetery had reopened to the next generation of contestants.

"Rose!" Sawyer called out again. "Bella!"

The tunnel seemed endless. It was an illusion Holly recalled from her first visit. How long had she and Sawyer been down here? Had time already distorted? Would their experiences be non-linear? Though the crypt hadn't seemed to change much in the past thirty years, Holly certainly had. Would her being a grown woman instead of a teenager change the crypt's approach to her? And what of

Sawyer? He was a man in a girl's playground. He didn't belong here. He served a purpose for Holly, but what could Madeline Goldman possibly want with him?

"Okay," he said, coming to a stop. "Enough's enough. We need to get the cops. Form a search party."

Holly tensed. "What?"

"I know we wanted to keep them out of this, but we've been down here for what seems like hours and haven't been able to find them. They could be trapped or hurt. The more people looking for them, the better."

"We can't do that."

"The way I see it, we don't have any choice."

But Holly felt it was she who didn't have a choice. She couldn't allow Sawyer to bring the police into this. It would dig up parts of her past she needed to stay buried, and more importantly, there was no way of knowing what Bella had done in her time in the crypt. She may have committed serious crimes of her own.

"You can't just call 911," she said. "We can't get a signal down here."

"I know. I'm saying we turn back and get the hell outta here. Go to the police station."

"No," she said, a little too sharply. "We have to keep looking for them."

"Damn it, we aren't getting anywhere. We haven't found any trace of the girls. What if they're not down here at all?"

"They are. I know they are."

Sawyer's face hardened. "And *how* do you know this?"

"I just do."

He took a step toward her. "All right. What's really going on here?"

"Sawyer—"

"All this weird shit that's been going on . . . you seem to understand it all. Only you. *You* brought us down here. *You* were welcomed in like royalty. Why is that?"

"There's no time to explain."

"Bullshit!" he said, pointing in her face. "Fess up to what you know. I deserve that much."

"Oh, *deserve*? What is it you think you *deserve*, huh? *The truth*? I mean, is the truth what you always told me? Is it what you always told your wife?"

Sawyer's jaw shifted. "Is that what this is really about? You and me? Jesus, use your graveyard witchcraft on me all you want, but don't fuck around when it comes to my kid."

"*Witchcraft?*" Holly's eyes widened. "You think *I'm* doing all this?"

"I don't know what to think! All I know is there's something really strange about this place, you refuse to explain it, and you brought me here and seduced me."

"Are you *kidding me*? I fell under the same spell as you did back there. I'm not a witch, but even if I was, I wouldn't need to put a spell on you to get you to fuck me. All I'd have to do is ask."

"I'm just saying all this weirdness tonight involves you in some way or another. If you're not gonna tell me why that is, I'm gonna search for the girls on my own, and that starts with getting the hell outta here."

With a huff, Sawyer turned around and started walking back. A mean heat was spreading through Holly's chest, but she couldn't lash out at him. For whatever reason, Madeline's spirit seemed to want them here together. Holly needed Sawyer more than ever, right?

"Wait," she said, swallowing her pride. "Please, don't go. You're not really going to leave me down here alone, are you?"

Sawyer turned around. "I'd rather not. Please, come with me."

"No."

Her bluntness made Sawyer grimace. "You're a very selfish woman, you know that?"

"How dare you say that to me?"

"You play with my emotions to get what you want, when you want it—"

"You son of a bitch."

"—and dump me for no reason when—"

She walked up so they were face to face. "Shut your mouth, you asshole!"

Anger coursed through Holly in a sudden hurricane. The audacity for him to put things on her after all she'd gone through because of him—all the guilt and longing, the feelings of inadequacy and indecency, the torture of knowing he would never leave his wife, never love her the way he loved Trisha. In the back of her mind, Holly knew her rage was more than what was called for, but just like her lust for him, she was unable to control it or reason with herself. Judging by the redness in Sawyer's face, he was feeling similarly.

"You always have to have everything your way," he said. "You can never compromise, never apologize."

"I don't owe you a damn thing."

"You wanna know something?" he said, sneering. "There's a reason you're alone."

Holly's stomach went hollow with hurt. "Don't . . ."

"You're just a miserable cunt, impossible to love. So you're gonna die alone."

Tears filling her eyes, Holly reared back and hit Sawyer in the jaw. Not a slap, but a closed fist punch that smarted her hand. Sawyer winced but seemed more shocked than injured, so Holly hit him again. He turned his head away and her fist caught his ear. When she came at him a third time, he grabbed her wrist and shoved her back against the wall—*hard*. Holly's neck snapped back, and she hit her head on the limestone. Stars obscured her vision, but the impact brought her out of her rage for a moment of clarity.

This hostility and distrust were part of the game. Madeline was testing the true feelings of the contestants, but Holly had thought the ghost wasn't making her and Sawyer play. There'd been no questions, only actions, the crypt bringing out all the mixed feelings the former lovers had for each other and amplifying them. Holly was a returning champion, but down here, all was a twisted game.

"Stop," she said, hoping to reason with him.

But Sawyer's fury was explosive. He shoved her again. Holly's breath left her as her back hit the wall.

"Fucking bitch," he snarled. "You've been wasting my time all night. This is all some silly game to you, huh? I've always been nothing but a toy to amuse you. Well, this time you've gone too far. My daughter's lost somewhere, and you've led me on a wild goose chase."

"Listen to what you're saying," she said, holding up her hands passively. "After everything you've seen down here, how can you think that?"

"You don't get to tell me what to think," he said, poking her chest. "All this time you've been telling me how to feel—about you, about us. Don't you *dare* tell me how to think. Not when it comes to my little girl."

"My little girl is lost too."

He suddenly grabbed Holly's collar, making her gasp. Sawyer had never been violent with her, but right now she feared him. Something was pulling them down to their most basic anger, the reptilian brain taking charge.

THE PRETTIEST GIRL IN THE GRAVE

"Fuck your little girl," Sawyer said. "You think Trisha and I haven't noticed how Bella's changed for the worse? All this goth shit. We don't need her around our daughter, trying to drag Rose down to her level. Your little girl's a basket case. A basket case on her way to being a total failure as an adult. With you and Justin for parents, I can hardly blame the girl, but fuck her anyway. Fuck the both of you."

The rage that had faded bloomed within Holly again until it was all she could feel.

"Get your hands off me, you dick," she said. She shoved him away, seething. "You ever talk about my daughter like that again, and I'll fucking kill you."

He smirked. "Yeah, I'm real scared."

Holly's hand dipped into her pocket without her even realizing it. "Tell me . . ." she said. "What is it you're really afraid of?"

His brow furrowed.

"We already know it's Trisha you really love," she said. "So, what happens when you die?"

Sawyer bared his teeth and stepped into her, but this time when he grabbed Holly by the collar, she didn't fear him anymore, and didn't hear what he said. She only heard herself whispering a single word repeatedly as she unfolded the knife in her pocket.

"Sacrifice."

TWENTY-FIVE

THE FURNACE SOUND FLARED, FILLING the hallway. Bella and Aubrey turned to the crackling roar of it, and at the other end of the tunnel saw a flickering glow. It started small, like candlelight, but quickly blossomed into a bright burst that washed across the walls. Bella and Aubrey froze, watching the strange spectacle from a distance as a smoky odor filled the corridor. It smelled like barbeque.

That's no furnace, Bella realized.

A pillar of flame coasted down the hallway, igniting the walls of the shaft as it passed through. The smell of charred steak grew stronger, the smoke thicker. It wasn't until the burning thing started screaming that Bella realized there was a person beneath all that fire.

"Oh my God," Aubrey said.

She tugged on Bella, but she was in a state of horrified awe and didn't move. The scream was high-pitched and piercing—the scream of a girl. It cut through the whooshing sound of the spreading flames even as they grew louder, the phantasmic figure drawing nearer. Realizing what she smelled was burning human flesh, Bella covered her nose and mouth with her hand.

"C'mon!" Aubrey said, pulling Bella back toward the theater.

The girls ran. Bella pounded the concrete so hard her feet hurt, but she ignored the pain. There would be time to nurse their wounds later, if they survived. That was all that mattered now—survival. But it was seeming less and less likely as the horrors continued to transform. Smoke burned Bella's eyes and filled her lungs, but still she ran, the flaming girl racing through the shaft behind them, screaming. The hall shook as it overheated. Hope drew dim as everything else brightened white with flame to the point of blindness. Bella heard Aubrey's terrified cries but could make no such sound to vent her own horror. Fear left her mute. The whiteness forced her to shut her eyes, and she sprinted forward until she felt as if she were falling, the hard concrete beneath her feet seeming to vanish, and for a moment Bella was drifting through space before she and Aubrey stumbled into the theater.

The brightness of the fire was gone, but the theater was no longer cast in blue and black shadows. It was as well lit as any normal theater, the warm illumination coming from nowhere. The rows of patrons had been resituated, the corpses back in their contorted seats, waiting for the show that lay hidden behind the curtains of tanned flesh. And as Aubrey and Bella entered, they were welcomed with a fierce round of applause.

The house lights darkened as the spotlights hit them. The girls clutched each other.

"It's been a heck of a contest, hasn't it folks?" the ghostly voice asked the crowd.

The audience hooted and cheered as the curtains came open. Savannah and Marnie remained propped up like gory scarecrows. Beside them was the corpse of Celeste. Her bloody face stared blankly into the crowd, head tilted to one side, eyes half closed. The wooden plank was still inside her, jutting out of her midsection like an extra limb.

"We've had many tests and tribulations," said the phantom hostess, "but now it's time for the beauty part of our show. This is a beauty pageant, after all."

The audience chuckled, and this time Bella thought she saw the mouths of the skeletons open and close in the darkness, cackling from beyond the grave.

"Ladies and gentlemen," the ghost said, "please join me in welcoming Rose Peterson to the stage."

Bella gasped. The spotlight swirled and landed on the front row where Rose sat in one of the chair sculptures with her back to Bella, her blonde hair all she could see. Then she stood. Her letterman jacket and jeans had been replaced by a long, black dress. It was riddled with holes and tears, patches of decay having worn through the material. A gray coating of dust surrounded the bottom of the skirt that covered her feet and cobwebs stained the sleeves and shoulders. Rose turned around and smiled, waving at the crowd, and the applause grew thunderous, a few male voices hooting and whistling. As she walked toward the stage, the spotlight followed her, revealing Rose's clothes on the floor beside a skeleton that had been stripped down to its withered undergarments. One of its arms had been broken off. Bella winced. Rose must have grown impatient while struggling to remove the dress.

On stage, Rose's gaze fell upon Bella and Aubrey, and she curled her upper lip. Even when the poltergeist hostess appeared like smoke from a volcano, Rose's eyes stayed on the two girls, projecting silent malice.

"I'd say dressing for the occasion has given Rose extra points," the ghost said into the microphone in her hand. "But Aubrey has gone so far as to eliminate another contestant."

The spotlight fell on Celeste's impaled carcass, and as if on cue a stream of blood bubbled and poured out of the dead girl's nostrils and slack mouth. The audience cheered and the spotlight swirled again, landing on Aubrey, and even with the light in her eyes Bella could see the heads of the dead turn their way.

"No," Aubrey said. "I didn't mean to . . ."

The ghost of Madeline Goldman guffawed. "Murderous *and* modest. You're going to make some fellow very happy one day . . . if you make it out of here."

More chuckles from the audience, their ashy jaws opening and closing like bear traps in the shadows. Bella tugged on Aubrey. They couldn't stay here. They had to keep running. With Rose on the stage, they might be able to make it to the hallway and head back to the ossuary, then the tomb. At this point, she'd rather face the bear than Rose, the undead, and the sadistic ghost of Madeline Goldman.

The ghost's face was still dark and obscured as she returned her attention to Rose. Bella realized the microphone she was holding was actually a femur with a length of yellowed, mummifying wrap hanging down like a cord.

"Final round, Rose," the hostess said. "Time to show us some gumption. Let's see what you have to offer, darling."

Suddenly Rose sprinted to the edge of the stage and leapt into the air in full basketball player style. Her dress fluttered like moth wings as she soared over the two rows of corpses and landed hard in her bare feet, staring down Bella and Aubrey like a lioness preying upon gazelles. She snarled and her eyes flashed, a feral thing.

"All girls are equal," she growled, "when they're down in this cave. Until *just one* is left standing—the prettiest girl in the grave."

Bella looked upon her best friend in abject horror, wondering if this could really be her. Rose was now so alien to Bella she almost seemed possessed. The evil of the crypt had soaked into her like blood seeping into a mattress. And if Bella and Aubrey were going to head back to the tomb, they would have to go through her. While they outnumbered Rose, her size and fierceness more than compensated for it.

"You betrayed me," Rose said.

Bella shivered. Did Rose know about that night with Tyson? Had she always known, or had the crypt bestowed her with special insight?

"Rose," she said. "Please. Whatever it is you're thinking of doing, please don't."

"You were supposed to be my best friend, and you betrayed me."

Tears filled Bella's eyes. "I'm sorry . . . it was just a mistake."

"No. You knew what you were doing. Admit it."

The tears fell and Bella caved inward. Maybe Rose was right. Maybe this was what she had to do—confess her sins. Madeline Goldman wanted honesty from the pageant's contestants, didn't she? Lying only made the ghost test them with greater viciousness.

"Alright," Bella said, nearly choking on the words. "I admit it. I had sex with Tyson."

Rose's face dropped, the snarling anger giving way to teary-eyed shock. "You . . . you what?"

Bella realized her mistake instantly.

Rose hadn't known. When she spoke of betrayal, she was referring to Bella leading her to the graveyard tonight. She'd said she thought Bella had brought her here as some sort of sacrificial lamb, choosing her new friends' witchcraft over her and Rose's decade of friendship. That she'd had sex with Tyson remained a closely guarded secret until now.

"I'm sorry. It just happened."

Rose glowered. "Well . . . the apple doesn't fall far from the whore tree."

Bella almost asked what Rose meant by that, but then it hit her. Rose knew about her father and Bella's mother. Had she caught them in the act too? Had she kept the hurt internal as Bella had, or had she confronted the lovers? If only Bella had known Rose was aware of the affair, they could have talked about it and consoled one another. Perhaps they could have even come up with a plan to bring their families together the way Bella wanted. Now it was too late, too late for so many things.

"Stay away from us!" Aubrey said as Rose stepped closer.

But Rose kept coming, slow but steady. "You should really take this opportunity to run and hide, Aubrey. I'm coming for you next. But first I want some quality time with my best friend here, to pay her back for all she's done for me."

"Don't," Bella said. "We can still get out of this together."

"There is no 'together' anymore," Rose said. "It's all broken. Broken apart."

Then she came at her.

TWENTY-SIX

SAWYER DROPPED TO HIS KNEES, blood oozing through his fingers as he clutched his belly. Holly stood over him with the knife tight in her trembling fist. She put her flashlight on him, watching his cheeks shudder as he turned pink, spit dangling from his lower lip.

This is why she let him in, Holly thought. *Madeline doesn't want to just watch me with him, she wants a beau of her own.*

What better offering could Holly make than to end Madeline's decades of loneliness by giving her a male companion, a Handsomest Boy in the Grave? She'd hoped being a former winner was enough to grant her reentry to the crypt, but everything had its price, all highways a toll. She couldn't expect to pull her daughter out of the game without offering a trade.

"Holly . . ." Sawyer groaned.

When he gazed up at her for help, she reared back and drove the knife into the side of his neck. Her hand was bathed in warm redness as she twisted the blade deeper.

Sawyer was too surprised to defend himself. Falling, he put out his hand to catch himself, and the knife came out of his neck. Blood spurted from a severed vein, and Sawyer coughed a crimson mist and curled forward, exposing the wide target of his back.

Holly stabbed and stabbed again. Jets of blood burst from Sawyer like water pistols.

You stabbed me in the back, she thought, *now I repay the favor.*

But she had trouble following her own logic. Had Sawyer really betrayed her? How so? By loving his wife too much to leave her but not enough to stop him from seeing Holly? By leading her on, making her think there could be more to this, that maybe she wouldn't have to die alone?

Though she hated to admit it to herself, she'd thought Sawyer Peterson might take the pain away. After a failed marriage, a shitty job, and the unbearable weight of what she'd done to her friends decades ago, all Holly wanted was love. With Sawyer, she'd at least had some semblance of it. But it had all been an illusion. His harsh words had proven that. Even if he'd been influenced by the black magic that permeated every inch of this necropolis, his words stemmed from hard nuggets of truth he kept locked in the secret chasms of his heart. He did resent her. He did think little of her. Holly realized now, with brutal clarity, that she was little more to him than a piece of ass on the side. She wasn't even girlfriend material to Sawyer, let alone wife material. She was just an easy lay, someone to entertain his desires now that he'd grown tired of sleeping with his wife. Holly probably wasn't even the first. Sawyer might have even been screwing around with other women at the same time he and Holly were having their affair. She didn't think she deserved much, but she deserved better than that. Several times in her life she'd dared to ask for companionship and every time had ended in staggering heartbreak, and as she stabbed now, she saw not only Sawyer but also her husband Justin, and every other man who'd failed her, cheated on her, used her. She let the anger flow as she raised the knife up and down.

It was just easier if she hated him.

~

The sound of girls screaming pulled Holly out of her dark thoughts. She blinked back to reality to see Sawyer Peterson crumpled at her feet like a groveling worshipper. His eyes were wide, but he saw nothing. A rich pool of blood had spread beneath him. His limbs had gone slack. He'd stopped breathing, stopped living.

Holly nearly dropped the knife. She remembered what she'd done.

THE PRETTIEST GIRL IN THE GRAVE

She hadn't blacked out. But the gravity of her actions pulled her back into her real life, the life outside this horrible place. Everything was in jeopardy now, but even her freedom was trivial when compared to the life of her daughter, so when Holly distinctly heard Bella's cries, she gripped the knife tighter and ran down the hall toward the sound, leaving Sawyer in the blood pool where he lay, a problem to be dealt with later.

A light at the end of the tunnel became fuller as Holly approached. When she finally reached the expansive theater, she was taken aback by the sight of it. When she'd been in this crypt as a teenager, she and her friends hadn't stumbled upon this place. How many other secret rooms were hidden in Madeline's lair? But despite the propped-up skeletons and mangled bodies on the stage, Holly's attention went directly to the three girls thrashing under the spotlights. Rose was on top of Bella, pummeling her with blows. A third girl was trying to pull Rose off Bella, but when she got close Rose slugged her away. The third girl's foot slipped into a crack in the floor, and she fell hard, crying out in pain. Seeing Bella at war with her best friend made Holly want to cry. Madeline had already turned them against one another. It made her wonder what unspoken resentments the girls had held for each other before they'd even come down here.

Holly ran toward them. "Rose, stop!"

Rose glanced up at Holly with eyes gone cold and mean, then went right back to pummeling, hitting Bella so hard her nose snapped to one side in a burst of blood.

"Get away from her!" Holly shouted.

She'd come into the crypt wanting to save both girls, if possible, but now only one truly mattered. She didn't want to harm Rose but wouldn't hesitate to destroy her if that's what it took to keep her daughter safe. She flipped the bloody blade downward, then kicked Rose off Bella and raised the knife in warning.

"Stop it!" Holly told her.

Rose glared up at her. She was wearing a decayed dress. Something had darkened behind the girl's eyes and her lips were peeled back in an animal snarl. She was nearly unrecognizable. The sweet girl next door had been deconstructed by the sorcery of the crypt and rebuilt upon the darkest elements of her personality.

"Stop or I'll be forced to hurt you," Holly said. "Don't think I won't."

Rose locked eyes with her, then looked to the knife. Seeing the blood, the anger on her face gave way to a look of pale horror.

"Where's my dad?" she asked in a shaky voice.

Holly paled. "He's . . . um . . . not here."

Rose slowly got to her feet. Holly was too stunned to stop her.

"Where is he?" Rose asked. "What have you done with him?"

As tears flooded Rose's eyes, she moved in on Holly, and though Holly raised the knife, the girl seemed completely unfazed. Rose wasn't scared for herself; she was scared for her father.

"Calm down," Holly said. "We need to work together if we're gonna get out of here alive."

But Holly knew there would be no partnership. Rose's father was just outside the theater, dead by Holly's hand. There was no coming back from that. She could try to deny she'd been the killer but doubted Rose would believe her. The girl had already come to the right conclusion.

"Where's my daddy?" Rose said, her face turning pink. "Answer me!"

Even if Holly had wanted to tell her, Rose didn't give her the chance. The girl lunged and Holly slashed at the air between them, trying to keep her back without seriously hurting her. Despite everything, she was still fond of Rose. She'd watched the girl grow up and cared for her like a loving aunt. Rose had always been good for Bella. She had a promising future. Holly didn't want it all to be destroyed because of the nightmare Madeline Goldman put her through.

But Rose was less sentimental. Though the knife cut into her arm, she dove into Holly's waist, grabbed her behind the legs, and lifted her into the air. Holly dropped her flashlight. She had no choice but to try to stab the girl, but as Rose flipped her upside down over her back, Holly was forced to put her hands out to keep from falling face-first onto the concrete floor, and the knife spun away under the back row of skeletons. Strange applause swelled and bounced off the walls of the crypt.

Rose was on her in a second. Before Holly could turn over, Rose sat on her back, took her hair in her hands, and started bashing her head into the floor.

"You hurt my daddy!" she cried. "I'll kill you!"

Holly's forehead split open, and her thoughts grew scrambled as blood filled her eyes. She struggled to fight back, feeling she might vomit or faint. When her head came up, she could just make out the girl she didn't know crawling toward her to help, but then Holly's face was smashed into the concrete again, filling her head with stars as three of her front teeth broke. As the certainty of her death began to take hold, Holly gasped for air, her head lifted for another blow, but then there was a loud shriek and her hair was released. Hot wetness splashed across the back of her neck. The weight of Rose suddenly left her, and Holly blinked away blood to see the girl roll onto the floor, a figure in black looming over her.

TWENTY-SEVEN

BELLA PAWED UNDER THE SEATS where her mother's knife had landed. In her hurry, the blade cut into her hand, but she ignored the pain. Mom was on the verge of being murdered. She had to stop Rose and the only way to overpower her was with the advantage of a weapon.

Her best friend's back was to her as she bashed her mother's head in. If she moved quickly, Bella might be able to take Rose by surprise. From the floor, Aubrey spotted Bella and started crawling toward Rose to distract her. But Rose was too focused on her violence to care. With Aubrey's ankle twisted, she posed little threat. But Bella was ready to fight back. She knew if she only tried to hurt Rose, eventually Rose would get the upper hand. If she were going to stop her, Bella would have to do serious damage. She would have to stop her for good.

Sprinting silently in her combat boots, Bella snuck up behind Rose, grabbed her by the hair, and before Rose could respond Bella put the knife to her best friend's throat, dug the blade in, and sliced deep, dragging the blade from below one ear to the other. Bella screamed as she slit Rose's throat open, a primal cry of heartache. It echoed off the walls, hushing the roar of the undead crowd. Blood sprayed from an open artery in Rose's neck and spattered across Mom. Rose clutched her throat, more blood leaking through her fingers, coating her hands and chest, and her screams came out as choking gurgles as she fell off her victim and onto her side, convulsing in fear for her life. Tears spilled down Bella's cheeks. She looked away, not wanting to see her best friend die, and went to her mother, who was still conscious despite her beating.

"C'mon, Mom," Bella said.

She pocketed the knife so she could lift her under the armpits. Her mother wobbled but Bella managed to support her. Having snatched Mom's flashlight from the floor, Aubrey braced herself on the row of seats but struggled to put weight on her injured foot. Though she too was now a killer, she'd gone pale seeing what Bella had done.

"Oh my God . . ." she muttered.

Rose made horrid gasps for life, gargling blood. Bella was tempted to get out of the theater as quickly as they could, but knew it was best to make sure Rose was finished. Anything was possible in this crypt, even the resurgence of a girl with a slit throat. If Rose somehow survived, she might sabotage them as they tried to escape, maybe even kill them. It was best to watch her die.

Rose bled out quickly. Her hands left her throat and fell to her sides, her chest rising and falling in one final plea for breath. Bella looked into her friend's eyes as they glassed over. She hoped to see peace in them. Instead, she saw only malice. In her last moments, Rose Peterson seemed to feel only hatred for the Whitman women and passed into death staring deep into the eyes of a girl who'd been like a sister to her most of her life, a girl who'd betrayed her, a girl who'd killed her.

The dead roared.

Festive, celebratory music played, and the rotted skeletons began to move. Aubrey limped away from them, and she and Bella watched in horror as the corpses rose from their seats. Their bones popped and crackled, their backs bent, knees buckling. They moved sluggishly, years of dust falling out of their sleeves and pants legs. One of the females tilted her head, and black liquid dribbled from her eye sockets. A dead man snapped in half from the effort of getting up, his torso falling off his lower body and hitting the floor with a sound like a bundle of snapping twigs. Though they struggled to do so, the crowd gave Bella a standing ovation. Warm light blossomed on the stage, and Bella's mouth fell open when she saw Celeste, Savannah, and Marnie clapping their hands and smiling with what was left of their faces. Aubrey huddled close to Bella and her mother as the voice boomed over the cheers of the dead.

"What a show!" Madeline Goldman said. "I don't hesitate to say this is the most exciting contest yet!"

Bella looked to Aubrey. "Can you walk?"

"I have no choice," Aubrey said.

Mom spat a wad of blood and tiny chips of teeth. She was starting to regain her balance and moved to Aubrey's side, putting her in the middle of the trio so Aubrey could put her arms across their shoulders.

"D-don't look back," Mom said, lisping from her injuries.

Aubrey gave the flashlight back to her and they shuffled through the theater as briskly as they could, Aubrey hopping on one leg to keep up.

"The show must go on," the ghost said cheerfully. "The show must go on."

The audience continued their praise as the trio reached the hallway, exiting the theater of horrors. It pained Bella to just leave Rose's body behind, but there was nothing she could do. This mass grave was her friend's only burial. Would Rose be reanimated like the others? Would she become part of the audience, her corpse bloating and liquifying upon a chair made of trash until her flesh fell away? Bella mourned not just Rose's lost life but also her abandoned spirit. Rose and the others were part of the sepulture now. They would forever remain runners up in a pageant from beyond the boundaries of eternal sleep. Bella could vow to never forget them and always honor their memories, but what good is sentiment to the damned?

TWENTY-EIGHT

HOLLY'S VISION BEGAN TO CLEAR. The spinning in her head faded as she and the girls made their way down the hall. Tonguing her mouth, she realized she'd lost teeth and cut her lip. Her nose throbbed, likely broken. She wondered if her face would ever look the same, then told herself it didn't matter. All that mattered was she had her daughter again.

Bella's cheek was bruised, and blood had dried around her nostrils, but she was all right. Holly knew all too well how the memories of this underground hellscape would torture her daughter, but a troubled life is better than no life at all. Bella was young. She could move on from this. Maybe with her mother's help, she could come to terms with what she'd had no choice but to do. Perhaps Bella could help her mother too. Now Holly had someone who understood, someone who knew she wasn't crazy, that the crypt wasn't imagined.

But then there was this other girl who limped in their arms. What of her? How did she play into this, and what was to be done?

The girl groaned as they passed over an uneven stretch of ground, and Holly turned her flashlight on her, seeing her clearly for the first time. Holly screamed. She backed away from the girl and grabbed Bella, pulling her away too. The limping girl struggled on one foot until she leaned on the wall.

"What?" Bella asked. "What is it?"

Bella tried to return to the girl to help her, but Holly pulled her back. She stared at the girl in disbelief, her mouth going dry as sawdust.

"Bridget . . ." Holly murmured.

Her old friend was young again, looking almost like she had when they'd entered this terrible place so long ago. Though Holly hadn't seen Bridget since then, she could never forget her face. That hair so dark it was almost black; those feline eyes; that olive skin. Though she hadn't died in the crypt, she had somehow returned here.

At the sound of her name, the girl furrowed her brow as if confused to be identified. "Did you . . . did you just call me Bridget?"

Holly held Bella closer.

Her daughter looked at her in total befuddlement. "Mom?"

"Stay away from her, Bella."

Bridget hobbled. "You think I'm . . ."

"I don't know what you want, Bridget, but leave my daughter out of it. What happened back then was between you, me, and Faith. Bella has nothing to do with our past."

Bridget's eyes widened. "Wait a second. Who are you?"

Holly tensed. Was it possible Bridget didn't recognize her after all these years? No, she must know who she was. Why else would Bridget become involved with her daughter? Her vengeful spirit had seized upon the opportunity to invade Bella's life. Holly couldn't understand how it had all come together, but she certainly understood why. She'd left Bridget down here to die, and when she'd managed to escape, Holly let the world think Bridget was insane. Now Holly's old friend intended to put her daughter through the same Hell.

"You brought the girls down here, didn't you?" Holly asked. "You led my daughter and Rose into this pit. You want to get back at me? Well, what else was I supposed to do, huh? I didn't want to kill you and Faith, but damn it, you can't blame me for trying to save my own life."

Bridget glared at her with those deadly cat eyes, her jaw dropping. "Oh my God. You're Holly Clark."

"Leave my daughter alone," Holly said.

"I'm not Bridget! I'm Aubrey—Bridget's daughter!"

Holly gasped. She blinked to steady her vision and held the flashlight out to better illuminate the girl's face. She looked so much like Bridget, and yet there were slight differences. Her face was more symmetrical and oval shaped. Her eyes were darker, lips fuller. And when Holly did the math, what she guessed to be the girl's age lined up with the twenty years that had passed since she'd heard about Bridget having a baby.

"You left my mother to die," Aubrey said. "You burned that other girl alive and left my mom to bleed to death in this fucking crypt. You're a monster." She looked to Bella, but Bella couldn't meet her gaze. "And you knew all along."

~

"I didn't know," Bella said. "I swear, I didn't know about any of this until you told me. And I couldn't tell you who my mom was then. Not while we were still down here trying to escape."

Aubrey sniffed back tears. Bella couldn't tell if she believed her or not. If she could just reason with Aubrey, they might still get out of this. Mom was right. Whatever happened when she was a teenager was between her and Aubrey's mother. The grudge didn't have to be inherited by their daughters, especially now that they'd come so far as a team.

"You really didn't know?" Aubrey asked.

"I swear to you, I didn't."

She still wasn't sure if Aubrey believed her, but she would have to trust Bella to get out of here. Aubrey could barely stand on her own. Without help, she would practically have to crawl out of the crypt— *just like her mother had*—and even if she made it, she would still have to get down the mountain.

"Please, Aubrey," Bella said. "Let's get out of here, together."

Aubrey glared at Mom, not needing to say anything to get her point across. Even if Bella regained Aubrey's trust, her mother never would.

The hallway suddenly swelled with the ethereal blue glow. Dreamy, old-fashioned music swirled and crackled, carrying with it the murmurs of the dead. Something splashed across Bella's feet and when she looked down, she realized she was standing in a puddle of blood.

Then she saw the body.

Rose's father was in a fetal position, having left life the same way he'd begun it. Multiple stab wounds left red streaks across his body.

His skin was white as cotton.

Bella shrieked and jumped out of the pool of gore. She looked at her mother, and the expression on her face was frightening.

"Mom?" Bella said.

Eyes misting, her mother didn't speak. She was caught. Guilty.

"Rose's father?" Aubrey asked, more statement than question. "She was right. You killed him."

Aubrey crept away from them.

"Wait," Bella said.

"No," Aubrey said. "Your mom is a *serial killer.*"

Mom shook her head. "That's not true!"

Aubrey crept faster, bracing herself on the wall so she could hop away. She winced in pain with every leap, and her tears devolved into sobs.

"You don't understand," Mom told her. "This place does things to you. I'm not a monster. I had no choice but to do the things I did."

Aubrey continued down the tunnel. Bella tried to go to her, but her mother snatched her by the arm and whispered in her ear.

"I had no choice. And neither do you."

A chill coursed through Bella. She stared at her mother, and her mother stared back, never averting her stern gaze. Bella tried to shake free of her, but Mom held her arm tight and whispered.

"I did what I had to. To survive—to end the game. The contest doesn't end until there is a winner."

The furnace sound returned, blending with the big band music and murmuring audience to create a hellish cacophony.

Mom set that girl on fire, Bella thought, remembering the flaming figure in the hall. *And she killed Rose's father too.*

It was too much to process. The strange blueness surged, giving a slow, cyclonic appearance to the crypt. Aubrey glanced back with terrified eyes but kept moving.

"I spent years afraid that her mother would tell people what I did," Mom said. "I don't want you to have to live with that same fear. You'll already have enough trauma without that paranoia to make things worse." Her mother reached into Bella's coat pocket, withdrew the knife, and put it in Bella's hand. It was still tacky with her best friend's blood. "She knows too much. She saw you kill Rose. She knows I . . . okay, I killed Sawyer. I admit it. But please believe me when I say I had to. I had to make an offering—a *sacrifice*. And so do you."

Bella trembled. "I already did . . . I sacrificed my best friend."

"But that sacrifice is not enough. If you want to get out, you must *win*. You have to become The Prettiest Girl in the Grave."

Bella knew Mom's old friend Bridget had managed to escape the crypt too. Aubrey could survive this just as well as they could. Bella shouldn't have to kill again. But what Mom was saying was true. Aubrey did know too much. Though Aubrey had killed Celeste in self-defense, making her just as accountable as Bella was for the murder of Rose, could they really trust her now that she knew what Mom had done to her mother all those years ago? Wouldn't she want vengeance? It'd be easy enough for her to tell the police Mom was responsible for the murder of Sawyer Peterson. Bella didn't want to see her mother go to prison. She didn't fully understand what Mom had done, but she trusted her more than she trusted Aubrey, who she barely knew. And Mom had been the one to win this contest in her day. She understood the rules of this crypt better than anyone. She said Bella had to take out Aubrey to win, and everything Bella had experienced tonight seemed to suggest the same thing.

"You have to do it," Mom said. "I can't do it for you. If I did, you wouldn't win, and you might be stuck down here forever."

Fingers closing around the handle of the knife, Bella shivered intensely, as if her body was rejecting what she was telling it to do. The furnace sound became crackling flames as the dead howled and whistled, and as the blue radiance surged, it seemed to home in on Aubrey like a bullseye, and inside the spinning rays the phantasmic visages of lost souls appeared and disappeared, watching on.

Bella came after Aubrey.

Seeing the knife in Bella's hand, Aubrey's eyes went wide. "No . . ."

She pleaded and tried to reason with Bella, saying everything the doomed were bound to, as if reading off a desperate checklist. Bella forced herself to ignore Aubrey's cries. She swallowed back the tears and suppressed preemptive regret. Aubrey hopped along quickly, and Bella stalked behind her, trying to build up the nerve to attack, but something within her was holding her back. The conscience she'd come down here with had been broken but wasn't gone for good. Rose had been manslaughter. This would be murder.

I love the dead, she thought. That's what Aubrey had said when answering her own question about love—*I love the dead*.

At the end of the blue tornado, Bella spotted an assortment of skeletal bodies. But what she first took to be the reanimated audience members were actually the human remains of the ossuary. Aubrey reached the entryway and stumbled, crawling on her hands and knees toward a mounted casket so she could brace herself and get up. The light of the ossuary grew brighter as Bella entered, revealing the cavalcade of carcasses that lined the ceiling. The fresh faces drew Bella's eye.

Savannah chuckled in the highest corner, her mauled head like a rotting jack-o'-lantern. Marnie bounced and hollered like a cheerleader but remained stuck to the ceiling. From the other corner, Celeste watched with black eyes, the smirk on her face crusted over with dried blood. And hovering above them—a human spider in a webbing of desiccated flesh—was Rose Peterson. She grinned sadistically, her slit throat like a second smiling mouth. Bella wasn't sure if her dead friends were rooting for her or mocking her, but she knew the wrath that germinated within her was not limited to the living. Madeline Goldman's dark influence was felt even by the dead. This crypt was her eternal home. Her power here was irrefutable. The ghost knew how to intensify lust and prey upon phobias. And she knew how to encourage the primal instinct for violence. While aware of the crypt's evil influence, Bella now understood that it was not a curse, but a tool. It gave her what she needed and kept the game moving toward its inevitable conclusion.

As Aubrey braced herself on the coffin, Bella raised the knife.

TWENTY-NINE

BY THE TIME HOLLY REACHED the ossuary, the deed was already done. She'd lagged, knowing Bella would have to do this on her own. The sound of screams and cries for help sent shivers down Holly's spine, but those shivers were accompanied by a profound sense of relief. She hadn't been sure her daughter was strong enough to do what must be done. Bella had always been meek and non-confrontational, the opposite of Rose Peterson in that regard. But Holly had never been violent before coming here either. In this sepulture, the need to kill was an infectious disease. It was not just an unavoidable result of the game, but an absolute prerequisite. The lives of all contestants counted on murder.

Bella stood above Aubrey. The knife was lodged in Aubrey's breast. One stab had been enough.

Clearly, this was fate. This was what Madeline wanted, and Holly realized it was what she wanted too. It was the best scenario they could have reasonably hoped for. Even while trenching down here with Sawyer in search of their daughters, she'd known in the back of her mind—no matter how hard she tried to deny it to herself—that the night would end in blood. She'd hoped things had changed and they could all get out alive. She'd hoped Madeline's spirit had been satiated and was finally at rest. But some things never change, and there is no rest for the wicked. In her heart, Holly had known these truths. They were bitter facts she'd learned thirty years ago, when she'd been crowned with a tiara of human remains.

"Bella," Holly said, approaching her.

Her daughter took deep, long breaths. The violence that had filled her moments ago had been released as she'd plunged the blade into Aubrey's chest. With her fury spent, reality came crashing in, bringing the horror with it. Bella appeared pale and wan, as if she'd been trapped down here for weeks. Holly slowly put her arms around her daughter. As they embraced, the dead flesh confetti started falling, and the ossuary echoed with applause. Celebrating, the bodies writhed and slithered in their eternal resting places, animating the ceiling and walls. A plume of dust appeared out of the ether, causing Holly and Bella to flinch, and as the fog cleared the silhouette of their hostess took shape between the mounted coffins. In one hand she held the collar of Sawyer's coat, dragging his bloody body into the ossuary like a hunter with a slain deer. She dropped him and raised both arms in a celebratory gesture.

"What a legacy!" the ghost said in a booming voice. "The daughter of our former beauty queen has become the new Prettiest Girl in the Grave!"

The dead cheered, but when Holly looked up at them, she saw endless horror in the eyes of the recently deceased girls. They were not cheering—they were screaming. But the sound blended with the celebration, the ritzy music and happy crowd drowning them out.

Out of the corner of her eye, Holly saw movement, and she gasped when she turned to look.

Aubrey was moving.

At first Holly thought the girl was still alive, but one look at her slack face assured her she was gone. She wasn't moving—she was *being moved*. Slender, black arms emerged from the floor and dragged Aubrey's carcass toward the wall of stacked bones. A charred head poked through, much of its red hair singed away, leaving scabby bald spots. As the body emerged in full, Holly could only watch in dread as the corpse of Faith Johnson glimmered with an orange crust like hot coals. Her seared flesh split with tiny flames as her empty eye sockets turned toward her killer.

Holly gritted her teeth. "I only did what I had to do, Faith."

If Faith understood her, she showed no emotion and made no reply. She hoisted Aubrey, and a litany of skeletal arms pushed out of the wall to snatch the girl's body. The dead hauled Aubrey into their terrible world, welcoming her to an eternity of darkness.

"C'mon," Holly told Bella through busted teeth. "Let's get outta here."

Bella sniffed back her tears, but as they started to leave, she did something that made her mother proud. Before Aubrey could be hoisted any higher, Bella went to her corpse, put both hands around the handle of the knife, and pulled it free.

"No murder weapon," Bella said, deadpan. "No evidence. Just in case."

Putting her arm around her daughter, Holly led her toward the exit, but the ossuary wasn't through with them yet. A spotlight struck down like a flash of lightning and the shadows swarmed. Bella cried out. Holly held her tight.

"It's okay," Holly said, knowing what was coming. "It's just part of the ceremony."

~

Bella was unable to turn away. Somehow, she knew she had to bear witness to the grotesque ballet unfolding before her.

Savannah dropped to the floor like a pile of wet rags and dug her fingers into her gaping wounds, tearing strips of flesh and sinew from her body, the sound like duct tape slowly being ripped from the roll. Her sister Marnie landed on her feet and bobbed on her tiptoes, smiling and clapping for Bella's victory. She jabbed herself in her remaining eye with the nails of her thumb and middle finger, and plucked it loose, tugging the optic nerve until it snapped free.

Bella couldn't even scream anymore. She was throttled by shock.

Celeste pushed out of the wall as if she were moving through mud. Her eyes were now entirely black, her skin purpling with rigor mortis. She pulled the wooden stake out of her chest and reached into the concavity it left beneath her sternum. The force of her fist shattered her ribcage, and she dug deeper until she found what she wanted, then tore the chunk of lung out of her chest.

Halfway up the wall, Aubrey suddenly reanimated, twitching as she dropped like a marionette. Her coat hung open, and she tore her bloody bra down to finger the stab mark, then ripped her wounded breast from her body and let it fall to the floor where it rapidly decomposed. She reached into herself and snapped a rib, then used it to cut a path out of her chest.

The older corpses joined the new in ritual self-mutilation. Bones snapped and dead skin peeled. Bodily dandruff rained down, fluttering like butterflies in the spotlight's beam. The music reached a crescendo that shook the crypt, and the cheers of the crowd were underlined by distinct cries of anguish.

A guttural voice called from above. "Congratulations, Bella."

She looked up just as Rose descended from the ceiling.

Bella stepped away but her mother told her it would be all right, that it was almost over. Rose's smile doubled, her sliced neck opening as if to sing. Her neck poured blood, sousing her as she put her fist through the wound in her throat. She twisted her arm so her elbow faced upward, then shoved her forearm down her gullet. Pushing further, Rose's shoulder dislocated with a loud snap. Bella wept as her friend contorted, Rose breaking her arm in several places to force it all the way down her throat. Her chest bulged and rippled. Blood dribbled from her mouth. Unseen things cracked within her as her eyes rolled back, and Bella's mother had to support her daughter so she wouldn't collapse in horror.

Slowly, Rose withdrew her twisted arm from her insides, holding a large hunk of red meat in her hand. Strings of flesh dangled from it like shredded tubes.

It was Rose's heart, and Bella could finally scream.

The dead girls gathered around Rose, adding their own body parts to the heart and warping its shape. Aubrey's rib pierced the muscle. Celeste's lung fused with it. Savannah's flesh hardened into a base and Marnie's eye was lodged in the center of the meat like a jewel. The bones of the other lost girls were peppered through the sculpture, forming a grotesque tiara. Rose raised it over Bella's head, and she was too paralyzed by fear to run, and though Rose's words were garbled Bella understood what she said.

"Congratulations to my best friend."

THIRTY

THEY MADE IT TO A tomb.

Bella looked around the strange, concrete room, confused and discombobulated. When she and her friends had first entered the crypt, there'd only been one long, descending hallway. She hadn't seen this place before, had she? There were supposed to be many passageways that led in and out of the crypt. And yet, she recognized the door. The piece of plywood Rose had put in the jamb was still there. Madeline's illusions had been tricking them from the very beginning.

Bella wanted to remove the bloody tiara, but Mom told her to keep it on until they escaped. She seemed to think it was important not to dishonor the crown. Bella did as she was told, desperate for any kind of guidance. She was too exhausted and traumatized to keep her racing thoughts together. They toppled over each other before any of them could finish. But soon this would all be over. This was the finish line, their exit to the normal world. Bella wondered if it would ever feel normal again. Would home provide the comfort it once had, even under the crushing weight of all they were bringing home with them? She'd survived this nightmare. Now she had to survive its memory.

Seeing the door to the tomb was still propped open, tears of relief rolled down Bella's cheeks, but a sudden movement in the corner startled her. She flinched, thinking of the bear, but a small, white light appeared, followed by a familiar voice.

"Bella?" the male voice asked.

Mom shined the flashlight toward the speaker. "Who's there?"

Bella's eyes went wide. Rose's boyfriend, Tyson, stood before them, holding his hand up to protect his eyes from the glare. The white light she'd seen was that of the phone he'd been using to see his way through the tomb.

"Thank God," Tyson said. "I'm so glad I found you. I've been looking around this graveyard all night."

Bella only stared at him, the hairs on her neck standing up.

"Where's Rose?" Tyson asked. When Bella and her mother didn't reply, the boy stepped forward. "God, are you hurt? It's okay. I came for you."

Came for you, Bella thought. *I'm coming. Bella, I'm coming!*

The words no longer conjured the memory of Tyson panting them in her ear as they'd made cheap love in a bathroom. Now they reminded her of the last time she'd heard them, down in the darkness of the tunnels where her desire for Tyson had been used against her, and the hideous ghost had emerged from the shadows, her dead fingers reaching for Bella.

It isn't over, Bella realized with dread. *She isn't done with me.*

The illusion of Tyson came closer. "Where is Ro—"

Bella didn't allow him to finish. The knife flashed as she drove it into his belly. He gasped. Her mother shrieked. When Tyson tried to grab her, she stabbed him once more, just beneath his belly button, then thrust the knife downward, opening his insides. She expected the shadow of Madeline Goldman to appear, revealing this was a repeated ruse, but the black void of her face never replaced Tyson's pale one of shock. Blood gushed over Bella's hand and splattered across her boots.

"Oh my God," she whispered as Tyson collapsed.

Tyson spat red. He clutched his stomach but was losing too much blood for it to make any difference.

"Oh my God!" Bella said as fresh horror set in. "Tyson?"

As the realization of her fatal error hit Bella, her mother took the knife away. Without a word, she went to Tyson and stabbed him in the jugular, finishing him off.

"No!" Bella cried.

Mom took her hands, both slick with blood. "Let's go."

"But . . ."

"But nothin'. It's too late. No evidence. No witnesses. No survivors."

~

The first hint of daylight was breaking when they reached the car.

Holly had sealed up the tomb, leaving Rose's boyfriend to bleed out in the dark alone, despite her daughter's objections. There was no need to take him into the labyrinth. Madeline would harvest him for her ossuary, leaving no trace.

Holly wasn't sure why Bella had attacked the boy. Maybe it was just nerves and confusion. Maybe she thought he was one of the crypt's bizarre tricks. They could discuss it later—if they dared bring it up at all.

On their way out of the tomb, Holly handed the knife back to Bella and led her to the wall just behind Madeline Goldman's coffin.

"Carve somethin'," she told her, still struggling to speak with a busted mouth. "You gotta write somethin' for the next contestants. A lil' tip or clue 'bout what needs to happen."

Bella had given her a dazed look but brought the blade to the wall and etched two words into it just where the gateway to the labyrinth had appeared.

No Survivors.

They drove home in silence. Bella held the tiara in her lap, knowing better than to discard it in the woods where someone might find it. She'd wept as they descended the mountain, but now she seemed all cried out, though grief hung about her like a hangman's noose. The haunted look she wore was painfully familiar to Holly. She'd seen it in the mirror for decades. She put her hand on her daughter's head, then ran it down her neck. The caress woke something in Bella, and she put her head on Holly's shoulder.

"It's gonna be okay now," Holly told her. "You won."

Bella spoke soft and low. "No, I didn't. Neither of us did. No one ever does."

Holly's heart sank. Though she hated to admit it, her daughter was right. Their victory was no victory at all, for to achieve it they'd lost too much—their friends, their lovers, their innocence, their humanity. Their only consolation was they'd survived, but the life they would return to would be forever tainted, which was a death in itself. While The Prettiest Girl in the Grave was released from the crypt, she could never truly escape it.

Holly checked her phone for the date. It was only the next day, not several days later as it had been when she'd come out of the tomb thirty years ago. It had seemed like such a long night, but time had no meaning in the crypt. Madeline Goldman bent time and space in whatever ways she wished. This time it would be to Holly's advantage. With little time having passed, it was possible no one had called the police yet.

Arriving home, she and Bella stripped, and Holly put all their clothes into a garbage bag to be burned in the backyard fire pit. Holly would wipe down the knife and throw it in the river at the edge of town. Bella wanted to shower but didn't want to be alone, so Holly came into the bathroom too and inspected her injuries in the mirror.

You fell, she told herself. *When you go to the emergency room, tell the doctors you fell down the front steps.*

She helped Bella into her pajamas and gave her two Valiums to ease the tension. The medication had done wonders for Holly over the years, as had the Trazadone and Zoloft. Alcohol did the rest, with mixed results. She escorted her daughter to the master bedroom and tucked her in, sitting on the edge and patting Bella until she drifted off to sleep. She sat there with her for a long time.

After leaving Bella a note in case she woke up in a panic, Holly went downstairs to the garbage bag full of bloody clothes. Bella had thrown the tiara of flesh in with them to be destroyed. Holly removed it from the bag and carried it into the detached garage. The door to the attic was just above the washer and dryer. She pulled it down and climbed up, carrying the tiara with her, and turned on the light so she could find the safe. This attic was the one place her husband and daughter never went into, so she'd hidden the small safe here under boxes filled with things she normally would have thrown away—old magazines and clothes that didn't fit anymore, items that would discourage someone from digging further. Uncovering the safe, Holly dialed the combination and opened the door.

Her old tiara sat on the velvet pillow she'd purchased just for it. The flesh had withered but the brittle hair remained intact, keeping the pieces together. At the tip of the crown, Faith's blackened teeth flashed their winning smile.

Holly moved her tiara to the side to make room for her daughter's.

THE PRETTIEST GIRL IN THE GRAVE

Though she may not realize it now, Bella would come to not only accept what she'd done but take pride in it. That's what had happened to Holly. She'd learned that to forgive herself she had to condone her actions. She'd played Madeline's game and won fair and square. In a deadly situation, she'd saved her own life. It was the greatest victory she would ever achieve. Sure, it wasn't exactly a happy life. Her marriage was a failure, and her job was a dead end. Her days were riddled with sadness and her nights with loneliness. But she was alive. And her spirit, however broken, wasn't trapped beneath a graveyard, doomed to watch other young girls suffer the same fate.

Holly would teach Bella to cope just as she had. They'd earned these trophies.

Closing the safe, Holly climbed down the ladder and sealed the attic, hiding their family secret. She took a deep breath. It was almost over. She desperately wanted that warm bath and glass of wine but had to be at work soon. Maybe she would call out after all. It was vital they keep up appearances, but her face was too bruised to just go about as if nothing had happened. And there was still one more challenge left to wrap up the game.

No evidence.

Holly went to the corkboard where the tools hung and selected the handheld hatchet her husband had bought to chop kindling when they went camping, then never used because he never took the family anywhere. She carried the hatchet outside, got in her car, and drove down the street until she saw the house. Dawn had broken, but the red sedan was still in the driveway, right next to the pickup truck. She walked to the front porch and just as she was about to ring the bell the door came open.

No witnesses.

Trisha Peterson stood in a beige pantsuit with a briefcase in her hand, ready for that morning meeting. She flinched when she saw Holly, having not realized she was there. In shock, she looked her up and down, gawking at the ghastly sight of Holly's battered face. Trisha glanced at the tool in Holly's hand. Before she could ask about it, Holly shoved her back into the house and closed the door behind them.

No survivors.

ACKNOWLEDGMENTS

Thanks to C.V. Hunt and Andersen Prunty, who are my friends as well as my publishers at Grindhouse Press. Special thanks to my dear friend Mona Kabbani for beta reading this manuscript and offering her invaluable feedback—this one's for you. Thanks to Brian Keene, Ryan Harding, Bryan Smith, Edward Lee, Aron Beauregard, John Wayne Comunale, Daniel J. Volpe, Ronald Kelly, Gregg Kirby, Josh Doherty, Bernard DeBenedictis, Wesley Southard, Wile E. Young, S.C. Mendes, Jonathan Butcher, Christine Morgan, John McNee, and Bear.

Extra special thanks to Jay Wilburn. Rest well, my friend.

Thank you to all my readers and fans, who have shown me more love than I could have ever imagined. I cherish you all.

One big thank you to goth girls everywhere. Never change.

And special thanks to Tom Mumme—always.

BIO

Kristopher Triana is the Splatterpunk Award-winning author of *Gone to See the River Man, Full Brutal, Blood Relations, The Long Shadows of October,* and many other terrifying books. His work has been published in multiple languages and has appeared in many anthologies and magazines, drawing praise from Rue Morgue Magazine, Cemetery Dance, Scream Magazine, and many more.

He lives in New England.

Shop: TRIANAHORROR.COM
Kristophertriana.com
Twitter: Koyotekris
Facebook: Kristopher Triana
Instagram: Kristopher_Triana
TikTok: Kristophertriana
Podcast: krisandjohnwayne.com

Other Grindhouse Press Titles

Made in the USA
Monee, IL
11 October 2024